"I want to…park."

In the moonlight, Chessie sent her husband a sultry look.

"As in…?"

"As in teenage-just-got-the-license park." She flipped up the armrest, then slid across the front seat to snuggle next to him.

Nick glanced at his watch.

"Not on this date, mister!" she exclaimed, pulling the watch from his wrist and tossing it into the back seat.

"You folks need to move along." The gruff voice seemed to be right in the car with them.

"What the hell!" Nick raised his hand to shield his eyes from the brightness.

"Nick?" The voice behind the blinding light boomed with amusement. "Chessie? For the love of Mike, you'd think the two of you could take it home." The police officer lowered his flashlight. It was George Weiss. Their neighbor. "Or at least a hotel room."

"We were watching the moon rise," Chessie explained sweetly.

"Among other things," George added. "I'm going to give you kids my usual safe-sex lecture." He dug into his pockets. "And these." He handed Nick a couple packets of condoms.

"Save the lecture, George," Nick muttered. "We're heading home."

"Don't let me come back in an hour and find you here." George grinned as if he were really enjoying this. "I'd have to write you up."

Dear Reader,

Independence Day was probably the most difficult book I've written. It's not about a traditional courtship, the kind that always provides me with such a lovely escape. This is a book that addresses the question "What happens *after* happily-ever-after?" More often than not, it's a roller-coaster ride of peaks and valleys. Sometimes the romance fades. Sometimes the passion gets lost in careers and families and pressing responsibility. This could be my life—and writing about issues that cut so close to the bone was very uncomfortable....

But is the rosy glow of courtship retrievable in a marriage? Absolutely, yes! Or so believes my heroine, Chessie McCabe. But for her, it will take a revolution. Little does she know that her quest to rekindle the passion in her workaholic, emotionally AWOL husband, Nick, will throw her family into turmoil and lead to a journey of self-discovery. Chessie and Nick learn that as great as the need for food and shelter is the need to be seen and heard.

Married twenty-nine years, I learned a lot from Chessie.

All my best,

Amy Frazier

P.S. So involved was I with this fictional couple that my daughter began to worry about them, too, calling from college for updates.... So, Sarah, did I guide them safely through the storm?

INDEPENDENCE DAY
Amy Frazier

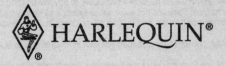

TORONTO • NEW YORK • LONDON
AMSTERDAM • PARIS • SYDNEY • HAMBURG
STOCKHOLM • ATHENS • TOKYO • MILAN • MADRID
PRAGUE • WARSAW • BUDAPEST • AUCKLAND

ISBN 0-373-78043-5

INDEPENDENCE DAY

This edition published by arrangement with Harlequin Books S.A.

® and TM are trademarks of the publisher. Trademarks indicated with
® are registered in the United States Patent and Trademark Office, the
Canadian Trade Marks Office and in other countries.

www.eHarlequin.com

Printed in U.S.A.

INDEPENDENCE DAY

CHAPTER ONE

"ON STRIKE, I SAID!" Exhilaration racing through her veins, Chessie McCabe threw another armload of dirty laundry from the bedroom window. "I'm on strike until my needs are met!"

Crumpled socks, T-shirts, shorts and underwear surrounding them like some freak snowfall on the summer-green grass below, Chessie's husband and two teenage daughters gaped up at her. She didn't blame them. This wasn't her usual behavior.

Her usual behavior involved patience. Large dollops of nurturing. Calmly maintained family schedules. An abundance of behind-the-scenes hugs, kisses, back rubs, pep talks and emotional support. Not public hysteria.

Well, this might be public, but it wasn't hysteria. It was a personal Fourth-of-July rebellion. And long overdue.

"Mom!" Fourteen-year-old Gabriella seemed about to die of mortification. "What are we supposed to do with this stuff?"

"I don't care. Wash it in the harbor. Pound it on the rocks. String it from boat to boat to dry. It's your dirty laundry. From this day forward, I wash my hands of it."

Her husband, Nick, eyed her silently. Even from her perspective at the bedroom window, Chessie could see the muscle along his jaw twitch. Not a good sign. And normally one that would send her into peacemaker mode. But not today. Today, the three of them could try to smooth her ruffled feathers.

"Let me make one thing perfectly clear," she declared, empowered by her second-story podium and the resonant Maine air. "I love the three of you very much. But I've spoiled you all rotten. From this day forward, my needs are as important as yours." She held her fist aloft in a militant salute. "Chessie McCabe is a doormat no more!"

"Mom!" Gabriella jerked her head toward the sidewalk opposite the McCabe cottage. "People..."

Chessie noted with some satisfaction that several obvious out-of-towners, cameras slung round their necks, had stopped on their way to the planned festivities at the village square. Had stopped and begun to stare at the little drama playing out on the front lawn. A small crowd. How handy. Every woman on the verge of rediscovering herself should find an audience.

She grinned. They probably thought this was all part of the town-sanctioned fun, a quaint reenactment of some obscure New England history. Tourists always thought Down-Easters so colorful.

Well, she'd show them colorful.

She plucked Nick's jockstrap from the bedroom floor behind her. With a whoop of pure abandon, she snapped the strap slingshot style, sending it arcing over her family's heads to settle on the roof of the purple martin birdhouse in the corner rose garden.

Seventeen-year-old Isabel slouched against the white picket fence around the front yard, embarrassment clouding her sober features.

Nick glanced from the stranded athletic supporter to the smirking tourists to his daughters to his watch. That damned watch. Then, with the same practiced patience he'd use as high-school principal on any one of his recalcitrant students, he stared up at his wife and cleared his throat.

"Chessie," he said, enunciating carefully. "The parade starts in ten minutes. I have a speech to give in thirty. Could we discuss this later?"

Chessie took a deep breath for courage. Across the street her friend Martha Weiss stood in her doorway, a bemused expression on her face. "Could we discuss this later?" she repeated, returning her gaze to Nick. "I don't think so. What I want from the three of you is a little bit of now."

One of the tourists, a middle-aged woman wearing an enormous red hat and a purple jersey tunic, applauded.

Feeling a glorious sense of release, Chessie slammed the window shut. She picked up her empty coffee mug, then headed downstairs to her studio and her potter's wheel in the barn. Not that she expected to get any work done immediately. Nick and the girls wouldn't let her opening salvo go unanswered. Oh, no.

Hormonally charged Gabriella wouldn't lose this opportunity to tell her mother—yet again—how she was absolutely ruining the teenager's life. While sweet, sensitive and poetic Isabel would take the opportunity to watch life unfold before her, ever the observer, marginally the participant.

And Nick...

Nick. Nick. Nick.

Nick, the proud and virile man Chessie had married eighteen years ago, would inwardly seethe at this inconvenient show of emotion, this lack of family solidarity. Nick, the workaholic and determined provider she'd followed around the country as he'd climbed his way from beginner teacher to full-fledged-high-school-principal-on-the-fast-track-to-superintendent...this Nick wouldn't be amused by her rebellion. Her husband, the now restrained and emotionally distant man she loved as a part of herself, but no longer understood, would instantly go into denial.

He'd try to find a way to minimize her outburst, pull his family together in a semblance of greeting-card perfection and still make his speech in the village square with five minutes to spare for schmoozing.

Well, not today. Today spin control wasn't going to cut it, not when the new and improved Chessie refused to be spun.

In the dining room, Chessie glanced out

the window and saw her family in the yard, trotting in line toward the barn. Grim Father Goose and his irate goslings. They knew her well enough to anticipate her destination.

Working her way through the cluttered kitchen, she placed her empty coffee mug precariously on top of the mound of unwashed dishes in the sink and sighed. The dirty dish fairy wasn't going to do the job this morning. Nope. She'd just wiped scullery duty from her priority list.

Steeling her will toward the revolution, she went out the kitchen door and through the furnace room. Oh, to get her hands in some therapeutic clay. As she opened the door into the barn's lower level, three stern faces brought her up short.

"What's all this about?" Nick asked, not without genuine concern.

Chessie moved toward the stairs leading to her studio and classroom. "I've chosen today to grant the three of you—and myself—emotional independence." She brushed past them. "Now, if you'll excuse me, the creative juices are flowing."

"But it's the Fourth of July," Gabriella

whined. "You'll miss the parade and Daddy's speech."

"I'll open the loft windows." Their cottage was only one door removed from the village square. "I'll hear the band and, with the PA system, Daddy's speech."

Isabel frowned. "But we won't be together."

Pausing, Chessie turned to her older daughter. "As cruel as it sounds, sweetie, we're none of us joined at the hip. And I need to work."

"Geez, Dad," Gabriella groused, "she was sane at breakfast."

Yes, she had been sane at breakfast.

It was after breakfast she'd needed to take fifteen minutes—fifteen minutes—for herself in her studio to sketch out the plans for the piece that had been buzzing inside her head for days now, the piece that might prove to be a significant advancement in a career that had never fully taken root because the family moved every couple years for Nick's career.

But noooo…her own fifteen minutes were not to be.

Nick couldn't find his red suspenders. Gabriella couldn't find her favorite jean shorts.

And Isabel couldn't find her iPod. All three looked to Chessie to produce the missing items as if by magic. When she'd finally got into the bathroom to wash her face and run a brush through her hair, she'd been met by the avalanche of dirty laundry.

The proverbial straw.

She was expected to be a 24/7 concierge for everyone else, but wasn't allowed fifteen uninterrupted minutes to be herself. Not someone's wife. Not someone's mother. Not someone's maid. Herself. A concept she'd almost forgotten the meaning of.

She felt her face go red with frustration.

"Mom?" Isabel's worried voice brought Chessie back to the barn and the present. "Are you all right?"

Nick glanced at his watch. Again with the watch. "Girls, for whatever reason, I think your mom needs some time alone. We can all meet up for the picnic later." He leaned over and kissed Chessie on the forehead. A very chaste kiss, infuriating in its total lack of passion.

"Do your thing," he murmured in a tone that bordered dangerously close to patronizing. "Get it all out of your system. Come to the parade later if you can make it. Either way, we'll have fun this afternoon on the islands." He delivered his lines with administrative deliberation. "I'm counting on you. As I always do."

Poor Nick. He didn't have a clue that the rules had changed this morning.

If his kiss hadn't been so platonic and his tone so dismissive, Chessie might've limited her initial declaration to the shower of dirty laundry. But it seemed her family still needed a more public nudge.

FROM THE PODIUM in front of the flagpole, Nick looked out over the attentive crowd. As he spotted his daughters and the rest of the McCabe clan—his father, Penn, his sister Mariah, and his brothers Jonas, Brad, with Emily and their four children, and Sean, with Kit and Alexandra—he felt very proud. He'd delivered a worthy speech—brief, patriotic and stirring—and he'd delivered it from the heart. Despite Chessie's unaccountable behavior earlier, he felt a real sense of hometown satisfaction.

"And in closing, I ask each and every one of you," he concluded with conviction, "as you enjoy today's activities, to count your blessings. There is no finer, freer place to live than Pritchard's Neck, Maine."

As the applause broke out around him, a flash of sunlight on metal captured his attention. Ever the principal, Nick worried that a brass player with the high-school band had gone AWOL for a smoke behind the library—until he saw Chessie in front of the library, adjusting a slapdash sandwich-board sign over her shoulders as she held aloft Nick's battered junior-high-school trumpet. The sign secure, she put the instrument to her lips and delivered one short, sour blast.

The band leader glowered at his brass section.

Nick's sense of hometown satisfaction sprang a leak.

It wasn't at all unusual for Pritchard's Neck residents and visitors to bring noise-makers to the Fourth of July parade and speech as part of the celebration and the local color. Chessie could toot her horn till the mackerel ran without raising an eyebrow. But the sign gave Nick pause.

In bold capital letters the board read, CHESSIE MCCABE ON STRIKE UNTIL HER NEEDS ARE MET. How many ways could that be taken? And how many people had noticed?

Nick felt the color drain from his face.

He heard a high-pitched, synchronized squeal from the front of the crowd. It appeared Gabriella and Isabel had just spotted their mother.

Damage control his middle name, Nick gave the band leader a curt nod. Quentin Landry, one of Nick's high-school faculty, responded immediately by having his students play a rousing exit march.

Snapping photos as if in pursuit of a Pulitzer, the tourists who'd witnessed the literal airing of McCabe dirty laundry earlier crowded around a sweetly smiling Chessie. It would be just Nick's luck if one of them worked for *The New York Times* Sunday magazine. His wife's behavior—today's behavior—certainly fit the eccentric mold outsiders often formed of Mainers, delighted in spreading in travel articles. But Nick—specifically, his career—couldn't afford eccentricity.

Grinding his teeth, he made his way off the bunting-trimmed podium.

Gabriella and Isabel assailed him. "Dad—"

"I'll take care of it." He gave each daughter a quick hug. "You know your mom—always on the cutting edge."

"But—"

"Go get the picnic hamper. We'll all four be on our way in just a sec." He could only hope.

The two girls stared at him.

"I promise," he said, grimacing.

What had gotten into his wife? Because of her artistic nature, he expected her to be occasionally, creatively quirky. In private. She'd always been sensible in public. Supportive.

Fully intending to keep his private and his public lives separate, Nick pushed through the crowd around the library entrance. "Excuse me," he said, grasping Chessie's arm and propelling her through the doorway into the small book drop foyer. "Show's over, folks." The sandwich board banged him in the shins.

Closing the outer door with difficulty, he turned to Chessie. Heatstroke might be a reasonable explanation for her bizarre behavior this morning. But she beamed up at him, her hazel eyes clear and purposeful.

"Performance art?" he asked, hopeful.

"Absolutely not," she replied with a seriousness that short-circuited his brief glimmer of optimism.

"Are you angry with me? With the girls?" Arguing on one of his rare days off wasn't his idea of fun. He hated confrontation on the home front. He relied on Chessie to negotiate peace.

She cocked her head. "Angry is such a negative word."

"What then? Pick a word, any word. As long as it explains why you threw our laundry onto the front lawn. Why you're wearing a…a picket sign."

"You noticed." She sighed. Her angelic expression hinted at sarcasm.

"Of course I noticed."

She patted his arm. "That's a start."

"A start?" In exasperation, he rubbed his hand across his forehead. "I have one day to relax before summer school begins. The driver's ed car's in the shop. The state accreditation team's making its first visit in two days. The air-conditioning in the science lab has been acting hinky. My best English teacher just told me she's pregnant and won't be back for the fall term…" He took a deep breath. "I wanted one day—one day—to recoup with my family."

"I needed fifteen minutes to work on an idea," she said, her voice barely above a whisper.

"An idea for a pot?"

"Sort of."

"And we didn't give it to you."

"That's what I thought at first. But then I realized you three wouldn't give it if I didn't take it. Couldn't take advantage of me if I didn't let you."

As he tried to digest this, she flashed him a grin. Her megawatt smiles never ceased to take his breath away, but this one felt like a shot to the solar plexus.

"And now that you've asserted yourself…" He hesitated, wary. "And now that we've taken notice…we'll kayak to the islands for a picnic?"

"Not exactly."

"Honey," his holiday slipping away, he glanced at his watch "the tide's only going to give us so much leeway."

"Ah, yes. Time and tide wait for no man." Her shoulders drooped slightly. "The high-school principal's credo."

"Are you trying to pick a fight? Is your p—"

The librarian poked her head into the foyer. "Is there something I could help you find?"

If only. "No, thank you," Nick replied. "We're okay."

As the librarian made her way back to her desk, Chessie glared at Nick. "No, my period isn't coming," she whispered, "if that's what you were about to suggest. It isn't always about hormones."

He backpedaled. "Chessie, give me some credit. Is your...pot you wanted to work on under deadline?"

Nice save. His wrist, the one with the watch on it, twitched.

"Not in the usual sense." She narrowed her eyes. "I told you a trustee for the Portland Museum of Art loved the idea for this piece. She wants it for her private collection. And she carries such influence in the New England art world that a successful sale might be the opening I've been looking for. The opening that could take my career to the next level."

"I didn't understand." A library patron tried to enter the cramped foyer with an armload of books, but the heavy sandwich board Chessie still wore got in the way.

"Sorry." Awkwardly, Nick and Chessie squeezed farther back into the corner.

"I know you didn't understand," Chessie continued, lowering her voice even more. "Neither did the girls. That's just the point. But you will."

Nick felt queasy. He liked explanations. Concise and logical explanations stripped of a storyteller's suspenseful pacing. He didn't like surprises. Pinching the bridge of his nose, he said, "Give me a hint."

"Let's just say I'm having my midlife crisis. I've worked hard for it. I deserve it. And I'm going to enjoy it."

"Chessie. You're only thirty-seven."

"And getting older by the minute." She reached for the door. "Go on. Take the girls to the islands. I'll spend the afternoon in my studio. We'll watch the fireworks together from the terrace tonight."

He stayed her hand on the knob. "You're kidding about the midlife crisis."

She paused. "If that explanation gets you thinking about the lopsided dynamics of our family life, so be it."

"What lopsided dynamics?"

"Hadn't noticed, had you?" Chessie bristled, an unusually combative look in her eyes. "How about my unappreciated backstage roles as the family's chief cook and bottle washer, laundress, taxi driver, mediator, cheerleader, nurse, convenient lover and general bend-over-till-I-can-touch-my-nose-to-my-behind Gumby?"

"You can't possibly think of yourself that way."

"I don't, but the rest of you—"

"Shh!" A child in the picture-book section put her finger to her lips.

With effort, Nick closed the door between the foyer and the main reading room. "What's gotten into you?" He wasn't a stupid person. He was the principal of a regional high school.

She paused, leveling him with her gray-green stare. "I have work. Work I need to do for myself. For a change. It's not as if I'm abandoning you. I don't always have to be the recreation director. It will do the three of you good to spend some time alone together. To have your routine jostled a bit."

His work routine was always being jostled. He didn't like upset in his personal life.

"We'll talk later," she offered. "There'll be a quiz on what you've learned this morning."

He didn't react to her attempt at humor. "I'll carry the sign home for you." He needed to take charge, even in this small way.

"Nick, Nick," she purred, "you always were my knight in shining armor."

"Were?" He stiffened. "So what am I now?"

"Your armor needs a little buffing." She wriggled out of the sandwich board.

Confused, Nick took the bulky sign from her and, with difficulty, turned it inside-out so the words were hidden. He opened the door as if nothing had happened.

But something had.

When they'd married eighteen years ago, they'd been in total agreement. He'd be the breadwinner. She'd keep home and hearth. Now Chessie wanted to change the agreement. It made Nick, a man who never tinkered with what worked, want to reach for the antacid tablets.

Chessie knew that, after her demonstration, Nick would want to make it home without attracting any more attention. But the sight of Penn, along with Sean, Kit and Alex waiting for them outside the library told her escape would be impossible. McCabes—

even in small groups—were notorious for practicing family by committee.

"So, this is what you had in mind when you said you had other plans and couldn't come to the family picnic," his father said.

Chessie saw Nick flinch. "I was going to take my family to the islands," he replied, a defensive edge to his voice. "I never have time to get out on the water. It seems I rarely have time to see my wife and daughters."

"Is that what Chessie's demanding?" With an amused twinkle in his eye, Penn indicated the now reversed sandwich board. "More attention?"

"Pop, butt out." Good-naturedly, Sean nudged their father.

"Hey, I'm just wondering if I should be wearing a protest sign," Penn retorted. "I'm his old man, and I never see him."

"I'm busy, Pop. Making a living."

"We all are," Sean noted. "So…great speech."

"Aunt Chessie, can I play your trumpet?" Sean's nine-year-old daughter Alex piped up. Nick looked relieved to be out of the spotlight for a moment.

"Sure." Chessie relinquished her noisemaker. "Do you think you can play it better than I did?"

"You weren't very good," Alex said with her typical candor. She put the trumpet to her lips, then blew till she was red in the face. Only a hiss of air came out. With a frown she lowered the instrument. "But you're better than me."

The adults laughed.

"Take it home with you," Nick urged. "You can practice."

"Oh, thanks." Sean ruffled Alex's hair. "Just what we need. More noise in the house."

"Your Uncle Nick's afraid Aunt Chessie might try to make a point with it again," Penn declared dryly.

"So…" Kit indicated both the trumpet and the sandwich board. "Are we talking about this?"

"Sure," Chessie replied as Nick said, "No."

If anyone would understand her mission, it was Kit. At twenty-five, her sister-in-law had been on her own for nine years—nine unconventional years—until Sean convinced her that loving him and Alex didn't mean she had to give up her individuality.

Nick looked at his watch. "The tide…"

"You know McCabe parties go on forever," Sean said. "Stop by when you get in."

"Thanks." Nick smiled, but he didn't say they'd be there.

Chessie wondered about that as they made their way home. Nick had told her that moving this last time was a good idea because they'd settle into a ready-made family. She and the girls had done the settling, but Nick remained strangely aloof.

"Are you and your family okay?" she asked.

"Why wouldn't we be?"

She didn't pursue the issue. Nick's relationship with his family had always been... special. His mother had died when he was twelve and Jonas, his youngest brother, just one. Nick had been old enough at the time to shoulder some of the responsibility of looking after the kids. She could see where the experience had honed his deeply ingrained provider instinct. But when he'd left for college nineteen years ago, he'd left for a future away from Pritchard's Neck. And when they'd returned last year, Nick had never seemed completely at ease with either his father or his siblings.

He seemed as emotionally AWOL with them as he was with her.

Chessie couldn't control his relationships with others, but if her strike woke her husband up, she might not be the only one whose needs were met.

CHAPTER TWO

"CHESSIE?" Nick glanced at his watch. Seven-thirty. "We're home!"

"I'm up in the bedroom."

She sounded rational. With some sense of relief that she hadn't ambushed him with more laundry, he climbed the stairs. Yet today's explosion—having gone beyond anything she'd ever pulled on them before—still worried him. He was tired from exploring the islands with the girls, but he needed to get to the bottom of this before the situation escalated.

But what was the situation? What did she really want from them? From him? She'd spoken in riddles.

Chessie had mentioned a project that was important to her. He'd always liked her interest in ceramics because it seemed to relax her, but maybe the self-imposed pressure to excel had gotten out of hand. Maybe she actually needed to lay off the pottery for a while.

Maybe he could engineer a short break for the two of them, since he'd chosen not to take his scheduled vacation this year. The AP science teacher had promised his spring term students a bus trip to Lake Winnipesaukee in New Hampshire next week. A reward for passing their Advanced Placement exams. Maybe he and Chessie could hook up as chaperones. It wouldn't be a real vacation, it wasn't an overnight trip, but it would be a change of scene. Maybe he could afford one more day off work. If he could only get next fall's hiring completed this week.

There were far too many ifs and maybes.

He found himself stalled in the upstairs hallway.

"Do you plan to step over the threshold?" Chessie leaned against the bedroom door frame, looking up at him. Lost in thought, he hadn't even noticed her. "I won't bite," she added.

"I wasn't sure."

"I said we'd talk later. Now's good."

"The fireworks start at nine."

"Oh, we have plenty of time before the

fireworks start." With a gleam in her eye that could itself be described as pyrotechnic, she pulled him into their bedroom and closed the door firmly behind them.

Things were looking up.

He moved to take her in his arms.

"Talk," she said, pushing him down to sit on the bed while she remained standing. "So...what did you learn today?"

He was in treacherous, uncharted territory. "Chessie—"

"Maaaa!" The adolescent shriek careened up the stairwell and through the closed door. "Are there any strawberries and whipped cream left over from breakfast?" Gabriella.

With a shudder, Chessie opened the door. "Miss McCabe, unless you broke both legs and at least one arm on your trip to the islands, you can open the refrigerator door and check for yourself." Her shoulders seemed to droop. "Please don't interrupt. Your father and I are in the middle of an important conversation."

"It won't interfere with us watching the fireworks, will it?"

"If you don't give us ten minutes, the fireworks will begin early, I promise."

Even from upstairs, Nick could hear Gabriella stomping off to the kitchen. He'd always admired Chessie's infinite patience with their daughters, especially Gabby, who was proving a handful. This evening, however, that patience showed signs of wear and tear.

Breathing deeply, Chessie turned back into the room. "Where was I?"

"You wanted to know what I'd learned today." He chose his words carefully. "I think perhaps you want more time to yourself."

"Not quite. It's more that I don't believe you and the girls see me as being a self. I'm your wife, their mom. Outside of that, I think I'm a bit of a blur."

"How can you say that?"

"Okay. What was I wearing this morning?"

A trick question. Was she wearing the shorts and T-shirt she had on now?

"Besides a sandwich board?" he asked, stalling.

Clearly impatient now, she crossed her arms over her chest. "Underneath the sandwich board."

He frowned. Before she'd surprised him with her strike sign, she'd shown every intention of working on her pots. He hazarded a guess. "Shorts. A smock."

"What color were my toenails?"

He glanced quickly at her feet. She wore sneakers. "Red, white and blue?"

"Have you ever seen me paint my nails? Ever? The girls, yes, but me? I don't think so." With an unexpected snort of laughter, she picked up a pillow from the window seat and threw it at him. "Red, white and blue. I'll give you C+ for creativity."

The fact that she didn't appear angry seemed to augur the return of the old, familiar Chessie, mischievous but sweet. His exact opposite. Perhaps that's why he'd been drawn to her back in high school—

Another pillow hit him in the head. "No daydreaming in class."

"Then can we cut to the chase? My day off is almost gone. I'd like to spend the rest of it with my family. With you."

"About this morning—"

"You're forgiven." He grinned, then immediately regretted his ill-timed humor as another pillow whizzed by his head.

"You and the girls mustn't take me for granted any longer." The renewed rebellion in her eyes told him this was no joke. "There are times I feel invisible."

"Sweetheart." He opened his arms to her. "You are the most colorful, least invisible woman I know. The girls and I love every quirky bone in your body." Okay, so it wasn't Robert Browning. He was a high-school principal—a weary high-school principal—not a poet.

"Do you understand how important my work is to me?" she asked.

"If there were a Maine Mom-and-Wife-of-the-Year Award, I'd nominate you in a heartbeat."

"And my pottery?"

"I love your pots." Better keep it simple. Talk of arts and crafts dragged him out of his league.

"Do you know how much money I put away from my teaching and sales last year?"

"I never asked because that's your mad money."

"Mad money? After taxes last year I added twelve thousand dollars to the girls' college fund."

Twelve thousand dollars? He nearly choked. He had no idea a hobby could be so lucrative.

"Mad money, indeed," Chessie muttered as she closed in on him. "The negotiating price for this new piece alone is fifteen hundred dollars. This is art, Nick, not Play-Doh."

"Fifteen—" He did choke. And sputtered. Chessie whacked him on the back. A little too hard, if you asked him. "We need to have a talk with our tax man. Have we declared your earnings?"

She sighed. "I filed separate forms as a self-employed businesswoman. I've kept my own books. I've joined the Better Business Bureau. Taken an Internet workshop on finances and investments."

He seemed to recall their tax man mentioning the separate filing, but the news had been overshadowed at the time by the threat of a sports-injury lawsuit at school.

"When did you do all this?" Her secret life astounded him.

"While the girls were in school. Any night you worked late."

That could've been any night of the week.

"And you didn't think I'd be interested?"

"I tried to tell you a dozen times," she insisted, "but you weren't listening."

With a sinking heart, he took her point.

"Aha!" she exclaimed when she saw he understood. "And did you know I'm very close to opening that gallery I've always wanted? In the barn on the ground floor."

He looked hard at this woman he'd underestimated. What else had she been up to in his absence? The possibilities racing though his mind made Nick feel—for the first time in his life—blown off course.

"How do you expect me to take you seriously when we haven't talked about any of this?"

She seemed taken aback by his question, but only briefly. "So much of our ever-shrinking time together is spent discussing your job and how it affects our future. The rest of the time it's the girls—"

"That's a cop-out, Chessie, and you know it. You want recognition, but you're not communicating."

Her nostrils widened as she inhaled sharply. "Maybe you're right...but today I woke up. I won't ever be satisfied if I don't tell you why I'm dissatisfied."

"And how." Smiling ruefully, he rubbed the back of his neck. "So...your pots can bring in that much?" Here he thought she'd been having a few friends over for coffee and crafts. "I'm impressed, Chessie."

"Impressed with the idea of a real business, are you? But do you appreciate the woman behind the work?"

"Of course we do," he replied.

"Let's leave the girls out of this. I'll deal with them separately. Do you appreciate me? All of me."

Hell, yes. He gazed at her as she strode across the bedroom to stand in front of the window. She was tall and still had a great figure after two children. Her long unruly auburn hair was partially held back by a ribbon. Her skin seemed otherworldly. Creamy. Smooth. Cool, most likely. She was always blessedly cool to the touch on even the hottest summer day. There was nothing cool about her eyes, though. Fire and ice. That was his Chessie. And ever since high school she'd had the power to excite him. He felt himself grow hard.

"If wanting you can be construed as appreciation," he ventured, "I'd say I recognize what a lucky man I am."

"So you want to make love to me?"

"Now that's a fact."

"Perhaps because we always make love on nights before you start your workweek?"

He didn't like this detour. "You make it sound like a routine."

"That's what I haven't quite figured out." Crossing her arms again, she began to tap her fingers restlessly on her elbows. "I'm not sure if you really want to make love to *me*... or whether you're simply after a bit of release from tension."

"You've been spoiling for a fight all day. It has to be hormones."

Low blow. And one he instantly regretted.

She glared at him.

He pulled his frustration in line. "Is it so awful I want to make love to my wife?"

"What about foreplay? What about romance? What about extending these concepts beyond the bedroom door?"

She was losing him again.

"I want to feel newly and thoroughly wooed," she explained. "No more school functions that do double duty as dates. No more chaste pecks on the forehead. No more checking your watch when I begin to talk."

"I had no idea—"

"Well, now you do. For a change, I want pizzazz instead of Friday night pizza. I want my toes to tingle and not because the Volvo needs a tune-up."

"Sounds good to me." He moved to embrace her, but she stepped aside.

"Seriously, Nick. Is it so awful I want to bring our relationship in for an inspection and tune-up?"

"I never thought there were two people who agreed more on how they wanted their life together to unfold. I promised to provide for you. You said you wanted to be a wife and mother."

"I did. Do." She seemed to search for words. "But I was nineteen when we married. I couldn't have anticipated how I'd grow. I love being a wife and mother, but I want to be other things as well. We need to rearrange our relationship a little bit to make room for all of me."

"But why today?" He made the mistake of glancing at his watch.

"Ooh!" She grabbed two fistfuls of her hair. "Some day I'm going to flush that watch down the toilet."

"Guys!" Isabel stood in the doorway. "I gotta use your bathroom. Gabriella's hogging ours."

Nick bristled. "Your mother and I are trying to have a conversation here."

"Go right ahead." Isabel whisked by them

into the master bath, then slammed the door, making the pictures on the walls rattle in their frames. Behind the closed door the teenager broke into a caterwauling song of love lost.

Nick suddenly felt ambushed by females. His office at school, even with the attendant troubles, now seemed like a haven. Even the boys' locker room would be a better hideout. An estrogen-free zone. Quelling his disloyal thoughts and mustering what little patience remained at his disposal, he stood. "Is it too much to ask for a little peace and quiet on my one day off?

Her husband's intransigence fueled Chessie's determination. He wasn't stupid. He wasn't selfish. He was maddeningly pre-occupied. But he'd been right about her needing to communicate if she wanted to be recognized—to be seen—and not simply as some competent mother of his children, some unobtrusive window dressing for his career.

"Some people are afraid of being fat and forty," she said, persevering. "Do you know what I'm afraid of? I'm afraid I'm headed straight toward faded and forty."

"It'll never happen." With obvious weariness Nick pinched the bridge of his nose.

"Fear of fading? After today? You're going to have to think of some other excuse to pick a fight."

"I'm not trying to pick a fight." She began to pace. "I'm trying to start a dialogue."

"I'm sensing lovemaking is fast becoming a long shot," Nick said, making sure Isabel couldn't hear him over her hurting song.

"I'll tell you what. Let's get kinky. Tonight let's perform that over-the-top sex act, listening. How about it?"

"Sarcasm doesn't become you, Chess."

A sudden overwhelming sadness sapped her energy. "I feel as if you're slipping away from me."

"Maybe that's because I'm tired and I have a full day tomorrow. Trying to provide for my family." His words sounded raw.

She knew this was how he showed love. By being responsible.

Crossing the room, she stood in front of him. "You are a wonderful provider, Nick."

"Then where have I failed you?"

"It's not a matter of failure." She placed her hands on his cheeks, felt his warmth. Gazed into dark eyes that had always mesmerized her with their depth and intelligence. "We've drifted into a relationship that's convenient. I want to rediscover the romance we shared when we were—"

"Hey, no time for gooey, guys." Gabriella burst into the room. "Mom, I need your hooded sweatshirt. It's getting chilly."

"Excuse me." Irritated, Chessie faced her daughter. "This is our bedroom. Please, knock. And you may borrow my hooded sweatshirt when you return the two tees you took last week."

"They're dirty…and out on the lawn."

"Then I guess you have yard work and laundry to do before the fireworks."

"Dad?"

"Your mother's asked you to do two things." Nick stood firm. "You have time before dark to start both. I suggest you get busy."

The bathroom door swung open. "Are you guys fighting?" Isabel stood wide-eyed in the doorway. Chessie knew this was her seventeen-year-old's biggest fear, that something would separate her family as it had too many of her friends.

"We're not fighting, love," Chessie denied. "We're having a discussion." Seizing the moment, she reached for the sheet of paper on her nightstand. "And I'll take this opportunity to explain our new cooking schedule."

Gabriella stepped to her father's side. "Dad, she's got that look in her eyes again."

Chessie ignored the perplexed expressions on her family's faces. "For a year now I've wanted to take the Art Guild's figure drawing class. Call it career advancement." She shot Nick a pointed glance. "But it's Wednesday right while I'm preparing dinner. So I need help. To that end, I've made up a meal schedule." She extended the paper to them, but the other three recoiled. "Each member of the family will be responsible for dinner on two assigned days of the week. Izzy and Gabby, you count as one person. I'll take the extra day, but never Wednesday. That should free me up to attend class, starting tomorrow. Girls, you begin the rotation."

"You expect us to cook?" Gabriella, her mouth working, looked like a beached fish gasping its last.

"You can start simple. Peanut butter sandwiches and milk. Carrot sticks. I'm not fussy."

"Honey…" Nick assumed his official negotiator voice. "They're just kids."

"And they'll remain children indefinitely if they don't begin to take on some responsibility."

"Tomorrow Mrs. Weiss promised to take Izzy and Keri and me to the mall." Keri was the neighbors'—George and Martha's—daughter and Gabriella's best friend. "Dad, switch days with us."

Nick's eyes widened in dawning recognition. He spread his hands, palms up to Chessie in a conciliatory gesture. "You can't expect me to—"

"Takeout. As I said, I'm not fussy. Now, I'll post this schedule on the refrigerator and then I'm assuming fireworks position on the terrace while you girls take care of the laundry in the yard." Amazed at how light she felt after this first transfer of duties, she smiled broadly. "Dibs on the hammock. But I'll share with a like-minded romantic." She could only hope.

Not waiting for further reaction from her shell-shocked family, she made her way downstairs, hoping she would draw Nick to her, not push him away.

"Maaaa!" Gabriella wailed behind her. "You've ruined the Fourth of July!"

"Oh, no, my dear," Chessie called from below. "I hope I've honored the spirit of the day."

"Well, I'm not watching any stupid fireworks now." Her younger daughter's grousing wafted down the stairwell, followed by an indistinguishable response from Nick.

Second thoughts stabbed her as she rummaged in the living room for her John Philip Sousa CD. Had she ruined a holiday with unreasonable demands? Had she mistaken wants for needs?

No, dammit.

She hadn't behaved selfishly today. She'd merely issued a wake-up call for Nick and the girls' own good, as well as her own. Growing up, she'd observed her workaholic father drive himself to an early grave. As an adult, she'd watched as too many of her friends had spoiled their children to the obnoxious stage. She'd seen husbands and wives grow to be strangers. If she lay down and became a doormat, what kind of a match was she for Nick? What kind of a role model for Izzy and Gabby?

Having found the desired CD, she headed for the furnace room where she tripped over the cat litter box, out of place and full to overflowing. Normally, she would stop what she was doing to clean it for the sake of the cats her daughters had begged to bring home from the shelter. ("We'll take care of them. Promise." Right.)

The new Chessie found a scrap of paper, a marker and a broken tomato stick. Skewering the paper with the stick, she wrote, "Yo! This ain't no toxic waste dump. Clean it up! The Cats." She jammed the stick in the corner of the litter and left the box in the middle of the floor.

Highly satisfied with no-holds-barred Chessie, she hunted up sparklers, the beach boombox and bug repellent, then forged ahead to the darkening terrace where she immediately began slathering on lotion. Despite the fact that the mosquito seemed to be the Maine state bird, she wondered if her family—should they choose to join her—would think to lather up without a motherly nag.

Ah, but she'd washed her hands of nagging, negotiating, coercing, reminding. She'd now moved into the fluid rinse cycle of mature communication. In the future, she would treat her family as individuals—as she wished them to treat her. She only hoped she hadn't hung herself out to dry.

Content that she'd protected every exposed inch of skin, she flipped on the Sousa CD. Perhaps if she seemed happy, her family would be lured to join her. She hadn't meant to drive them away. On the contrary, she was searching for a way to draw them closer. In a more equitable fashion.

She struck a match to a sparkler. The slender wand sprang to life, adding its cheery glow to that of the myriad fireflies dancing in the dusky gardens. Chessie raised her little torch to the heavens.

"Huzzah," she said softly, not sure whether she felt the proper revolutionary or one rather isolated wife and mother. An exile by her own design.

Footsteps crunched against the stones on the terrace. She turned to see Nick standing behind her.

"Truce?" he asked, his voice weary.

At the sight of him, her heart beat faster. "Care to join me in the hammock?"

"Sure." He smacked the side of his neck with the flat of his hand, a clear sign he hadn't put on bug lotion. Oh, well, he was a big boy.

As Chessie sat in the hammock, Isabel called from the kitchen window. "Mom, what did you do with my Zinc Noze Boyz CD? It was in my portable player."

The sharp pain in Chessie's backside told her exactly what someone had done with the player and headphones. "Isabel, you left it in the hammock. I hope it wasn't here overnight when it rained."

"Criminies!" The teenager's footsteps echoed through the house.

"Zinc Noze Boyz." Carefully sitting next to her in the hammock, Nick chuckled. "Now there's a recording I wouldn't want ruined."

Isabel burst onto the terrace, her arms outstretched. "Thanks," she mumbled, grasping the player and jamming the headphones over her ears. Leaning against the house, she quickly became lost in the music, with only occasional swats to various body parts. No bug lotion. Like father, like daughter.

Nick draped his arm over Chessie's shoulder, then lay back in the hammock, pulling her with him. "Nice perfume," he murmured.

Perfume? She never wore perfume. Oh, yeah, the bug lotion. If this was all the romance today's demonstration had gotten her, she needed to up the ante. Might even have to implement Plan B…

"This is nice," he added. His muffled words told her he'd be asleep before the fireworks started.

Plan B it was.

"Yes, this is nice," she agreed. "Emerging starlight. The scent of flowers. A cricket serenade. The closeness of two bodies." She stroked his thigh. "It's quite romantic."

"Couldn't agree more." He was fading fast.

"We need more romance in our marriage."

"Anything…you…say." He held to consciousness by a tenuous thread.

"And I have a plan." She walked her fingers up his chest. "I read in your *Sports Illustrated* that athletes try to imprint positive behavior. Good golf swing. Great slap shot. Terrific slam dunk."

"Soun's great."

"They try to memorize how the positive feels and then block out the negative or the extraneous, both mentally and physically." She stroked the stubble along his jaw.

"Mmmm…"

"So I thought, since we both agree this romantic feeling is nice, we could work on replicating it. Kind of like the athletes. We'd be in training, so to speak, in our relationship." She laid her cheek on his shoulder with her mouth close to his ear. "More romance. It could become our mantra."

His deep intake of breath sounded suspiciously like a snore.

"We need to recognize the difference between real romance and a convenient physical release." She ran her tongue along the rim of his ear. "Nick, while we're concentrating on the romance, I think we're going to have to can the sex."

On the verge of sleep or not, he sat bolt upright in the hammock. "No sex?" With the wild look of someone with one foot in dreams and the other in reality, he spotted his daughter lost in her music and lowered his voice. "Are you out of your mind?"

She seemed to have his attention now.

"Just till we're back on track as a couple, hon." She massaged the tense muscles of his back. "Sex can cloud the issue."

"Dammit, we're married."

"I'm well aware of that. But I'd like to feel as if we were courting. And I, for one, am embracing celibacy until that hearts-and-flowers feeling returns."

"What are you trying to do to me, Chess?"

"Us, Nick. Us. And I'm trying to make us better."

Angry, he stood up. "Well, it sure feels as if it's all about me. And none of it feels good." He stormed off the terrace, past Isabel, who appeared oblivious to her father's distress.

Chessie slumped back in the hammock as the first of the fireworks exploded overhead with a tremendous boom and a dizzying display of color.

CHAPTER THREE

TEN HOURS LATER Nick still fumed.

Last night, afraid he might say something he'd regret in the morning, he'd left Chessie on the terrace without discussing her ridiculous challenge. He'd been too frustrated to debate what he didn't understand. Besides, pure physical exhaustion had caught up with him. He'd headed to bed.

He hadn't slept, however, and his wife hadn't joined him in their bedroom.

Morning had dawned with confusion dogging his sleep-deprived brain. Even now, after all the words exchanged yesterday, he didn't see why she'd become dissatisfied with their marriage. And celibacy after eighteen years together? What a crock. He felt manipulated and hoped the old sofa in her studio, where she'd more than likely spent the night, had been lumpy.

He'd looked forward to reading the morning paper to see if he was still in the same universe he'd been in before the Fourth, but the new paper carrier had tossed it in the birdbath.

Aggravated before the work day had begun, he pounded the steering wheel of his old and cranky Volvo as he prepared to head to school. He empathized with cranky, wincing at the grinding sound the car's transmission made when he pulled out of the driveway. Not unlike the discordant, grating gears of his once well-oiled life.

He'd stop at Tindall's Service Center on the way to school and leave the car to be checked. John would give him a ride to work.

His thoughts crowded, Nick scratched the back of his neck in irritation. The mosquitoes had feasted on him last night, and now the nonstop itching was driving him nuts. At least something had been hungry for his body, he thought sourly.

Using extreme caution, he drove the short distance to the service center. As he pulled into the lot, he experienced a pang of envy for the automotive work of John Tindall, his former classmate. With machines, when something went wrong, the problem was real, physical and, for the most part, observable.

Unlike relationships.

As he stepped out of the car, Nick wished he could raise Chessie on a lift, hook her up to a diagnostic machine.

"Nick." John hailed him from the gas pumps where he was putting out pails of water and windshield cleaning squeegees. "How's it going?"

Nick shook his head. John didn't really want to know. "If I leave my car here, could you look at my transmission sometime today? I don't like what I'm hearing."

"What I'm hearing," John replied with a grin, "is that Chessie's set to reform you."

Just what Nick needed as he went about the delicate business of hiring new teachers, some new to the area. What if this gossip filtered through his staff to the recruits? How would it affect his image as a professional and a leader?

He spied Abigail, John's wife and book-keeper, peeking out from behind curtains in the office window, an unmistakable smile on her pretty face. Nick sighed heavily. "You know Chessie, John. Just some Fourth-of-July hijinks."

"If you say so." The mechanic wiped his hands on a rag.

"Oh, hell!" Nick ran his fingers through his hair. "Do you know what women really want?"

John snorted. "Abigail says all she wants is a little bit more than she's ever going to get."

"But what exactly is that little bit more?"

"In Abigail's case, money."

Nick shook his head. That wasn't the case with Chessie. Or was it? She'd said she wanted to be romanced. Did that mean expensive jewelry and exotic bouquets? Those things hadn't mattered to her in the past. But, as far as he'd been concerned, Chessie had seemed content, and look at how wrong he'd been on that score.

"What about romance?" he asked.

"Frankly, Abigail seems to get her kicks from a ledger in the black. But what do I know?"

"You're saying you haven't a clue."

"Not a one." John raised his hat, repositioned it, then set it back on his head in the age-old male gesture that begged to change the subject. "So, you want a ride to work?"

"Yeah. I hope you're better at figuring out transmissions than you are at figuring out women."

At the high school, Hattie St. Regis, his administrative assistant, met him with a fresh pot of coffee and a double-parked agenda. "Restful holiday?" she asked, her eyes betraying no sign of gossip-induced interest.

"Yes," he lied, trying to focus on the day planner on his desk, obscured with new paperwork.

"Good. We have quite a schedule today." She poured them each a cup of coffee. "I'm thinking of getting an espresso machine in this place. Regular coffee just doesn't spark my plugs any more."

What did spark women's plugs these days? He didn't dare ask Hattie's advice. For the past year the two of them had maintained a strictly professional relationship.

Shuffling papers, he spotted a petition from a large section of last year's female student body, requesting the addition of an elective course on women's studies.

"Hattie." He held up the petition. "I think we've been vigilant in updating our curriculum. We've tried to include important contributions, events, philosophies from all groups regardless of ethnicity or gender."

"Yes?"

"So why would we need a separate women's studies class?" He noted her sharply raised eyebrows. "I mean, if we're sincerely trying to appreciate the accomplishments of women in the curriculum at large, why would women want to segregate the issue? What do women want or need that's so different from what men want or need?"

She eyed him sharply without speaking, and he wondered if she didn't see clear through to his real question.

"Do you want a professional opinion or a personal one?"

He swallowed hard and took the plunge. "Personal."

"Women of any age want to be taken seriously. Need to be noticed for the whole of who and what we are." A hint of mischief warmed her eyes. "Sometimes we have to get demonstrative. With, say…petitions."

She picked up her coffee mug and turned to leave his office. Over her shoulder she added, "If I were you, I'd okay the women's studies course…and I'd pick up a big box of Chessie's favorite chocolates on your way home tonight. It's not a solution, but it's a start."

Nick rubbed his eyes. Everyone wanted to be taken seriously. To be noticed for their skills and accomplishments. Women couldn't claim that need as their own. But Chessie felt strongly enough about it that she was afraid of turning forty and faded.

How could his own red, white and blue trumpeter feel faded? She was Technicolor, for crying out loud. Neon. Hadn't he told her as much time and time again?

Hadn't he?

Hattie was right. He'd pick up chocolates on his way home from work. And he'd find out all about that pottery project the museum trustee had shown interest in—a fifteen hundred dollar interest, no less. Maybe then Chessie would forget about her ridiculous no-sex challenge.

And if she didn't? Well, Nick might just have to admit he had a problem. But wasn't solving problems his stock-in-trade?

CHESSIE SUPPRESSED A SCREAM and the urge to hose down her heel-dragging daughter, who didn't seem to care that her mother couldn't wait to hook up with the art class that would begin in fifteen minutes. Couldn't wait to be in the company of artists like herself. Self-motivated adults. As compared to her girls, who'd fought her at every turn today.

"Isabel," she said, trying desperately not to nag. "I'll be back in two hours. Your dad should be home from work by then. We can eat any time after that." With dismay she viewed the mountain of dirty Fourth-of-July dishes. Obviously, she needed to provide some impetus. Not nagging, but nudging. "You can't prepare supper, and we can't eat without clean recruits from the dish department."

"This is so unfair," the teenager complained.

"Unfair or not, dishes happen."

"But I have a headache." With a pained expression, Isabel sank against the counter.

Chessie felt no sympathy. Her elder daughter was prone to hypochondria and a sort of Victorian lethargy. "A lovely hand-soak in dishwater should cure it."

"We have to be the only house in Maine without a dishwasher. It's absolutely prehistoric."

"Nevertheless." Chessie heard Gabriella thumping down the stairs. "Ah, reinforcements. I'm sure you and your sister—" She gasped in shock.

Gabriella, whose wavy strawberry-blond hair had been her crowning glory, now sported a buzz cut with only a fringe of bangs, which she had dyed a startling lime-green.

"Gabriella!" Chessie squeaked. "What have you done?"

"Don't go ballistic." Her younger daughter shrugged. "You're not the only one in this family entitled to a little recognition."

"But your hair…" Even Isabel seemed stunned by her sister's daring.

Gabriella slouched against the door frame. "It's not as if I pierced anything."

"Oh, gawd! Just wait till Dad sees," Isabel drawled dramatically. "You do remember Dad. The principal of your school for the next four years. You might as well learn early he's a dictator when it comes to the dress code."

"It'll grow back by September."

The new Chessie bit her tongue. Let Gabby deal with her 'do and any consequences. Chessie was headed for professional development.

"Dishes and dinner, girls."

"We've got it covered," Gabriella replied, reaching into the Mason jar that held money for emergencies. "On our way back from the mall we'll stop at Boston Market and pick up supper."

More tongue biting on Chessie's part. She'd told Nick she didn't care if takeout was on the menu. "Okay," she conceded, "but feed the cats, please."

She had to leave quickly before she reverted to form.

Once outside and hustling toward the town square, she spied the Art Guild members coming out of the Atlantic Hall where the class was to convene in the huge community room above the library. "What's happening?" she called to Betsy O'Meara, a watercolorist.

"Our model canceled. She broke a leg, hiking."

Chessie's spirits fell. She had so looked forward to this, two hours of escape from worrying about her uncooperative daughters and the silent treatment Nick had given her since her declaration last night. She needed to test her fragile wings, to feel a part of a supportive like-minded community, if only temporarily. And, at this point, she didn't care how she engineered it.

"I'll take the model's place," she volunteered, jogging up to Betsy.

"You will?" The bushy white eyebrows of eighty-year-old sculptor Sandy Weston shot skyward.

"Not nude," Chessie clarified. "My college days are over. Draped will have to do. Is there anything I can use to wrap myself in?"

"Perhaps." Betsy looked dubious as she led the way up the stairs to the multipurpose room. "We share this space with so many other groups that we don't like to leave much behind. Things tend to disappear." She headed for the easels and stools pushed into the corner. "There's this backdrop fabric."

"Eew!" Glancing with dismay at the ratty piece of cloth, Chessie shivered at the thought of it against her skin. "I have an old white sheet that should make me look quite Greco-Roman. It won't take a minute to get it."

A chorus of thank-yous met her offer as she hastened downstairs and back across the square. It was the sheet she'd thrown over the studio sofa last night. Hopefully she could be in and out with it before anyone even knew she'd been back. So she didn't have to explain…. Suddenly she felt angry at herself for feeling furtive. She'd suggested posing draped, for pity's sake. Not nude. A big difference. She wasn't certain, however, that Nick would, should he hear of it, see the distinction. Well, he didn't have to hear of it.

The sheet fetched and bundled under her arm, she fairly flew back to the hall. It was so exciting to be part of an art class again.

"Chessie!" Thomas Crane, the UPS driver, called out to her from his truck parked in front of the hardware store. "Chasing Nick with leftover laundry?"

Exhilarated by the divergence from routine, she laughed. "No! I'm posing at the Art Guild," she replied over her shoulder as she gained the Atlantic Hall doorway, immediately regretting her words. Thomas was an awful gossip.

Maybe he hadn't heard her. Hope sprang eternal.

Hurrying up the stairs, she burst into the class as the members finished pushing the easels and stools into place.

Betsy came forward. "You're a love! This isn't much of a first day for you, but the rest of us appreciate it."

"No problem." Chessie ducked behind a screen set up for the model, slipped her arms out of her tank top so that it became a tube top, shed her capris and sandals, then began to drape, tuck and knot the sheet. "I'm just glad to be here. It beats making tuna casserole."

She might not be sitting behind an easel today as planned, but in front of one, she certainly wasn't invisible.

Satisfied with her impromptu toga, she emerged from behind the screen to perch on the model's stool in the center of the circle of artists. A peace descended on her as she shifted positions until the guild members chose one in particular.

The past two days hadn't gone smoothly, but she felt certain that with strength of purpose it was only a matter of time before her family realized her need for space and recognition. After that hurdle had been cleared, returning Nick to romance would be a snap.

SITTING BESIDE Felicity Kincaid in the town's one taxi, Nick pressed his foot to the floor as if he could increase the vehicle's speed from the passenger's seat. "Can't you go any faster?"

"I could," the cabbie replied, "but it would probably mean losing my license. What's the hurry anyway?"

Chessie.

Yesterday his wife had bared her soul publicly on a sandwich board. Today, according to Thomas Crane, she was planning to bare her body as well. Posing for the Art Guild.

Everyone knew that figure drawing classes used nudes. But not his nude, his wife. Call him a chauvinist, but Chessie's body was for his eyes only.

"It's a family emergency," he muttered.

"It wouldn't have to do with your wife throwing your laundry out the window, would it?"

"No." Nick bit back an oath. The laundry seemed tame compared to today's antics.

"Uh-huh." The normally loquacious cab driver seemed to suppress a grin. "We'll get you to your destination safe and sound. The Atlantic Hall, you said?"

"Right." He looked out the window as if he found the passing New England scenery fascinating, hoping Felicity would think conversation an intrusion.

Truth be told, he couldn't think straight. Chessie, with her unlikely behavior, had yanked out his emotional underpinnings, sending his senses and his thoughts reeling.

He could only await her next salvo. He'd always thought of himself as a proactive kind of guy. He hated feeling reactive.

Because Pritchard's Neck was a small community, it didn't take long before Felicity pulled up in front of the hall. Reaching in his pocket and withdrawing a twenty, Nick dropped it on the front seat, then vaulted from the taxi without waiting for change. The moment's urgency overrode any sense of frugality.

He had to get to Chessie before she took her clothes off. Or if she'd stripped already, he had to bundle her up and hustle her home, back to routine and sanity. He was prepared to bodily carry her away if necessary. Pressing through the hall's outer door, he charged up the stairs, up to the meeting room where his wife might even now be lounging in the altogether.

Chessie had posed, briefly, as a single college student. Back then, he'd thought her daring sexy. Now, the thought made him seethe. What in blazes did the woman think this stunt was going to do to two impressionable teenage daughters?

"Chessie!" His voice echoed on the upper

landing as he thrust the door to the meeting room open and caught the gaze of the lovely model in the circle of easels. Chessie. His Chessie.

She reclined against a stool, her arms, shoulders and feet bare, one slender leg emerging from the folds of a white sheet draped about her as if she was a Greek goddess. She'd swept her Titian hair up on top of her head, exposing her long, smooth neck. Surprisingly, she showed more flesh when she bicycled about town in tank top and gym shorts, but somehow the toga was more sultry, more suggestive. His wife was, in fact, unmistakably, breathtakingly beautiful.

And, having burst, like a Viking marauder on drugs, into the room full of fellow Pritchard's Neck residents, he felt the fool. Yet he still couldn't bring himself to let go of the unaccountable anger he felt.

Chessie beamed at him, then turned to the stunned little group. "It's about time to take a break, yes?"

The artists agreed with alacrity as if Nick might begin the pillage at any moment.

Swishing lightly toward him, Chessie seemed a different woman. Neither of this time or place. Certainly not the mother of two teenage girls.

For a minute Nick had thoughts of how her costume might play out in their bedroom. Abruptly, he reined in those thoughts. If he could be turned on by this getup, what about Sandy Weston over there, pretending to put the finishing touches on his sketch, or Patrick Goodall who seemed to pay a great deal of attention to the sharpening of his pencil?

Nick had always consigned jealousy to the knuckle-draggers, but now Chessie's exposure cut deep to a possessiveness he didn't know he had.

She drew him out on the landing, then closed the door behind them. "I'm assuming UPS delivered more than the usual school supplies."

"You assume right." Trying and failing to find a neutral tone of voice, he lifted the corner of her toga. "This isn't what I had in mind when you said you were joining a professional group."

"It's just for today. The model canceled. Next week I'll be on the other side of the easel. Fully clothed."

After today, with his all-too-public reaction to her participation, he didn't want her on either side of the easel with this group. He wondered if she even had anything on under that outfit.

She touched his cheek with her fingertips. Her eyes flashed mischief. "Were you about to carry me off, Nick?"

"If you were nude, yes." He felt like one of his students caught doing something rash and adolescent. And totally uncool.

"How politically incorrect," she sighed. "How impulsive. How almost romantic. Against my better judgment, I'm flattered."

She thought his actions romantic? She was flattered?

Comprehension dawned.

"So this is how you'd have me spice up our marriage?" he demanded. "Cut out of work early? Spend my last twenty on a cab? Barge like a fool into a group of residents, three of them with kids in my school?" Prickly heat rose up the back of his neck.

"You spent your last twenty on a cab?" she asked as if she hadn't heard anything else. "That's something my boyfriend Nick would do."

"Well, boyfriend Nick didn't have three

mouths to feed." He gestured toward the closed door. "That seems beside the point now. What are those people thinking?"

"Oh, for goodness' sake. They only know you're upset. We have two teenage daughters. It could be anything."

"But it was you."

"Yes." A dreamy look crept into her eyes. "You came for me—in a cab that wasn't in the budget, no less—because you were, what, intrigued? Jealous? Hot to get behind one of those easels yourself and take up a new career?"

"I was—am—ticked."

"That's better than preoccupied."

Suddenly weary, he turned away. "Don't expect me to play the town fool again to inject some fizz in a marriage that you, for some reason, seem to think has gone flat. I'm going home."

Chessie reached for him. "Just when we've begun to get to the heart of the matter?"

"Is that what you call it?" Eluding her touch, he started downstairs. "I thought we'd reached an impasse."

"You can't walk away, Nick!" She opened the door to the meeting room and called,

"Sorry, folks. Family emergency. See you next week," then followed her husband down the stairs and out the door into the town square.

Nick winced. Although he didn't pause to look over his shoulder, he could imagine how she looked, barefoot and determined, with that…that…toga flapping.

It was just his luck that Eban Hoffman, one of the local lobstermen, stood at the hardware store gas pumps, filling his pickup, watching with taciturn interest every movement on the square. Six hounds in the truck bed stood at attention as they spotted Chessie, who padded up alongside Nick.

"Would you slow down?" she asked, breathless, clutching fabric to her chest. "My sheet's unraveling."

Sure enough, great swaths of the makeshift robe flapped like pennants in the brisk coastal breeze. She was in danger of exposing more than shoulders and arms.

What did she have on under that thing?

Eban's dogs, excited by the movement, began to bark and pace the truck bed, eager to get out and join the fun. Their owner, more interested in the drama playing out before him than in controlling his dogs, stood staring and scratching his head.

Nick refused to prolong this public entertainment. With authority, he swept Chessie into his arms and began marching for the privacy of home, the sheet billowing out behind them.

"Oh, my," Chessie said as if this was just the afternoon's activity she'd had in mind.

Not about to waste breath explaining to her that his actions did not in any way constitute romance or a harbinger of marital changes to come, he picked up his pace. He simply wanted to get her off the square before disaster struck.

Too late.

"Come back he-ah this instant!" Eban shouted.

Nick heard the playful canine whines, heard the scrabble of claws on asphalt, heard the jingle of rabies tags before the dogs surrounded them. Yapping, jumping, snapping and intent on seizing whatever loose fabric they could reach in a frenzied game of tug o' war, they probably hadn't had this much fun since that crate of spider crabs got loose at the pier.

Chessie shrieked as two dogs, their toothy grip firm in a corner of trailing sheet, their eight combined feet planted in the roadside grass, threatened by sheer dog-headedness to unwrap her.

Nick broke into a jog.

Just as Eban and Hamilton Quick, owner of the hardware store, caught up with them, one of the dogs, leaped up and snapped. Instead of coming away with a prized hunk of fabric, he sank his teeth into Nick's left buttock.

CHAPTER FOUR

WERE HER PARENTS TRYING to screw up her life totally?

It sure seemed that way.

Having escaped to Keri's room, Gabriella wanted to disappear from the face of the earth. Pushing herself back into the mound of stuffed animals on her friend's bed, she tried to erase the awful memory of *them* in the square just now. Tried to focus on the perfectly normal trip to the mall beforehand. Focus on her new flavored lip gloss. On running into Danny Aiken, Keri's boyfriend. On Danny saying how phat Gabriella's haircut was...

Not on the ride home when—excruciating minutes ago—Mrs. Weiss had driven into the square and there they were: Dad carrying Mom. Mom wearing a sheet. That dog taking a bite of Dad's butt. Everybody running out of the hardware store. Yelling. Pointing.

At her parents.

They looked like they were trying out for some lame reality show.

Now, as she heard Mrs. Weiss's SUV pull out of the driveway below, taking Mom and Dad to the emergency room, she tried to think how she could make sure her parents' behavior didn't cross her new friends' radar.

Her new cool friends, thanks to Keri.

"Parents can be so…gross." Keri wasn't helping matters. If she thought Mom and Dad were gross, what would Danny think? Or Baylee Warner? Or Margot Hensley? Or anyone else in Danny's group. And now Keri's group by association.

Gabriella wanted this new crowd to be hers, as well. No such luck with her parents acting whack.

"Do you hear what I'm saying?" Keri was right in her face. "You have got to, like, prove you're not just as weird."

"As who?"

"As your parents." Keri made a face. "Wake up. You need damage control here."

As if she needed to be told.

"This is our freshman year coming up,

Gabs. Do you want to be in, or do you want to be out?"

She'd been so close to being out for the past year since moving to Pritchard's Neck. Keri had been her only real friend. Now Keri had moved into the winner's circle as Danny's girlfriend, and Gabriella knew Keri was trying not to leave her behind.

What scared Gabriella more than anything in the world was the thought of being left behind.

"Well?" Keri poked her in the ribs.

"Do I even have to answer that?"

"You'd better come up with some answers before we both find ourselves on the outside looking in." There was something like fear in Keri's eyes.

Gabriella knew Keri was on probation. Danny could only bring her so far into his circle. The group had to cast its approval, too. And if the group wanted to test Keri's loyalty by having her dump a former friend—a friend with even the whiff of geek or weirdo about her—well… The thought made Gabriella queasy.

"What can I do?"

"Make sure you're a whole lot cooler than your family."

Gabriella tried to bury herself in the stuffed animals again, but Keri yanked her upright. "The hair's a start," she said. "Brilliant even. Danny said so."

"The hair will be history by the time school starts. Remember the dress code?"

"Yeah. Your dad's dress code. Could it get any worse than your father as principal?"

"My mom, Fourth-of-July nutcase."

"Your dad, dog food."

Her dad on the way to the emergency room in Mrs. Weiss's SUV because his Volvo was AWOL and Mom's Mini Cooper was too tiny for him to lie on his stomach.

"Hey, Danny wasn't in the square, if that's what you're worried about," Gabriella pointed out in weak defense.

"No, but Kurt Ryan's dad was coming out of the hardware. And Baylee's mom works in the E.R. How soon do you figure before everyone knows?"

Gabriella pulled the comforter over her head. "I wish I was dead."

"There's no time for that." Keri pulled the cover aside. "You gotta think how to keep far away from all this before you get blackballed."

"How are we going to do that?"

Keri raised one eyebrow, and Gabriella realized there didn't have to be a *we*. This was her problem. Keri could wash her hands of it.

But Keri softened. Maybe it was because they were such good friends, or maybe Keri needed someone lower on the totem pole than her. "For the summer the hair's a good start. But we gotta keep people thinking you're out there."

Gabriella didn't feel out there. Not even with her new haircut. She felt miserable. Saddled with a lame family. And in over her head.

Keri jumped off the bed and began examining her face in her dresser mirror. "A boyfriend would be huge."

Gabriella didn't feel ready for a boyfriend. That Keri had met Danny two weeks ago at the beach and had chased him till he'd given her the time of day made Gabriella's jaw drop. She didn't want to think what Keri might've done to make Danny so loyal so quick. No, the idea of a boyfriend made Gabriella nervous.

"Boyfriends take time," she replied. "I need something quick."

"You gotta be fearless. You gotta act as if you don't care what your parents think."

Easy for Keri to say. She was an only child.

Her mom treated her more like a girlfriend than a daughter, and her dad treated her like a princess.

"You suggesting I start smoking and hanging around street corners?" Gabriella asked sarcastically.

"No," Keri replied, serious. "Everybody smokes and hangs around street corners. You need to be awesome. A standout. Plus, you don't need to waste attitude on just anybody. Save it for when you're hanging around Baylee or Margot or Kurt."

"As in?"

"As in when we're at the mall together, you might lift a lip gloss rather than pay for it."

"Shoplift? I don't need to steal." Besides, it was wrong. Just wrong. And Keri should know better. Gabriella's father might be a principal, but Keri's was a cop.

"Nobody needs to shoplift. It's just for kicks." Keri narrowed her eyes. "But you're right. You don't need to do it. It's not original. You need something fresh."

Something beyond smoking and theft? Gabriella didn't like the sound of the words *fearless* or *fresh*. "Couldn't I aim for something like best dressed?"

Keri looked at Gabriella's outfit. "Not when your mom makes your tops and you buy your jeans at a discount store. We're gonna take care of that, don't you worry, but first we gotta come up with a rep for you."

Gabriella's family hadn't stayed in one place long enough for her to get a reputation. She was always just the new kid.

"How about smart?"

"In high school?" Keri made as if to slit her throat. "Look at your sister, the brainy poet. Just another word for nerd."

If Isabel was a nerd, was Gabriella? She thought of her dad. Not making the honor roll had never been an option in their family. "Funny?"

"Funny walks a thin line with stupid. Some people might think what happened in the square this afternoon was funny. Do you want to be known that way?"

Gabriella absolutely did not.

"Don't worry." Keri flopped on the bed beside her. "I'm going to make you over this summer. I'm not a hundred percent sure how, but by the time school starts, everyone's going to be asking who Gabriella McCabe is. Hey, maybe not Gabriella!" Keri jumped to her feet. "Maybe Tiffany. Or Brianna. Or Kayla. Have you thought of changing your name?"

"Why?"

"'Cause Gabriella sounds like an old lady, and Gabby sounds like a cowboy on the retro western channel."

Change her name? Her parents would freak. "I don't know—"

"You don't know?" Her friend's look turned harsh. "Do you want to consider your options? Like the losers' lunch table? It's no different in high school than it was in junior high. Maybe worse."

That table with the fat kids. The picked-on, misunderstood and unattractive kids. The ones who fit in with no group whatsoever except losers. In a couple schools she'd been one of them.

She wasn't going back to that table. Not ever. A new name and identity suddenly appealed to her.

"Aside from picking a name, what do I have to do?"

"Nothing yet." Keri slipped her arm around Gabriella's shoulders. "Just leave everything to me."

With her future in Keri's hands, Gabriella's

thoughts slipped back to her parents. She wondered if her father had made it to the emergency room yet. And hoped that Baylee's mom wasn't on duty this afternoon.

"WOULD MUSIC HELP?" Martha asked from the driver's seat.

"No." Lying on his stomach in the back of the Weisses' SUV, Nick spoke between clenched teeth. "Thank you."

This day had turned out to be—literally— one big pain in the ass.

"We're almost there, honey," Chessie reassured him. "I can see the sign for the emergency room."

"Just drop me off." He knew the E.R. took cases in order of severity. Dog bite would be way down the priority list. He didn't need two women—one he was royally ticked at— hovering over him for a couple hours. "I'll call a cab when I'm done."

"Nonsense," Martha countered cheerfully. "You'll need moral support."

He thought he heard a suppressed giggle.

Shifting his weight, he groaned at the stab of pain. Cautiously, he felt his backside. The bleeding seemed to have stopped, but his trousers—his new trousers—were ripped badly, and the fabric stuck to his skin with what he could only assume was dried blood. He'd have to walk into the E.R. with an immodest patch of himself hanging out.

"Do you have anything I could tie around my waist?" he asked. "Just so I don't give the world a free show."

"Hold on," Martha replied, pulling to a stop under the hospital portico.

The back doors to the SUV opened, and Chessie handed him the sheet she'd been wearing. He nearly threw his back out, turning to see what she had on. A tank top and a pair of jeans with the store labels still hanging off them.

"Martha let me wear a pair she picked up at the mall," she explained. "Wrap the sheet around you."

"I'm not wearing that damned sheet." He struggled to slide backward out of the SUV. "What else do you have?"

"This," Martha replied briskly, tying a huge plastic Macy's bag around his waist. Empty, it flapped behind him like half a loincloth. "Now, lean on your wife. I'm going to park the car and wait in it. I picked up plenty of new magazines today, so don't think I'm in a rush."

Chessie threaded her arm under his and across his back, but he pulled away. "I don't need help."

"Nick, I'm sorry. No one could've anticipated this."

As he limped ahead of her through the emergency entrance, he winced at the pain dogging his every step. Warm moisture trickling down the back of his thigh told him the wound had reopened.

"May I help you?" the nurse behind the desk asked.

"A dog bit me," Nick replied. "I think I need stitches."

The nurse handed him a clipboard with a form attached. "Do you know if the dog had been immunized for rabies?"

"The owner assured me it had." Call that the only plus in this doggone day.

"Fill out the form, and a doctor will look at you as soon as possible." The nurse motioned to a row of chairs against the wall. "You can have a seat over there."

"He can't." Chessie pointed to his backside. "Sit, that is."

"Chessie," he growled, grabbing the clipboard. He headed for the corner.

"Mr. McCabe! What you doin' in here?"

Nick turned slowly to see Chris Filmore, the high school's star running back, hobbling on crutches out of the examination area. A bright white cast covered his left leg. The sight did not bode well for the upcoming football season.

"What happened, Chris?"

"Broke my leg." The kid looked sheepish. "Playing Frisbee at the beach. What are you in for?"

"A dog bit me."

"Where?"

"In the square."

"No, man. I mean where did he bite you?"

How did a high-school principal refer to that particular part of the anatomy with a student?

As Chris surveyed the plastic shopping bag draped over Nick's backside, understanding crept into his face. "Oh, the glute." The corner of his mouth twitched. "And here I was feelin' embarrassed."

"Glad I could ease your pain," Nick muttered and held up the clipboard to signal the end of the conversation.

"See you in September." Chris headed for the exit, amusement lacing his farewell.

Chessie stood wide-eyed before Nick.

"I suppose you find this all very funny, too," he said.

"I don't see humor in someone else's discomfort…but getting all tense isn't going to help the situation."

"Thank you, Doctor." He wedged himself in the corner of the waiting room and, standing, began to fill out the patient information sheet. It wasn't her butt all bruised and bleeding under a red, white and blue sale bag.

"I'm going to call the girls." She backed away. "Can I get you a soda?"

"No." He kept writing. The fluorescent glare made his head hurt.

When she left, he felt suddenly smaller that he was hanging on to his anger. He felt weary, too. Bone weary. He handed the completed form back to the desk nurse.

An hour and forty-five minutes later, he lay facedown on an examination table as a cheerful young resident stitched up his backside. "So, Mr. McCabe," she said, "how'd you happen to anger this particular dog?"

"He was rescuing me," Chessie piped up

from her spot at his head. "From a very large pack."

"Ah, a hero."

"Just a high-school principal," Nick replied. He'd given up rising to any bait.

"A high-school principal? How's your work schedule for next week?"

"I can't take it off if that's what you're asking."

"No. I was just curious how many meetings you have to attend."

"Way too many."

"Well, you're going to have to attend standing up. I don't think even a hemorrhoid doughnut would give you any relief."

Fine. He was going to have to do enough explaining as it was. He didn't need a shiny red rubber prop to add to the merriment.

"There. Finished." The resident backed away. "Mrs. McCabe, you're going to have to make sure this wound is kept—"

"I can handle it." Nick gingerly found the floor and stood.

"Not unless you have eyes in the back of your head," the resident countered. "Besides, you have a bigger task."

"What?"

"Thinking up a list of snappy comebacks." The woman flashed him a bright smile. "No doubt, you're going to be the butt of a lot of jokes this week."

"And you wanted to inaugurate the agony."

"My pleasure."

He pushed aside the curtain that separated him from his fellow E.R. sufferers and moved stiffly toward the exit. His left cheek felt numb. He no longer cared that the protective Macy's bag lay at the bottom of a hazardous waste can. He just wanted to get home. What he really wanted was a return to the day before the Fourth of July.

"Isabel said they saved us some of the dinner they picked up at Boston Market," Chessie informed him as she followed him to the parking lot.

"I'm not hungry."

"How long are you going to stay angry at me?"

"If you don't mind, I don't feel up for a long drawn-out discussion."

"What's really going on here, Nick?"

He stopped short of the SUV where Martha sat reading a magazine. Damn, he'd forgotten the neighbors were involved. He turned to his wife. "What's going on here? Frankly, I don't know. You seem to be the one with all the answers. Trouble is, I don't understand them."

He opened the double doors at the back of the SUV, and crawled in.

Feeling shut out, Chessie climbed in the passenger side.

"How'd it go?" Martha asked.

"He'll live."

"But will Eban's dog?"

"No jokes, Martha," Nick said from the back. He sounded like a principal presiding at a rowdy assembly. "I've reached my quota."

When Martha shot Chessie a questioning look, Chessie mouthed, "Later."

They rode home in silence. Nick didn't forget to thank Martha, but he didn't stick around for Chessie to follow him into the house.

"Call me if you need anything," Martha said before backing across the street into her own driveway.

It was eight-forty and starting to get dark, but there wasn't a light in the house. Chessie entered the kitchen to stare at a sink full of Fourth-of-July dishes and a table littered with paper plates and containers of half-consumed takeout. The girls were nowhere in sight.

She made her way upstairs. All three bedroom doors were closed. She knocked on the closest. Gabriella's.

"Go away!"

"Gabby, what's wrong?"

"As if you didn't know."

Chessie did know. Having witnessed the debacle on the square, her younger daughter would be mortified. She tried the knob only to find the door locked.

"I said go away."

Perhaps they all needed a little breathing room. A little perspective. But she couldn't resist the urge to reassure herself her family was at least minimally okay.

Isabel's door was cracked a hair and gave when Chessie knocked. Her older daughter, sprawled on her bed with the ubiquitous headphones stuck over her ears, sat up and turned off her CD player when her mother poked her head in the room.

"Are you and Dad all right?"

"He's just a little sore from the stitches."

"I mean are the two of you okay? You know…"

"Sure we are. It's just been a rough day."

Isabel looked down into her lap. "It's kind've been a rough year."

"How do you mean, sweetie?" Chessie sat on the edge of the bed.

"I don't know. I thought moving here would be easier. What with all the aunts and uncles and cousins. I thought you and Dad would be more, well, happy."

"It's been an adjustment for all of us." Chessie brushed a lock of hair from her daughter's eyes. She worried too much about things beyond her control. "But it's only going to get better. I promise."

Isabel turned soulful eyes on her mother. "Why did you go on strike? I don't understand."

"A strike is a negotiating tool. I'm trying to negotiate new family dynamics. I want you and Gabby and Dad to see me as the woman I am. An individual. I want you and Gabby to be strong and independent individuals, too. Enough to implement drastic measures."

"I don't know...."

"Know this. I love you all very much." Unwilling to engage in any more dramatic discourse, she gave Isabel a quick peck on the cheek.

Although Isabel didn't appear reassured, Chessie needed to touch base with her husband. They'd already gone to bed once without making up. She didn't want to go for a second straight night.

In the master bedroom Nick seemed to be asleep already. In fresh boxer shorts, he lay on his stomach diagonally across the bed, leaving no space for Chessie.

"Nick?" she said softly.

He didn't open his eyes. Didn't move or reply.

"I love you. I really do," she added, in case he was feigning sleep, and backed out of the room.

She headed for a good long think in her studio, which, although cluttered, was far more orderly than the house. After no more than five minutes behind the potter's wheel, she was startled to see someone in a Red Sox cap out of the corner of her eye.

"Friend or foe?" she demanded.

"Friend, I hope." Martha stood at the top of the stairwell. "Is it safe to come up? I brought coffee—decaf—and cinnamon buns." Martha made the very best cinnamon buns in southern Maine.

"Throw the buns up here, then go away!"

"Go chase yourself." Martha popped above the landing. "Just because you throw a mean jockstrap, you think you're better than the rest of us desperate housewives."

Chessie stopped work on the free-form clay prototype before her, a project she'd already entitled "Her Head Was in the Goddess Movement, but Her Feet Were Firmly Planted in the PTA." It was the piece the trustee at the Portland Museum of Art had expressed an interest in. "How'd you know I was up here?"

"Saw your light." Martha placed the plate of cinnamon buns and the coffeepot on the lobster trap that served as a table.

Reaching for two handmade mugs on a nearby shelf, Chessie sighed. "I sure could use a cigarette."

"You don't smoke."

"Yeah, well, I sure need something."

"Chessie, what's going on over here?"

"I'm not sure any more."

"I don't mean to pry...."

"Hell, there's no prying when I've put it out in public for everyone to see."

"The laundry."

"And the picket sign, yeah."

"And the dog bite."

"I don't take responsibility for that." Chessie sat on the lumpy sofa next to Martha and poured two cups of coffee. "Nick stuck his nose where he shouldn't have."

"What is it you want—really want—out of all this?"

"Respect. Attention. Space. Hey, it shifts with the moment." She rubbed her eyes. "After two days I'm not sure any more."

"Then apologize to your husband. Get it over with and move on."

Startled, Chessie looked at Martha.

"So you made a mistake," her friend continued. "Being stubborn isn't going to make it better."

"Capitulating isn't going to either. Besides, I don't think the strike is a mistake. Nick and I have talked more in the past couple of days than we have in the past few months."

"If you say so…but your confrontational stance makes it seem as if you see Nick as the enemy."

"No, this isn't a war."

"What is it then? Be fair to yourself, Chessie,

as well as your family. You need to be very clear about what you want before you draw a line in the sand."

"I want—I need—to be a part of this family, yes. A part of a couple, as well. But I also want to be seen as an individual. Not just someone who serves a function, a cog in the wheel."

"So this is less like a tantrum, more like a cause." Martha raised her fist in a militant salute. " 'I will not be a doormat!' I heard you."

"They needed a wake-up call."

"So you gave it. Now chill. Let a few things slide. Forgive them and start over."

"It's not about forgiveness." Chessie frowned as she blew on her hot coffee. "It's a matter of re-education. And that's not a one-step process."

"Uh-oh. You mean there's more coming?" Martha looked dubious.

"This is serious." Chessie had hoped for more support from her friend. She bit into a sticky bun and let the heavenly jolt of carbs give her a lift. "I haven't been a doormat exactly. I didn't do for Nick and the girls because they made me, or even because of any sense of duty. Sure, Nick and I planned a traditional family life, but I pampered them because I loved doing it. I didn't realize I was spoiling them and they were taking me for granted. I expected more from them. The fact that they don't reciprocate hurts. There are times I could use a little spoiling."

"Aw, don't be so hard on the girls," Martha urged. "If it's the laundry you're worried about, don't go there. All teenagers are slobs. It's not a worthy battle."

Keri was a great kid—smart and popular—but Martha and her husband, George, seemed to see her as a buddy. And sometimes Chessie winced at the things Keri got away with.

"It's more than laundry," Chessie insisted. "Gabby and Izzie have grown too dependent on me."

Suddenly on a roll, she sat up ramrod-straight. "And why should I ask for their help? Our family's a community. They shouldn't think of work around the house as helping out poor old Mom. Each and every task should be the equal responsibility of each and every family member."

"Perhaps…"

"No perhaps about it. I feel undervalued and overwhelmed. When we lived in Georgia, I heard a wise expression. 'When Mama ain't happy, ain't nobody happy.' Well, I ain't happy, Martha."

She saw genuine concern in Martha's face. "So what would make you happy?"

"One, I want my family to see my pottery as more than some little hobby. It's Nick's turn to support me. As an artist. This is the first move where I've had space to start a business, and I want to give it a try. Two, the girls need to see me as strong and purposeful, a mentor. Not their personal housekeeper."

"Hmm…" Martha didn't look convinced. "Maybe they need a friend as much as a mentor. I know if I came down on Keri like a drill sergeant, she'd be impossible."

"Am I really expecting too much of them?"

"If Nick weren't principal of their school, would you be so worried that his kids weren't perfect?"

Chessie inhaled sharply. "You may have a point." Nick's career had always been about more than just the job. It was always about community service and family values and reputation. And Nick wanted that reputation spotless. "Sometimes I feel as if we're under a microscope. We can't be just us. Nick and

I are more like a public institution. We seem to have lost the art of being a private couple, able to live on our own terms."

"He certainly loves you. You can see it in his eyes when he's with you."

"Yes, but does he love me madly, passionately, recklessly?"

"How many years have you been married?"

"That shouldn't matter."

"Be reasonable, Chess. You have a solid marriage. Security. Two things many women would envy. Nick's an upright man. A good provider and dad. And easy on the eyes."

"I know I have a good marriage." For the tiniest of moments, Chessie felt guilty about not being satisfied. "I simply want it to be better. Hell, I want it to be great."

"How are you going to get Nick to understand that without hurting his feelings? Without pushing him away? How are you going to win the battle without losing the war?"

Wasn't that the big question in any revolution? Chessie tried to subdue the niggling doubt in her gut.

CHAPTER FIVE

THE NEXT MORNING, carrying a shredded newspaper she'd fished out of the rambling rosebush, Chessie stumbled into the house. She'd fallen asleep on the sofa in her studio again. Another night like that, and she'd be ready for the chiropractor. Another night like that and her no-sex ultimatum would be a nonissue.

Gabriella and Keri, both dressed in bathing suits, were sitting at the kitchen table, picking at leftovers from last night's takeout and talking in excited whispers. They stopped when Chessie entered the room.

"You'll make yourself sick," Chessie remarked, unable to keep quiet. "That food hasn't been refrigerated."

Gabriella shot Keri a bored look.

"You're both up early," Chessie continued. "What do you have planned for the day?"

"We're going to bike to the beach," Keri replied.

"Just the two of you?"

A look of irritation passed over Keri's face. "We're going to meet some friends there."

"Do I know them?"

"Mom!" Gabriella's face flamed red. "Mrs. Weiss has met all of them. Now stop the third degree."

Chessie reached for the coffeepot. It seemed to be the only clean utensil in the kitchen. She remembered Martha's advice to let some things slide, and decided to cross the picket line for just a moment. "Let's clear away this food and do up these dishes. Together."

Gabriella glared at her.

"Since we're biking, we really wanted to get an early start," Keri said sweetly.

"We all have things we want to do today—"

"Okay!" Gabriella jumped from her seat. "If it will get me out of this house, I'll do the dishes. Keri, you can dry."

Keri's eyes grew wide. "They're not my dishes," she said in a low deliberate voice.

"But if they don't get done," Gabriella replied just as deliberately, "we won't be able to…go to the beach."

Gabriella's pointed look to her friend made Chessie wonder if the two were up to more than beaching.

"Morning." At Nick's terse greeting, Chessie turned to see him enter the kitchen, dressed in a three-piece suit. The summer schedule in the district required little more than casual attire.

"You look handsome," she offered.

"When I explain why I won't be sitting for a week, I figured I needed to look as dignified as possible."

"Good plan." She kissed him on the cheek, disappointed when he flinched. "Coffee will be ready in a sec."

"I'll get some at work. Could you drive me to John's to pick up the Volvo?"

"But you can't lie down in the Mini. Let me call Martha—"

"No!" He nodded at a pillow on the floor next to his briefcase. "If I stand at work all day, I'm sure I can tolerate five minutes sitting in the car. I'm not going to arrive at school backing out of the cargo space of my neighbor's SUV."

"Fair enough. Let me get my keys."

Knowing this injury wounded his pride more than anything else, she wanted to hug him. But the stiff set of his shoulders warned her off. As much as she needed the hug, he'd simply need a good routine day at work.

In her second concession of the morning, she allowed him his space. As she retrieved her keys and silently headed for her car, Nick, just as silently, followed.

When they pulled into John's service center, she could see the Volvo parked off to the side, something written in white on the rear window. She dropped Nick at the office, then pulled up next to his car. In paint kids used to write school spirit slogans all over their cars before football games, someone had written Go Dawgs! and drawn a cartoon bulldog, the school mascot. Except this bulldog held a ripped pair of pants between his clenched teeth.

Before she could rub out the graffiti, Nick walked over, and Chessie knew any chance of a routine day for him had evaporated.

GABRIELLA AND KERI pedaled their bicycles not toward the beach but to Baylee Warner's house.

"Are you sure her parents aren't going to be home?" Gabriella asked, a nervous knot in the pit of her stomach. Maybe Mom had been right about those leftovers.

"Positive. Both her parents work. Baylee's watching her little sister this summer, but she's at soccer camp today. We'll have the house to ourselves."

"I don't know about all this…"

"Look, if you're going to hang with me and my friends this year, you have to prove you're up to it. Getting into the Surf Club this Saturday will prove it for sure."

"Why the Surf Club?"

"'Cause mostly summer people and tourists hang there. Less chance someone will know our parents."

"And Baylee's going to make us look twenty-one? In your dreams." Gabriella actually hoped Baylee couldn't perform this particular miracle—the dress rehearsal was today—because, as much as she needed to be accepted, she was afraid to sneak into the over-twenty-one beach club. What if they got caught? "In case you've forgotten, we're fourteen."

"So? Half those models in *Marie Claire*

are under eighteen." Keri pedaled on. "You won't believe what Baylee can do. I've seen her secret stash of clothes and makeup."

If Baylee's stash was secret, Gabriella didn't want to ask where she'd got it.

"Margot's gonna be there, too. We're all going Saturday night."

Gabriella giggled nervously. "Girls' night out?"

"Oh, sure. Sometimes you can be so dense."

"What do you mean?"

"The guys are meeting us there. Our job is to look hot. They're getting everyone fake ID."

Gabriella sucked in air. Things were going too far, too fast.

"You chicken?" Keri stared at her. "I could always ask someone else. Margot and Baylee already have dates. Danny's gonna fix you up—if you want in—with Kurt Ryan."

"Omigod, he's so fierce!"

"It's just a fix-up. Nothing permanent. Unless you can convince him you're all that and then some." Keri turned into Baylee's driveway with Gabriella following. "Your friends can only do so much, Gabs. You gotta do the rest."

Baylee opened the door before the girls could knock. "I am so excited I could pee my pants." She gave Gabriella the once-over. "I gotta say I didn't think you had the stuff. But when Keri told me about your idea to sneak into the Surf Club, well, I thought, totally bitchin'."

Keri had told Baylee this was her idea?

"Come on upstairs. You're going to love your options." Baylee led the way to her bedroom. "Nobody's here, so you get to see my collection in all its glory."

Gabriella inhaled sharply as she looked around a room draped in piles of the latest outfits, accessories, makeup and lingerie. "What do you earn babysitting your sister?"

Baylee made a face. "Are you for real?"

"She's just kidding," Keri snapped, heading for a gorgeous pink lace bra Gabriella had seen in Victoria's Secret. She remembered it cost fifty-five dollars.

"Picked that little number up on a particularly good day at the mall." Baylee smiled angelically. "I even have a couple Wonder Bras for those of us who need a little extra."

"Dibs on this," Keri said, clutching the pink bra. "With this!" She held up a sheer turquoise blouse. "And this." A black paisley miniskirt.

Gabriella's mouth dropped open. Her parents would kill her if she went out in public dressed in any of those.

"But what about Gabs?" Keri turned toward her with a critical eye. "I think we need to concentrate on her first."

Baylee ran a hand over Gabriella's buzz cut. "Let's work from the hair. She needs to look tough but tender, if you know what I mean. I'm thinking biker chick meets Catholic schoolgirl. Make those old dudes checking ID drool all over themselves."

Gabriella suddenly felt unsure of her haircut. She'd done it to upset her parents. She hadn't anticipated she'd have to fill a role with her peers. "I was thinking more sophisticated. Maybe the hair needs toning down. If you had a wig—"

"You're too funny!" Baylee circled her as Keri dug through the clothes strewn about the room.

"This is so simple it's brilliant," Keri said, holding up a plaid pleated miniskirt, a plain white tank top, a man's tie and a pair of strappy sandals with four-inch heels.

"And no makeup except big sixties eyes," Baylee squealed. "Absolutely no one will recognize you."

Good. Because if they did, and her parents found out, Gabriella would be grounded till she was fifty.

STANDING IN HIS OFFICE at four that afternoon, Nick flicked paint dust off the sleeve of his suit. Despite the fact that he'd been brushing at his clothes all day, those minute flakes kept recurring like a bad case of dandruff. Earlier at the service center, Chessie and John had ordered him to stand back as they'd used old rags to erase most of the graffiti on his Volvo. He knew they were trying to do him a favor by hurrying, but he wished they'd used water. He and his custodians had far too much experience with the temporary water-based paint and soap concoction. It washed right off, but when it was dry erased, it turned into a static nightmare.

His suit badly needed a trip to the dry cleaners. So much for dignified.

Hattie—the one person who hadn't acknowledged with a grin or a nudge or a comment the McCabe family events of the past two days—came into the office and closed the door behind her. "Do you have time to see Richard Filmore?"

Richard was president of the board of education and a stickler for detail. Nick didn't know if he had enough energy this late in a very long day to engage in a debate with the man. But, then again, Nick was paid to engage in any debate that involved educating the town's children. "Send him in," he said at last.

"Coffee?" Hattie's eyes were filled with sympathy.

"I shouldn't."

"You look like you could use it."

"What the hell." What he could really use was a vacation. Or an extra pair of hands. Or a few uninterrupted minutes with his wife to sort out their differences. They appeared to have differences that hadn't even registered on his radar. There had been a tension in the house this morning, and he didn't like it. And not just with Chessie. With Gabriella and Isabel—

"Nick?"

He looked up to see Richard standing before him, two cups of coffee in his hands. "Hattie sent these in."

"Sorry. Lost in thought." He motioned to the seat across from his desk. "Make yourself comfortable. I'll need to stand."

"So I heard." Richard sat, then put one cup on Nick's blotter. "You must have a lot on your mind."

"Yeah. Filling the last few positions is the biggest headache. I can't seem to find a Latin teacher—"

"I was talking about your personal life." Richard leaned forward in his seat. "I like to think of our school system as one big family. As president of the board, it's my job to see that all the members are happy. Are you and Chessie happy here, Nick?"

That was a loaded question if he'd ever heard one.

"We are."

"I thought so, too. Your first year has been remarkable."

"I hear a 'but.'"

"No buts. I just want you to remain happy. You. And your wife."

"Chessie's fine," he said, trying to keep the edge out of his voice. "She's starting a pottery business. The girls are fine, too," he added in an attempt to steer the conversation. "They're both looking forward to the start of classes."

"I'm sorry, but I'm going to have to be

blunt." Richard put down his cup, rubbed his hands together. He looked uneasy. "Chessie seems to be a little…dissatisfied of late."

"If she's dissatisfied, it's with me." Nick didn't like acknowledging that much, but, as a public servant, he'd always been under scrutiny. "It doesn't have anything to do with this move. Or with my job."

"I don't mean to make you uncomfortable, Nick, but Chessie made it an issue with your job when she made her dissatisfaction so…public."

"Chessie's an artist. She can be very dramatic."

"Some people are concerned that she's… come a bit unglued."

"It's none of 'some people's' business."

"I'm not here to judge. I just stopped by to remind you the board provides our families with an excellent health care package…and that includes mental health."

"You think my wife is crazy?"

"No. No, I don't. But recent events have made her appear…let me return to my original description, for lack of a better word, dissatisfied. And counseling can very often put things back on track."

"We don't need counseling. We need time to sit down and talk, but time has been at a premium this past year. Chessie was trying to get my attention."

"I understand, but you have to understand how small towns—"

"Chessie and I grew up in this small town."

"Then you know that as much as people here live and let live, they're pretty eager to find out just how the other guy's living." Richard sighed heavily. "You're a wonderful principal. I'd hate to give the perennial malcontents who hang around board meetings any grist for their mill."

"This is nothing, Richard. Chessie, the girls and I are fine. You're married. You have kids." In fact Chris, the football running back who'd broken his leg, was Richard's son. "You know the ups and downs of family life."

"Only too well." Richard shook his head. "But we're in the public eye. We have to be careful."

"Point taken. But don't worry, everything's under control."

"Then give Chessie my best." Richard stood. "I hope to see her at the pops concert on Saturday."

Nick had forgotten about it. He hoped Chessie's strike didn't mean she wouldn't be at his side. "See you there," he replied with more confidence than he felt.

He hated this limbo of uncertainty. Hated, too, that at a time when he should be focusing his energies into laying the foundation for a new school year, he was caught in a web of damage control in his personal life.

Normally, he'd head out for a run to clear his head. But the stitches in his left cheek wouldn't allow it. Not a man to do much talking outside work, he felt an unaccustomed urge to talk to someone. He should talk to Chessie, but their conversations of late had only confused things more. His father? His brothers? He'd been on his own and away long enough that coming to them now with personal issues seemed cry-babyish. And he'd always been the strong one. Maybe the fewer words the better.

"Your wife is on line one," Hattie said over the intercom.

Nick pressed the button for line one and picked up the receiver. "Chess?"

"Hey, how's it going?"

"I've had better days."

"That's why I thought—since it's your night to cook—we could just have pizza."

His night to cook? Was she still serious about that rotation? "Okay," he said, irritated but not willing to begin another battle. "I'll order it before I leave, so it arrives just as I'm getting home."

Home. Before, always a safe haven. Now, somehow a minefield.

As CHESSIE WASHED the clay off her hands at the sink in the corner of her studio, she read the computer printout tacked to the wall. It was the roster for the pottery class she'd begin teaching next Monday, and it was a sizable enrollment, the best ever. If things kept up, she'd be able to divert a little of her earnings from the girls' college fund to getting the barn's first floor ready to open as a gallery. She wiped her hands on the back of her jeans and headed downstairs.

She didn't want to alter the space too drastically. It shouldn't be cluttered. The simple, rustic interior would show off her handcrafted crockery and her free-form sculpture to advantage. She really only needed some lumber for shelving. Penn and

Jonas had volunteered their carpentry skills. She and her sister-in-law Emily had picked up several antique tables at the flea market. And Emily's husband, Brad, said he'd gladly wire some track lighting. It was amazing how the various members of the McCabe family had supported her dream while her husband had just now realized she had one—

Chessie caught herself. He couldn't know what her dreams were if she didn't share them. It was hard to believe she'd told his family so much more than she'd told him. But somehow she always seemed to get pushed aside as they talked about Nick's job and the girls' lives. The new assertive Chessie needed to communicate to her husband.

Hugging herself at the thought of the expansion of her pottery enterprise, she twirled around to find Nick standing in the doorway.

"You were on my mind," she said, moving across the floor to wind her arms around his neck. "Kiss me."

He bent to administer a dutiful peck on the tip of her nose.

"A real kiss."

"Chessie, I'm tired."

Oh, no. He wasn't going to get off the hook that easily.

She pulled him to her and sought his mouth. Feeling slightly wanton for a wife of eighteen years and a mom of teenagers, she ran her tongue over his lips. Trailed her fingers down his neck to his tie. Loosened the knot. Pulled him even closer and deepened the kiss to where she felt warm and a little dizzy and not at all motherly. Nick was—when he let himself go—a great kisser. And surprisingly, he let himself go now. Held her tight. Prolonged the kiss.

When they came up for air, his eyes were glassy. "Now that's a welcome home."

"I couldn't agree more." Her arms around his waist, she laid her head on his shoulder. "You're home early."

"The day just kind of wore itself out. Richard Filmore stopping by put the cap on it."

"What did he want?" She felt him tense immediately.

"He wanted to know if he'd see us at the band camp's pops concert Saturday night."

"Why wouldn't he?"

"I don't know." Nick stepped back. "Would you go with me? I'm not quite sure what the parameters of this strike are."

"Are you asking me on a date?"

For a minute it appeared he might pull away altogether. But the lines at the corners of his eyes eased. "Would you like that?"

"Hmm. I hear the theme is big band music, dancing under the stars. I do love dancing."

"My dancing's definitely rusty."

"Oh, did you ever dance?"

One corner of his mouth twitched. "In another life."

"Let's see if we can resurrect you." She tugged on his tie so that he had to bend. So that she could sample another hot kiss. Just as he seemed to warm to this departure from the routine, she stepped away with a flirtatious grin. "Pizza's here."

Walking out of the barn to the delivery car, she hoped her husband was watching. The little extra sway in her backside was for him.

AFTER SUPPER Nick submerged himself in paperwork. After that kiss in the barn earlier, Chessie was disappointed he didn't want to spend a little time with her, especially since the project he was working on was her particular nemesis. The staff field day.

Every year, in every school where Nick had held an administrative position, he'd hosted a staff field day mid-summer. His idea. For teachers, administrators, para-professionals, custodians and lunchroom staff, the day was a series of physical and mental challenges designed to build team effort, mutual respect and trust in a fun environment. Nick went to a great deal of trouble to schedule a day when just about everyone could come, since it was voluntary. He promised his staff that anyone who gave up one vacation day for this event would reap the benefits of better team spirit throughout the school year. And they always did. That's why his people made an effort to show up.

Except Chessie. Every year he'd asked her to come with him. But because none of the other families attended and because she was an absolute klutz when it came to organized physical activities, she always declined. She knew he was disappointed, but she wouldn't humiliate herself. Or him. Or take the focus off the staff.

But the amount of time and research and scheduling and effort this monster of a project—wholly outside of his contract—took made Chessie view it as Nick's mistress.

She needed to step away from the competition.

Gabriella had gone to spend the night with Keri. Isabel was in her room, filling out applications to college. So Chessie decided to take a walk and visit Kit. If anyone could think outside the box and offer a fresh perspective on the situation Chessie had dug herself into, it would be this particular sister-in-law.

The evening air was softly redolent of marsh roses, and the walk down the Pier Road refreshed her with every step. At the head of the harbor, she stopped to watch the boats riding gently at their moorings. Yachts seemed to outnumber lobster boats three to one, making her think of a conversation she'd overheard in Branson's grocery about lobster fishing becoming increasingly squeezed with regulations, of lobstermen becoming a dying breed. She thought of her brother-in-law Sean and wondered how he was doing. While Nick had chased his living around the country, Sean had remained in their hometown, unfazed by climbing a career ladder.

On more than one occasion, Chessie had envied his decision.

"Chessie!" The call echoed from across the narrow head of the harbor.

Squinting into the setting sun, she could make out Kit on the wharf behind the Mc-Cabe lobster pound, surrounded by a colorful flotilla of kayaks, part of her summer coastal exploration business. She returned the greeting, then trotted around the bend.

"Hey, there!" Kit called as Chessie skirted the family pound to the wharf behind. "I can use some help."

"What are you doing?"

"Midseason maintenance."

Chessie grabbed a sponge out of a soapy bucket of water. "You look as if you're rescuing beached whales." She looked at the kayaks' bright colors. "Psychedelic whales. Beached during an acid flashback."

"Your imagination's more vivid than Alex's."

"Where is she? And Sean?"

"Playing poker with Adele Jenkins and Penn."

"For money?"

"For matchsticks."

"I was going to say, you and Sean could retire early." Alex's gaming skills were prodigious.

Kit chuckled. "What are you doing out and about without your brood?"

"I needed to talk to a person who might not think I'm nuts."

"So, the strike's still on?"

"Sort of." Chessie scrubbed hard at a dried patch of algae on the bottom of a yellow kayak. "Let's just say my revolution has developed a mind of its own."

"Ah."

"You sound as if you expected as much."

"I certainly know the danger of best-laid plans." Kit stopped working. "Last year I came back to Pritchard's Neck to settle my mother's affairs. Period. Today I stand before you a married woman with a nine-year-old daughter."

"Are you complaining?"

"Absolutely not. All I'm saying is sometimes you have to hold on and enjoy the ride."

"I think I could handle that, but Nick…"

"Needs to have a plan. Sean, too. When we first got together, he didn't like the feeling of losing control. Of his emotions, really."

"Is he any better at it? You sure have brought some changes to his life."

"Sure, he's adapted. But we're still honeymooning. He'd do anything for me. Ask again in twenty-five years."

Chessie sighed. "It's eighteen years for us, and I don't think Nick has ever really let go. It doesn't help that he's always had such a buttoned-down job."

"Is he getting grief for your performance?"

"That's the thing. I'm sure he is, but he isn't telling me. With me he's just prickly and distant. And getting worse."

"Maybe you intimidate him."

"Me?"

"Intimidate might not be the word. Threaten? Confuse?" Kit furrowed her brow in thought. "Are you angry with Nick?"

"No. I'm just trying to start a dialogue."

"Well, I bet he's translating your actions as anger. Men seem to think in terms of unequivocal emotion. It'd be a normal male response to erect a protective wall if he felt confused or threatened."

"But I've told him I'm not angry."

"Maybe you have to show him."

"I'm not following you."

"You know the old saying about catching more flies with honey." As she crouched by a kayak, soapy water dripping from the sponge in her hand, Kit shook her head. "I'm no expert in the art of sweetness, but you might be able to pull it off."

"What are you talking about?"

"I'm guessing you're waiting for Nick to make some moves. To fulfill some of those needs you mentioned on your picket sign."

"Yes."

"Well, I hope you're willing to wait till you-know-what freezes over."

Chessie frowned. "You think?"

"It's not that Nick doesn't want to please you. He needs a demonstration."

"We're going to the outdoor pops concert Saturday night. I think that has romantic potential."

"Then seduce him."

"Seduction." Chessie breathed the word and thought of the possibilities. "Perhaps a dab of makeup and perfume. A new hairdo. A slinky dress. That's so unlike me."

"You've got it. Seduction isn't about the same old same old." Kit moved on to scrub the bottom of the next kayak in the row. "A trip to the mall should set you up."

"Martha will want to be in on this, for sure. Will you come, too?"

"Right. You're asking a woman who knows zip about fashion. When Sean and I go out, I raid Frederica's attic for vintage clothes." Frederica was Kit's eighty-something friend.

Chessie gazed with affection at her outdoorsy sister-in-law who'd softened only slightly since she'd breezed into town a year ago and set the gossips buzzing with her motorcycle, her pierced eyebrow, tattoos and purple spiked hair. "Just come with me so I don't end up looking like June Cleaver."

"I can definitely make sure you don't take that route."

"Do you have a couple hours Saturday afternoon?"

"For you, I'll make time." Kit pointed at the row of kayaks. "Payment in advance."

As the two women set to the task in companionable silence, Chessie thought of Nick's kiss earlier in the barn. She'd taken the initiative, and he'd responded. That course of action hadn't been in her original plan, but it had definitely been a romantic moment and had seemed to inch them closer to her goal. So, how did she justify a plan of seduction with her no-sex rule? How did she demonstrate the spark she craved without appearing the tease? And, biggest question of all, if she felt sexy, would she want to refrain from sex with Nick?

She liked sex. She was married to a sexy man. And now she was finding that her no-sex ultimatum was a lot like going on a diet. She had good intentions, but when you put the cookies in front of her, would she crumble?

THIS MOVE TO Pritchard's Neck wasn't at all what Isabel had expected.

Surrounded by applications to colleges, she couldn't concentrate on her future. The present took up too much of her energy.

She'd thought because Dad's big family was here things would feel more familiar, more comfortable. Instead, she had never felt so confused and unsettled. Dad had always thrown himself into his job. Isabel guessed he was trying to prove himself so he could get an even better job down the road. That was the way it had worked all her life, but this past year it had seemed worse. She'd seen him more at school than she had at home.

Then…Gabriella was headed for trouble. Keri was an okay friend, but the crowd those two were trying to hang with was fast and shallow. In no way real friends. There wasn't anything Isabel could do about it, though. Her sister wouldn't listen to her. She'd have to find her own way.

And Mom? Mom had been a different person this past year. She seemed more interested in her own stuff—her pottery, her classes—than in what Isabel and Gabriella were doing. Did she think they didn't need her anymore? Last year when they'd started visiting colleges, Isabel had felt like an adult. Now, a year older and filling out applications for out-of-state schools, she wasn't so sure. How was an adult supposed to feel and act?

Mom wasn't helping. Her mother's freaky behavior lately was selfish. She didn't see or chose not to see how she affected the rest of the family. Like dominoes lined up. Dad was even more tense than usual. Gabriella was more set on separating herself from the family. And Isabel wondered how she could leave for college when she seemed to be the only one who saw things clearly.

She knew what she had to do, but she didn't like it.

With a heavy heart, she collected the applications spread across her bed. After long hours of deliberation, she'd made her short list. Boston University, the University of Miami, Duke, Oberlin College, Furman University. She'd spent so much time poring over their features, they were like old friends to her. Now, as if saying goodbye, she looked at each application in turn. Then she shredded them into scraps so tiny she'd be unable to change her mind.

CHAPTER SIX

"I LOOK LIKE a hootchie-mama!" Chessie exclaimed as she looked at the woman in the changing stall mirror. It couldn't be her reflection because she'd never in her life worn a pair of tight low-rider leather pants, nor a sequined off-the-shoulder sweater. It was the umpteenth outfit she'd tried on this afternoon. None of them felt right to her. She might never make it to the pops concert tonight.

"You said you didn't want to look like June Cleaver," Kit replied from the banquette outside the dressing room where she and Martha sat ready to voice their opinions. "Let's see."

Chessie opened the door. "Who wears this stuff?"

"Well, if you did," Martha replied, "Nick would certainly sit up and take notice."

"As would the board of ed and the PTA." Chessie tried unsuccessfully to execute a deep-knee bend. "This is a school function, ladies. I'm looking for something that says to Nick, 'Come and get me,' while not making the rest of the world think I've lost my mind."

"I see the sales clerk rehanging something that might do," Kit suggested, standing. Up until now, Martha had chosen the clothing, forcefully, as she'd engineered the whole makeover outing. "Let me get it."

As Kit left the dressing room, Martha appraised Chessie. "You should get that outfit. It's not at all hootchie-mama. It's very sexy and it fits you beautifully."

"It's not me."

"I thought the point of this makeover was to push the envelope. Update the earth-mother Chessie. Now, that's an update."

"I'd wear it once and my girls would take it over."

"The price you'd pay for looking hip."

"Am I hip or just a woman trying to act young?"

"Try this," Kit said, returning. She held up a silky dress in a bronze-colored fabric.

Martha wrinkled her nose. "Boring."

"Look at the color with her hair," Kit insisted, thrusting it into Chessie's arms. "I brought these, too." Strappy high-heeled sandals in peacock green. "Go. Try them on."

Chessie retreated to the changing stall. After the sticky warmth of the leather pants and the scratchiness of the sequined sweater, the dress felt liquid-smooth and cool. When she looked in the mirror, she held her breath. The dress skimmed her body perfectly. The deep V-neck showed a little cleavage without giving away the store. The floaty capped sleeves hid her upper-arm tan line. The skirt flared at the waist into a tulip hem that swirled softly at her knees. But it was the color that took her breath away. At first glance it was bronze, but as Chessie moved, blues and greens shimmered below the surface in a subtle moiré.

"What's going on in there?" Martha asked. "You're awfully quiet."

Chessie opened the door.

"Wow!" the two exclaimed together.

"I feel like a new woman," Chessie whispered, stepping to the three-way mirror. "This is me, but a me I didn't know existed."

"We have a winner," Martha declared. "Let's see the shoes with it."

"I don't know about dressy sandals." Chessie

came back to reality. "I'm afraid I have Birkenstock feet."

"And that's why we're all getting pedicures while you get your hair styled." Martha stood up with finality. "The owner of the salon is a dear friend of mine. He's pulling out all the stops for us. Come on. Let's pay for this stuff."

Although Chessie loved the dress, she felt a tiny twinge as she forked over a hefty chunk of her pottery earnings. She had never spent so much on herself at one time, and for an outfit she might wear once.

"I see that guilty look, Chessie," Martha said sharply, "and I will not have it. You deserve this dress."

"It's not so much that," Chessie replied as the three women made their way through the mall to the salon and day spa. "With the clothes and the hair and all, I feel as if I'm…I don't know…baiting a trap. I didn't go through this much primping when I went out with Nick in high school."

"Honey, when you're sixteen, pheromones do all the work for you." Martha laughed. "After a certain age and so many years of marriage, a woman must use all the help she can get."

"I feel like I'm chasing Nick."

"So?"

"Did you chase George?"

"Oh, he chased me till I caught him, and, believe me, I used every trick in the book."

Chessie turned to Kit. "You've been awfully quiet. Did you use your feminine wiles on Sean?"

"Ha!" Kit grinned broadly. "My entire wardrobe consisted of tank tops and cargo shorts. Moreover, I did everything I could to drive him away. I pushed him off my porch. I slapped his face in public. I told him dating was bourgeois romanticism."

"And he kept coming back for more."

"Thank God."

"You see," Martha interjected, "if you don't have any fashion sense, offer them excitement. Men are simple creatures. They respond to bright colors and movement. I swear that's why George still watches cartoons."

"That doesn't describe Nick." Chessie sighed. "I'm not sure what does anymore."

"Hey, hey," Martha cautioned. "I thought you were just trying to attract him. Understanding him, now that's another seminar."

"If you're trying to understand men,

you've come to the right place." Lee, the owner of the salon, came forward as the three women walked in. "That's all anyone ever discusses here, morning, noon and night. I could write a book."

Martha and Lee air kissed.

"So, who's getting the makeover today?"

Tentatively, Chessie raised her hand.

Lee swooped away the scarf she'd used to tie back her unruly curls. "Oh, yes!" he exclaimed. "We're going to get rid of this Cousin Itt look!"

He had that hair *cut* look in his eyes that made Chessie's blood go cold. "Just a trim and shaping," she said weakly. "I've worn my hair this way since high school."

"And does it show," Lee retorted. "Time for an update."

"But my husband likes it."

"But he's going to love it when I'm finished."

"This is what you're working with," Martha said, pulling the new dress and shoes out of the bag.

Lee's eyes lit up. "I have a vision," he declared, pulling Chessie toward the back of the salon where an assistant waited with three footbaths. "Come on, ladies. It's pedicures, gossip and one fabulous transformation."

Chessie's pulse began to race. What had she gotten herself into?

BEFORE THE MOVE back to Pritchard's Neck, he'd promised himself weekends would be devoted to family, but so far Nick hadn't been able to avoid working most of every Saturday.

He glanced at his watch as he headed for the Volvo in the school parking lot. Five-fifty. He'd lost track of time as he and the custodians had moved hundreds of boxes of cleaning and paper supplies off the loading dock where a new trucking company had dumped them into the storage closets. Left outside, they would have disappeared by dawn tomorrow. He might have an advanced administrative degree, but when a job needed doing, a job needed doing. Including manual labor.

Now, hot and sweaty, he had to get home, shower and change, and get back to the football field with Chessie for the pops concert. It was the last thing he wanted to do, and, technically, it was the duty of Eleanor Adams, his assistant principal, to put in an appearance tonight. Nick didn't really need to go. Sure, he'd told Richard he'd show up, but shouldn't the dog bite get him a bye? And while Chessie had talked about a date, wouldn't she just as soon have some quality time at home? Maybe they could rent a movie that the girls would enjoy too. It seemed like ages since the four of them had spent an evening together.

Besides, Isabel and Gabriella would act as a buffer. It wasn't as if he needed or wanted to hide behind his daughters, but he thought he and Chessie needed some neutral time to restore a sort of equilibrium. There'd been so much *sturm und drang* of late. Far too noticeable turmoil. As they were moving boxes, one of the custodians had actually asked him if he was getting a divorce.

Good God, that couldn't be on Chessie's mind, could it?

Not if the kiss she'd delivered the day before yesterday signaled her intent. See, that was the crazy part. Why would she push him away when she'd declared she wanted to be wooed? And why would she tell him no sex, then turn around and lay a kiss on him that made him feel like the pursued? Whatever, Nick wanted to work it out in private. Too many people in town had now logged in an opinion. He definitely wanted to stay in tonight.

Pulling in to the driveway, he was pleased to see the Mini Cooper. It would mean—might mean—his wife was safely home and not out and about fomenting revolution. Gingerly, he got out of his car. The dog bite was healing nicely.

No sign of the girls, except that the house was a mess. He needed to have a talk with them. In that Chessie was right. The girls were old enough to take on more responsibilities.

He headed upstairs, the thought of a hot shower already beginning to relax his aching muscles. "Chess? You home?"

"In here," she called from their bedroom.

"Change of plans," he said. "Would you mind—"

Who was that woman coming out of their bathroom?

"Chessie?"

"What do you think?"

She indicated the dress—she rarely wore a dress—but he couldn't take his eyes off her hair.

Where the hell was it?

She turned around slowly, and his heart sank as he saw that her hair was neither pulled back with a tie nor piled on top of her head. He loved her long hair. But now it was gone. Mostly. Cropped and sophisticated and nothing like his free-spirited Chessie.

She tentatively touched the blunt cut that came to her jawline. "It will grow," she tried to reassure him. "But I kind of like it."

He was shocked speechless. The color and curls were still there, but in a style that made her look as if she'd just stepped off a plane from New York, ten years younger. It made him feel as if he were standing in the room with a stranger. A gorgeous stranger, but a stranger nonetheless.

"Well?" she said. "Say something. I'm losing courage."

He took in the rest of her. The figure-revealing dress. The every-man's-fantasy heels. The glint of copper nail polish on her toes. "It's going to take some getting used to."

And it was going to take some getting used to in public. The eager look on his wife's face said she wasn't going to settle for a night in.

"I'll shower," he said, brushing by her, suddenly uneasy in her presence. Out of the corner of his eye, he caught the disappointment on her face.

When he emerged from the bathroom fifteen minutes later, she was no longer in their bedroom. He threw on a clean shirt and trousers and ran his fingers through his damp hair. Before heading downstairs he steeled himself for the prospect of making conversation with a woman he wasn't sure he knew any more.

He found her on the terrace, standing very still and gazing absently at the flowers. She held a large basket.

When she heard his footstep, she turned. "I packed a picnic supper." She also seemed unsure of herself, and the moment felt awkward.

"Where are the girls?" It seemed strange talking about their daughters when this felt so much like a first date.

"Gabriella's spending the night with Keri."

"Again?"

"She seems to live across the street, I know, but Martha doesn't mind."

"And Isabel?"

"Gone for a walk. She says she's going to work on her poetry tonight."

He didn't know what else to say.

"Would you feel more comfortable taking your car?" she asked at last.

"Yeah. More room. And the pillow's still in it. Well, we'd better get going."

They drove in uncomfortable silence to the high school. What could he say? That she looked gorgeous? She did. That he liked her hair? He didn't. It wasn't so much the cut. It suited her. More than suited. It made her features stand out. Made her come alive. But it had been such a big decision, and knowing how he loved her long wild curls, how could she spring this on him? One more change in five days of what seemed like endless and incomprehensible changes.

Parking in the spot reserved for him, Nick started for the stadium, then realized Chessie wasn't beside him. She sat in the Volvo's passenger seat and waited. He felt like a fool. When was the last time he'd opened the car door for her? She'd made her point.

"Hey, Nick." John and Abigail Tindall came up alongside him. "Where's Chessie?"

"Right here." As Nick opened the car door, she emerged—long, shapely, tanned legs first.

"Put your eyes back in your head, dear." Abigail chuckled and poked her husband in the ribs. "You'd think he'd never seen a pair of—oh, my goodness! Chessie, you look fabulous! Who cut your hair?"

"Lee Barnes. Like it?"

"Love it," Abigail raved.

"You've got my vote," John added, giving Nick a sly look. "Bet it makes you feel as if you're stepping out on your wife."

"You could say that." For the life of him, he didn't know why the Tindalls' enthusiasm made him so testy.

"We've got to run," Abigail said, holding up a folder. "Wendy forgot her music. Catch you later."

Nick put his hand on Chessie's elbow and moved her through the gathering crowd toward the stadium. He nodded and smiled at people he knew—just about everyone—and tried to ignore the surprised looks. The appreciative looks. The thumbs up, even. They were all for Chessie. Were people wondering if that's what her picket sign had meant by having her needs met? Did they think she'd been lobbying for a day at the spa and an extreme makeover? And why did he care what they thought?

"Oh, Nick, look." Chessie stopped at the football field. "The kids and the band boosters have done such a lovely job."

You wouldn't know this was the same guts and glory arena of football season. Midfield before a portable acoustic shell trimmed in twinkling lights, the band played a lively forties jitterbug number. Fanned out from the stage and a large dance floor, a hundred or more banquet tables covered in white linen dotted the grass. People were quickly finding places to put picnic hampers and coolers, greeting friends and family, lighting candles as centerpieces and settling down to enjoy their children's music.

"Nick! Chessie! Come join us!" Betsy O'Meara called from a table in the middle of the crowd. Nick recognized Sandy Weston and Patrick Goodall and the rest of the Art Guild group along with their spouses. Although there was no alcohol at this school function, he thought he saw eighty-year-old Sandy surreptitiously pour something from a flask into a plastic cup. Great. As an administrator, he was here to police students, not the senior citizens. And if he had to be here, he'd feel more comfortable with a table of faculty members. He tried to steer Chessie in the other direction toward Hattie St. Regis and her husband.

"We'd love to join you," Chessie called back to Betsy, and he could do nothing now but follow her.

"Wow!" Sandy exclaimed as they approached. "Chessie, you've emerged from your cocoon! Nick, you have one beautiful dance partner tonight."

Nick winced. "I'm not sure how much dancing I'll be doing."

"Ah, your…injury." Sandy stood, then held out a chair for Chessie right next to his own. "I'll be glad to help fill your dance card, my dear."

Chessie beamed up at the old coot as if she was actually enjoying his outrageous flirtation.

As Nick stood behind his wife's chair, the group discussion broke into small talk about art and technique and the best tourist-free spots for open-air sketching. Chessie, her cropped head bobbing with enthusiasm, joined in the discussion as if he wasn't there.

He looked around at the crowd enjoying themselves in the gathering dusk and resigned himself to a very long evening.

BAREFOOT, ISABEL CLIMBED down the rocks near the pier to the high water mark where the outgoing tide had left an undulating berm of treasure. Seaweed in every shape and color. Gull feathers. An occasional float from a lobster trap's line. Smooth pebbles. Driftwood. And sea glass. She liked the sea glass with its frosted surfaces best of all.

She often came here to collect random objects to serve as inspiration for her poems. Clutching her notebook in one hand, she bent to examine what the latest tide had left behind. Usually, she felt peaceful here, even with the continual activity at the pier. By day, the lobstermen ruled. But they were a generally taciturn bunch. Unless Uncle Sean spotted her, she was left alone. By evening, the owners and crews of the pleasure boats came ashore. But they were mostly tourists or summer residents who might take her picture as she mucked about at the water's edge, but who never pressed themselves into her world.

That was the way she liked it. The solitude gave her a chance to think. A chance she got less and less at home lately. She didn't know what she was going to do about home. About her family. And she didn't know what she was going to do about the pain she felt inside.

Usually her poems helped. Would the hurt

go away when she got older? Most adults acted as if they didn't remember the agony of growing up. Until that forgetfulness descended, Isabel wrote poems. Notebooks and notebooks full of them. Some of them she put to music. But she couldn't concentrate on her music lately.

It was hard enough to concentrate on her writing.

In fact it was hard to feel peaceful even in her favorite spot tonight. Too many troubling thoughts kept vying for her attention. Too many problems kept vying for solutions she didn't have.

Take Gabriella.

Please.

This afternoon she'd tried to have a serious conversation with her sister about Mom and Dad. About how she and Gabby needed to make things easier for their parents right now because they seemed to be going through a rough patch. A potentially dangerous rough patch. Isabel had seen her friends' parents split over less.

As she saw it, with Mom acting out, the two sisters needed to keep things copacetic. As much as she'd cried over ripping up her college applications, she knew she'd done the right thing. She needed to stay home, attend a community college in Portland and keep an eye on her parents.

But when she'd tried to find her sister earlier, she'd been holed up in her bedroom with Keri. They were on about how they were joining up with Baylee Warner and Margot Hensley for a makeover tonight. As if there hadn't been enough makeovers already.

Isabel thought bitterly about her mother's haircut. More than Gabriella's buzz, her mother's radical new look bothered her. It bothered her that her mother could look so young and so…sexual. And didn't she know that Dad loved her long hair? Why would she take that away from him? It was like a slap in the face.

When she'd tried to discuss it with Gabriella, her sister had just shrugged. She'd said the more outrageous Mom acted, the less right she'd have to complain about what Gabby was planning.

That was when Isabel knew Gabriella wasn't just going to hang out with the girls and experiment with makeup and hair. But when she'd confronted her, Gabriella had shut down. Keri had looked at Isabel as if she were an infant.

A seagull landing on a nearby rock startled her. She needed to get home. It looked as if she wasn't going to find any poetic inspiration here this evening, and, if she stayed, her sour mood might just ruin the karma of the place. As she stepped over a pile of seaweed, pain sliced through her heel. She looked down to see blood oozing from the sole of her foot. A jagged piece of glass—not the beautiful sea glass, but a fragment from some nasty beer bottle—poked out of the rock-strewn shore. For a moment, Isabel stood absolutely still, her foot slightly raised, a detached part of herself fascinated by the red blood, the green glass. And the physical pain. So different from her emotional pain.

For an instant, the physical pain blotted out the pain of her emotional chaos.

And then all the first aid her mother had ever drummed into her surfaced. She hobbled to the shoreline where she stood ankle-deep in the cold Atlantic. The salt and the iodine would naturally cleanse the wound. The cold would anesthetize it.

But as the physical pain receded, the confusing jumble of emotions returned. She stood with the harbor stretching before her and felt so alone.

She thought of the red blood and the green glass.

As if sleepwalking, she made her way back up to the rocks and found the broken shard. Held it up in front of her like a talisman. Grasped it firmly, then, very deliberately, drew its razor-sharp edge along the soft flesh of her upper arm.

CHAPTER SEVEN

CHESSIE HADN'T MISSED a dance.

While Nick had mingled as only an administrator would, Chessie had accepted any and all dance invitations. And they'd come in a steady stream. It seemed the new and improved Chessie had the power to turn heads. All but her husband's.

His underwhelming response to the effort she'd put into looking attractive for him had hurt. Big time. So she'd decided to look attractive for herself—how liberating—and had left him to stew in his own juices.

But now that she'd tasted adulation, she realized it wasn't her goal. Not in the least. Bringing Nick closer to her was. So, as the band took a break and the stars began to come out in force, she threaded her way through the crowd, two soft drinks in hand. Obviously, she needed to take a different tack, and she'd finally thought of one.

She found him just leaving a group of parents.

"Hi. I was watching you from across the way." She held up a can. "Can I buy you a drink?"

"Sure." As he reached for it, she held on.

"I'm Chessie. I'm a potter. I like moonlit walks, long conversations and men who aren't afraid to commit."

He looked puzzled.

"Humor me," she said, releasing the soda.

"Okay…" He took a swig and gazed at her over the rim of the can. "I'm Nick. I'm a high-school principal."

"So, Nick, what do you like to do when you're not being a high-school principal?"

"What? There's supposed to be time beyond the job? Nobody told me that when I hired on."

Chessie chuckled, pleased he was going along with her little game. Then she saw Richard Filmore heading their way. This wouldn't do. She wanted Nick to herself.

"Can we talk? Somewhere it's not so crowded?" she asked.

He touched her arm—this time his touch lingered—and steered her beyond the tables to where the track circled the football field. There were no adults here, only small groups of young children playing tag and letting off steam away from their parents.

"This better?" he asked, his voice husky.

"Yes." She fell into step beside him, aware of the tension between them. Not the stress of the previous week, of husband and wife at odds, but a sort of just-having-met electricity. Their relationship needed some first-date jitters, some searching for who the other person was, what he or she wanted.

They walked in silence until they were far enough away to feel alone under the night sky. He'd rolled up the sleeves of his shirt, and when his arm brushed hers by chance, she could feel the coarse hairs and the warmth of the flesh beneath. The sensation felt new to her.

"So, Mr. Principal," she said at last, "if you had any spare time, how would you like to spend it?"

"I'm a basic no-frills guy. Aside from running to let off steam, I like to spend time with my loved ones. Pretty boring, huh?"

"I wouldn't say that." She looked at him as if she were seeing him for the first time. Would she be interested in him if she had just met him tonight? "But you do look as if you could use a little fun."

"Ouch. I look that bad?"

She stopped and reached out to touch the scowl line between his eyebrows.

"I've had a tough week," he said.

"Anything I can do to help?"

He started at her question.

"I know we just met," she offered with what she hoped was a come-hither look, "but do you want to party?"

"When I first saw you tonight—" a slow grin softened his features "—I thought, 'There's a woman who knows her way around a good time.'"

"And why did you think that?"

He paused and seemed to see her, really see her. "You…look…hot."

His comment, along with the intensity of his gaze, made her shiver.

"You think?" She turned slowly in front of him as she'd imagined turning—preening—earlier at home. "So why didn't you ask me to dance?"

He shook his head ruefully. "The competition was tough."

"And you let a little thing like competition scare you off?" She trailed her fingers down his shirtfront. "I may have just met you, but already I would have expected more of you."

A strange thing happened as they stood close together on the track at the far end of the football field, under the stars. Nick the administrator was replaced by Nick the man. A tall and handsome man with a look of longing in his dark eyes.

At that moment the band began to play again. A slow number.

"May I?" Before she could answer, Nick slid his arm around her waist, pulled her close and began to move to the music.

She wrapped her arms around his neck, felt the heat of his cheek next to hers, let the rhythm of their bodies take over. Would she be attracted to him if she had just met him tonight? Yes. If for the chemistry alone.

Nick smelled the exotic scent of a perfume he didn't recognize. Felt the wind blow a short errant curl across his cheek. Felt the woman in his arms respond to the music and his body with a sensuality that was new. And exciting.

This was Chessie?

The thought unnerved him. As much as he loved the old, nurturing Chessie, this new woman turned him on. Was that okay?

"Chessie," he said, fighting to hold on to reality, "about this week…"

"Let's not talk about this week," she whispered in his ear. "Let's stay in the moment."

All right. He could handle the moment because it sure felt fine. But, in light of this past week, what would she expect beyond this moment?

"What do you want?" he persisted. "From me."

She pulled away slightly and laid a finger across his lips. "This is an excellent start."

If that was true, maybe this basic no-frills guy had a chance.

FOR WHAT SEEMED like the millionth time, Gabriella brushed Kurt's hands away as they slid up her sides too close to her breasts while they danced, her back to his front. Surrounded by the throbbing beat, the pulsing lights, she found it easier to turn away from him—to pretend he wasn't there—but harder to anticipate his unwanted moves.

"What's the matter?" he shouted in her ear from behind. "You need a drink to loosen up?"

She shook her head. If she kept Kurt dancing out here on the floor with everyone else, she might just make it through the night. What time was it? It seemed like they'd been here forever. The glistening bodies, the smell of sweat mingled with perfumes and alcohol had seemed edgy and bold when they'd first arrived. Now it seemed stale and cheesy. No big deal.

Just why had they gone through so much to get here?

Gabriella had told her mom she was spending the night with Keri. Keri had told her mom they'd been invited to spend the night at Baylee's, and Mrs. Weiss had driven them to the Warners'. Baylee had packed their outfits in an overnight bag and had her dad drive them to Margot's, which was right on the beach within walking distance of the Surf Club. The guys met them at the entrance.

For all the build-up, getting into the club had been a snap. Whether it was the clothes and makeup—Baylee had done a fabulous job—or the fake IDs, the checkers waved them right through. This might be a club for summer residents and tourists, but Dad would have a cow if he could see how many Coastal High kids were in here right now.

The DJ changed songs—the music never stopped—and Gabriella felt Kurt's hands slip over her hips. Gently. He'd suddenly become a much smoother dancer, shadowing her every move. Surprised, she turned her head to find herself dancing with some other guy who was definitely not Kurt. He was kind of goofy-looking and somehow familiar, but she stayed with him, turned to face him, because he didn't try to paw her as Kurt had all night. Besides, Kurt was nowhere in sight.

Neither were any of the other kids she'd come with.

Suddenly nervous, she looked around. She hadn't seen Keri in a while.

"What's wrong?" her dance partner mouthed.

"I can't find my friends!" she yelled at him, but the music was so loud he shook his head in confusion.

She stood on tiptoe and tried to see over the crowd looking for Keri, Baylee or Margot. Quite frankly, the guys they'd come with made her nervous. Including Danny. She didn't mind if they'd split.

"Come on!" The guy who wasn't Kurt edged her toward the doors leading out to a huge deck.

She sure didn't want to be alone with him, but because she could see people out there, she didn't resist. Maybe one of her group had gone out to catch some air.

There wasn't a sound system out on the deck—Gabriella could imagine the beachfront property owners had something to do with that—but it was still loud. She could, however, hear herself think for the first time that night.

"Something wrong?" the guy asked as they found a space by the railing.

"I can't find my friends."

"Who are you looking for?"

When she told him the names of the seven people she'd come with, he made a face.

"What?"

"It's a free country," was all he'd say. He was tall and thin and had grown a really scraggly soul patch. He looked at her as if he could see right into her skull. Not in a pervy way, but nosy. "How old are you?" he asked.

The nerve. "How old are you?"

He laughed and Gabriella could see he had nice white teeth, if a little crooked.

"I gotta find my friends."

"Suit yourself," he replied as she pushed away from the railing. "Thanks for the dance. You're good."

There was something kind of old-fashioned about the comment. Gabriella couldn't imagine Kurt thanking her for one lousy dance. In any event, she couldn't switch partners. Actually, she didn't want a partner. She needed to find Keri and see if they could leave. By getting in here, they'd made their point. Whatever the heck it had been. Now her head hurt. She didn't feel like sticking around till someone with authority found out how old they really were.

"Hey, what's your name?" the guy called after her. "I'm Owen."

Geez, Owen was the name of someone's grandfather. Gabriella suddenly felt sorry for him, and pictured him younger. At the losers' table in junior high. "Madison," she replied. Now was as good a time as any to try on a new identity. She headed back into the noise of the club.

But once inside, she felt alone and unprotected, nervous without the skinny guy watching her back. Somehow he'd made her feel safer than Kurt. As she made her way around the dance floor, guys reached out to cop a feel even as they were dancing with another girl. This was cool? Call her a nerd, but she thought it was lame. It was time to leave. But where was Keri?

If the others wanted to stay, let them, but she needed to tell her best friend. Maybe she'd come with her. Keri had a cell phone. They could call Mrs. Weiss and wait for her outside Margot's house. They'd make up something about how they ended up there. Mrs. Weiss always seemed to believe whatever Keri told her. Maybe they could buy some sympathy and say Gabriella felt sick and wanted to sleep in her own bed. That was kind of true. Gabriella needed the familiarity of her own room about now. Being over twenty-one wasn't what it was cracked up to be.

She saw Kurt over at the end of the bar, sucking face with some girl as if he hadn't come with someone else. Gross. What a jerk.

By the restrooms, she saw Danny and a

couple guys she didn't recognize. He should know where Keri was.

Pushing her way through the crowd, she saw Danny palm something to one of the other guys before they turned and disappeared into the crowd, leaving Danny looking around as if he expected someone else.

"Hey, Gabs. Wassup?"

"Where's Keri?"

"How should I know?"

"Geez, Danny, you're her date."

"Date. How quaint." He looked at her funny. "You're something else."

"Then have you seen Baylee or Margot?"

"Do I look like directory assistance?" He seemed irritated. "Hey, Gabs, nice talkin' to ya. But if you don't mind, I got business."

"What business?" He was giving off the same pervy vibes as Kurt.

Danny pulled his hand only slightly out of his pocket, and Gabriella could see a bunch of little plastic bags with pills. "You interested? You look like an E kinda girl."

Now she knew she had to find Keri.

Pushing her way into the women's restroom, she scanned the row of girls in front of the mirrors. "Keri?"

"Check to see if your friend's the one in the last stall," a girl drying her hands said. "She's been in there a while. She might be sick."

Peering under the door, Gabriella didn't recognize the shoes, but they were all wearing new stuff. Baylee's stuff. "Keri?"

There was no response. No movement even.

She turned to go, but a bad feeling stopped her. Whoever occupied the stall, Keri or not, was too silent. Too still.

"Are you okay?" Gabriella asked, rapping on the door. She would've welcomed an expletive-laced order to go away, but behind the door the toes in the platform sandals never even twitched.

Panicking, Gabriella knelt to look under the door.

Keri sat slumped on the toilet seat, her face flushed, her eyes half open.

"Keri!"

She didn't move.

Gabriella tried the door. Of course it was locked. "Keri! Open up!"

Keri didn't respond.

The others in the restroom backed away uneasily.

Not caring what they thought, Gabriella

crawled under the door and into the stall. "Keri?"

As her head lolled backward, Keri's eyelids fluttered. She was hot to the touch. Burning up hot. As if she had a fever.

"Help!" Gabriella unlocked the stall door, but couldn't open it in the cramped space. She had to crawl back out underneath.

"Help me get her out of there," she pleaded as a dozen faces stared blankly at her. "She needs air."

Finally, one of the girls stepped forward and helped Gabriella lift Keri out of the stall and into the larger room where they laid her on the floor.

"Omigod," someone muttered. "She must have taken some bad shit."

Gabriella looked up. "What are you talking about?"

"Ask Danny Aiken. He's her boyfriend, isn't he?"

Had Danny given Keri drugs? Had he slipped them in her drink? Had she taken them on her own?

At that moment, Keri turned on her side and retched. Her cell phone fell off her belt.

Without thinking, Gabriella grabbed the phone and punched in 911.

NICK FELT more alive than he had in a long time.

After a slow start the evening had turned out to be fun. Now there was a word he hadn't used recently. Chessie was right. He'd needed to loosen up a little. And loosen up he had with this new, sexy woman. They'd danced and flirted as if they'd just met. And, as one of the last couples to leave, they'd closed down the pops concert. Not in an administrative capacity, but as two people who didn't want the evening to end.

"Turn here!" At the light Chessie pointed down the Sea Road. "Let's ride around the beach."

Turning the Volvo, he glanced in her direction. She had her window open and was letting her hand glide on the soft night air. As she rested her head back against the seat, her short tousled curls played about the smile on her lips. He couldn't remember when he'd seen her so relaxed. And happy.

"Did you have a good time tonight?"

"You're not supposed to ask me. Not on

our first date." Her voice was light and teasing. "I'm supposed to tell you."

"Well?" He stroked her thigh under that silky dress and felt a jolt of longing.

She ran her hand lightly over his. "I had a terrific time tonight. Let's run away together."

That's how he felt, too.

He followed the bend in the road and came out on the stretch where the beach was separated from the pavement by a ribbon of sidewalk and a low seawall.

"Oh, how beautiful!" Chessie exclaimed as the stars and the moon reflected off the ocean's surface. "Pull over!"

"Do you want to get out and walk?" he asked as he turned off the ignition.

"No. I want to…park." In the moonlight, she sent him a sultry look.

"As in…?"

"As in teenage-just-got-the-license park." She flipped up the armrest, then slid across the front seat to snuggle next to him.

"On the first date?"

"As you said, I'm a girl who knows my way around a good time."

"In the family sedan?"

"The parents will never know."

He glanced at his watch.

"Not on this date, mister!" she exclaimed, pulling the watch from his wrist and tossing it in the back seat.

"You mean business."

She giggled, then turned on the seat to face him. It was amazing how perfectly her body fit up against his. "I mean business."

He slid the steering wheel up and the seat back.

"Mm," she purred as she twirled a bit of his hair between her fingers. "That's more like it."

The moon shone through the open window, illuminating her face. With her silvered features and the short haircut, she didn't quite look like his wife.

He didn't feel quite like himself.

Tentatively, he kissed the corner of her mouth.

"Oh, no," she murmured, sliding her hand behind his neck and pulling him to her. "Like this."

She nipped his lower lip once before her kiss became passionate and deep and insistent. It was not a kiss to be dismissed as fun and games. It sent serious desire through his body.

He ran his hand over her hip. Over the

swell of her bottom. The silky fabric of her dress felt like a second skin, and in the dark interior of the car, it felt as if she might have nothing on. He closed his eyes and groaned.

"I've been wanting to get you alone for a very long time," she whispered huskily in his ear.

At that moment he thought he glimpsed a part of what she'd been trying to tell him with the laundry, with the picket sign. Of the need for intimacy.

He cupped her face in both his hands and held her so that he could look in her eyes. "I'm sorry," he said.

"Don't be." She smiled. "Be mine."

Words wouldn't come. Instead, he pulled her to him in a kiss.

With it, Chessie felt a change in Nick.

For the first time in ages, he was with her, truly with her. In fact, she'd bet he wasn't thinking at all, but was humming on pure physical auto-pilot. And all because of her.

Oh, my, but he could kiss!

She felt light-headed. Perhaps it was the short haircut and the unaccustomed feel of the night air against her neck. Perhaps it was the teasing silk of her dress against her skin.

More likely it was Nick's undivided attention. He'd really seen her tonight, for the first time in a very long while. And now he wanted her.

Breathless, she pulled away, almost expecting to see a stranger next to her. But it was Nick. Handsome and strong and looking at her as if he could eat her alive.

"You are so beautiful," he murmured, running his fingers down the deep vee of her neckline, trailing shivers of pleasure along her skin.

She demurred and shook her head as if to disagree.

"You can't tell me you thought those guys were asking you to dance because they took pity on you." Gently, as if in awe, he touched her hair. "You're a knockout."

"Thank you," she said, feeling truly beautiful under his gaze. And powerful.

She leaned across his lap, buried her face in the curve of his neck. And felt him inhale sharply.

"Oh, no! I forgot about the dog bite!" She tried to shift her weight, but he held her tightly. "Does it hurt?"

He chuckled and the sound reverberated through his chest. "Honey, I'm feeling no pain."

She began a gentle massage of his chest, moving her hand in slow circles, lower and lower still until she slid her fingers between the buttons of his shirt just above his belt buckle and felt his warm skin. "What are you feeling?"

"I'm..."

She slid her fingers below his belt and felt the trickle of hair that dipped directly from his navel south.

"...feeling..."

"Yes?" She ran the flat of her palm over his erection.

"...like this." Starting at her knee, he ran his hand between her thighs. Slowly. Under the fabric of her dress. Stopping just as his thumb grazed her panties.

"Are you wearing a thong?" Incredulity threaded his words.

"And if I am?"

"Toto, we're not in Kansas anymore."

With a shiver of anticipation, she unbuckled his belt...just as a light blinded her.

"You folks need to move along." The gruff voice seemed to come from right in the car with them.

Her heart in her throat, Chessie started and

hit the steering wheel with her elbow, sounding the horn.

"What the hell!" Nick raised his hand to shield his eyes from the brightness.

Chessie adjusted her skirt over her legs.

"Nick?" The voice behind the blinding light boomed with amusement. "Chessie?"

Now she noticed the flashing blue lights behind the Volvo.

"For the love of Mike, you'd think the two of you could take it home." The police officer lowered his flashlight. It was George Weiss. Their neighbor. "Or at least get a hotel room."

As Chessie quickly moved to the passenger seat, she noticed Nick's unbuckled belt. She gave him a sharp nod.

Abruptly he shifted his hips away from the window. "Ow!" Apparently, as foreplay disappeared, so went the local anesthetic.

George laughed right out loud. "As if you two needed any more notoriety."

"We were watching the moon rise," Chessie explained sweetly.

"Among other things," George added, apparently unable to restrain his mirth. "I'm going to give you kids my usual safe-sex lecture." He dug into his pockets. "And these." He handed Nick a couple packets of condoms.

"Save the lecture, George," Nick muttered. "We're heading home."

"Don't let me come back in an hour and find you here." George grinned as if he were really enjoying this. "I'd have to write you up."

"You'd love that."

"I would. But if you keep your nose clean and get this girl home safely…I'll restrict the report to Thursday night poker—"

The radio in the squad car crackled with urgency.

"Gotta run," George said. "Sounds like they need back-up at the Surf Club. God, I hate drunks." He thumped the side of the Volvo with the flat of his hand. "Drive safe now."

Chessie suppressed a giggle. Nick's face had been in shadow, so she'd been unable to read his mood. They'd been communing so exquisitely until George's interruption. Would this development set them back?

"Whose idea was this?" he asked, turning the key in the ignition.

"Mine?"

"And a damned good one it was," he declared as he put the car in gear and accelerated so quickly she swore the old Volvo left a patch of rubber. Right in front of officer George Weiss's cruiser. Martha wasn't going to let them live this down.

Nick extended his right arm. "Come here, woman." He laughed. A deep, rich, heartfelt laugh.

Joyfully, she slid across the seat again and buckled up in the center. Then she laid her head on his shoulder and sighed. The silence on the way home wasn't from tension. It was from contentment. Life was good. If Nick could find humor in tonight's turn of events, there was hope for them.

"You know," he said at last, caressing her arm, "just because we're changing venue, doesn't mean the night has to end."

"I like the sound of that." Did she just say that? Dear Lord, give her strength. What was happening to her no-sex diet? The husky tone of Nick's voice wasn't offering cookies. It was offering a deluxe hot fudge sundae.

"Besides, an officer of the law gave me these." He pulled the condom packets out of his shirt pocket. "Now why would he do that if he didn't mean for us to use—"

He stopped speaking so abruptly, Chessie

sat bolt upright. They were about to turn in to their driveway, but another police car blocked their way. Nick pulled over to the side of the road. As he did, officer Ken Nadick got out of one side of the cruiser, and Gabriella got out of the other.

CHAPTER EIGHT

NICK COULDN'T BELIEVE his eyes.

The kid getting out of the squad car didn't look like his fourteen-year-old daughter. She looked like a hooker.

"What happened?"

"Gabby, are you okay?" Chessie was right behind him.

Silent and sullen, Gabriella made no move toward them.

"We picked her up with about a dozen other underage kids at the Surf Club," Ken Nadick said.

"The Surf Club!" Chessie exclaimed. "You were supposed to be spending the night with—"

"Mom! I've already been read the riot act." Gabriella started for the house, but Ken stopped her.

"Not so fast, young lady," he said. "You've

got a lot to explain to your parents. Later. But right now you're going to stay while I tell them the facts as I know them. Then you can all start on the same page."

Gabriella slouched against the squad car. Nick had seen that part-tough, part-scared look a hundred times in his office. On other people's kids. He'd hear her side of the story, as Ken said, later. With a heavy heart he turned to the officer who headed up the substance abuse program for the high school. "What do you know?"

"We got a 911 call from the Surf Club. Drug overdose. Turns into a drug bust with a bunch of underage drinkers as postscript."

"I wasn't drinking!" Gabriella protested.

With a severe look, Ken silenced her. "Your daughter had fake ID on her, but she passed the breathalyzer and the field sobriety test. I thought it best just to bring her home."

"How did you get to the Surf Club?" Chessie turned to Gabriella, astonishment and hurt written on her face.

"You guys are going to have to work out the details," Ken replied. "I'm sorry but it's going to be a long night." Opening the driver's door of the cruiser, he nodded his head toward the Weiss's house. "Consider yourself lucky. George had to follow his daughter to the hospital. She was the drug overdose."

"Keri?" Tears welled up in Chessie's eyes. "Gabriella—"

But their daughter had fled into the house. Chessie followed, leaving the two men in the driveway.

"Thanks, Ken," Nick said. "I wasn't looking for special treatment."

"I wasn't giving any," Ken replied, getting into the squad car. "As I said, Gabriella was clean. She was just where she wasn't supposed to be."

An understatement if Nick had ever heard one. He headed into the house to get to the bottom of this mess.

Before he reached the kitchen, he heard Gabriella's bedroom door slam.

"Unlock this door at once," Chessie ordered from above.

He charged up the stairs. When he got to the top, Gabriella still hadn't unlocked the door. "Open the door," he said, trying to keep his anger in check. It was amazing how much easier it was dealing with other parents' kids' problems. "We're going to talk."

Silence.

"What's she doing in there?" Chessie asked. "What's she capable of?"

Yesterday he might've been able to give his wife an answer. Today he couldn't. "If you don't open this door, I will," he threatened. God, he felt like kicking it down.

"Wait, Dad." As if she read his thoughts, Isabel appeared from her room, a coat hanger in her hand. With the hook end, she jabbed the hole in the middle of the doorknob, releasing the lock.

He and Chessie pushed into Gabriella's room at the same time.

Their daughter lay on her bed, her face buried in a pillow. He sat on one side, Chessie on the other. "Tell us what happened," he said.

Gabriella didn't respond.

"Gabby…" Chessie put a hand on Gabriella's shoulder, but the girl jerked away.

"We're going to get to the bottom of this," Nick insisted. "It's time to own up."

Gabriella rolled to a sitting position, then scooted back against the headboard as if she wanted to get as far away from her parents as possible. Thick black mascara smudged her eyes.

"You were supposed to be spending the night with Keri," Chessie began. "What happened?"

"We got invited to hang out with Baylee and Margot."

"How'd you get to the Surf Club?" Nick couldn't believe he'd become one of the parents who lost track of his teenager.

"Mrs. Weiss drove us."

"To the club?"

Gabriella refused to look him in the eye. "To Baylee's."

"And why didn't you call your mother or tell us your change in plans? We both have cell phones."

"Mrs. Weiss knows them. Knows their parents. It wasn't a big deal."

"Obviously, it was. You still haven't told us how you got to the Surf Club."

"We walked."

This was like pulling teeth, but he persisted. "From Baylee's house?"

"No. Baylee's dad drove us to Margot's."

"So far you've lied to us, to Mrs. Weiss and to Baylee's dad, and you're not even at the club." He paused to let the full import of his words sink in. To her mind or to his, he couldn't be sure. "How did you get to the club from Margot's?"

"We walked."

"Where did you get fake ID?"

"Some guys."

"Names?"

"I don't know their names."

She was lying. He knew it. His daughter was lying to his face.

"Where did Keri get the drugs?"

"I don't know."

Another lie.

"Where did you get these clothes?" Chessie broke in.

The clothes. Neither Chessie nor he would ever allow either girl out of the house in an outfit like that. Nick hated to think what the men at the club had thought of this girl-woman in those clothes.

Gabriella didn't respond.

"Three questions you don't know the answers to." Nick rose from the bed. "We can wait. You're grounded until you can tell us the whole story."

"That's so unfair!" Gabriella shouted. "I wasn't drinking! I wasn't doing drugs! I was just dancing!"

Nick looked at her buzz cut and the heavy makeup. The skimpy outfit. There was far more than dancing going on tonight. This was a girl—his girl—who stood on the threshold of womanhood.

"If everything was so innocent," Chessie remarked, "why did you sneak behind our backs?"

Gabriella looked as if her mother had slapped her. "You have some nerve dissing me," she muttered.

"I beg your pardon?" It was Chessie's turn to look slapped.

"I just went dancing with my friends!" Gabriella yelled. "You've been acting all weird in public! Before strangers! You embarrassed me and Dad and Isabel! I didn't do anything worse than you've been doing all week!"

She stopped suddenly as if she knew she'd stepped over the line.

Quietly, Chessie rose from the bed, her eyes glittering. "Gabriella, you are grounded until we get some answers…and until I get an apology from you. I'm going to call the hospital to see how Keri's doing."

She brushed past Nick as the first tear rolled down her cheek.

With one final look at his unrepentant daughter, Nick followed his wife. When had family life become this difficult?

As soon as her parents had gone downstairs, Isabel slipped into Gabriella's room. Her sister was a mess, that was for sure.

"Go away," Gabby said. "I don't need any more grief."

"I'm not here to give you grief. I thought you might want to talk."

"Sure. So you can blab to Mom and Dad."

"I wouldn't do that." Isabel sat on the edge of the bed. "It's just that I know you'd normally turn to Keri."

"Oh, Izzy!" Gabriella threw herself on Isabel. "She's got to be okay! She just has to be!"

"What happened?"

"I don't know. We got separated. When I finally found her in the restroom, she was so out of it. So hot. Like she had a fever." Gabriella began to cry great gulping sobs as her story spilled out in ragged chunks. "I called 911. Now everyone's gonna think I got the place raided. But it was Keri I was worried about."

"Of course. You couldn't have done anything else." Isabel rubbed her sister's back. "Gabby…how did Keri get the drugs?"

"I don't know for sure, but I think it was her boyfriend. Danny. Danny Aiken. Just before I found Keri, I saw him with some pills in his pocket."

"Why didn't you tell the police?"

"He was the one they busted. Caught him trying to flush the pills down a toilet. I figured they could put two and two together." Gabriella flung herself on the bed. "I'm already dead meat for calling the cops."

"Get a grip!" Isabel pulled her sister upright, looked her in the eyes. "If you haven't figured it out already, that crowd is trouble."

"You don't understand what it's like to always be on the outside."

"Hello. I moved as many times as you did. I was the new kid, too."

"Yeah, but you don't need people. You stick to yourself and your poetry. You don't care what people say. Besides, in a year you'll be away at college and out of here."

Isabel flinched. That's what she'd thought too. Once. Seemed like an eternity ago.

"God, Izzy, you're so lucky. You're getting out just in time, and I'm stuck here." Gabriella groaned dramatically. "Mom and Dad are going to ruin my life."

"Did you ever stop and think you might ruin theirs?"

Gabriella narrowed her eyes. "If only."

"Don't say what you don't mean." Isabel glanced over her shoulder. "Hey, I don't know where they are right now or what they're talking about, but I bet you put a bug in Dad's ear about Mom. He's not real happy with her lately, and you go and accuse her of setting a bad example."

"I said she embarrassed us. I only said the truth. Deny it."

Isabel couldn't, but she needed to get her sister to see the bigger picture. "Well, we don't need to draw attention to it. What do you want, Gabby? Mom and Dad to split up?"

Gabriella's look was hard and cold. "All I can say is my friends who come from divorces don't have their parents breathing down their necks all the time."

"Seeing as how tonight turned out," Isabel snapped, standing, "maybe you need your parents to breathe down your neck a little harder."

"This conversation is over." Gabriella rolled on her side.

"Fine." Frustrated, Isabel stalked out of the room, closing the door behind her.

Her parents' door was open and a bedside light was on, but no one was there. Pausing on the landing to listen, she could hear them in the kitchen. It didn't sound as if they were fighting. She went downstairs.

"Isabel," Dad said when he saw her in the kitchen doorway. He and Mom were sitting at the table. They looked as if they'd been hit by a bus. "I thought you'd be in bed."

"I'm not sleepy. Did you find out anything on Keri?"

Mom shook her head. "I called the hospital. They only release information to family members. No one's home across the street, so we still don't know anything."

"We'll go to the hospital tomorrow," Dad said. "If she's still there, she'll be able to have visitors."

Isabel fought back tears. It could have been Gabriella in that hospital. "I love you," she blurted out.

"We love you, too," Dad replied. "Now try to get some sleep."

Isabel went upstairs, but she doubted she could even close her eyes. Things were so, so wrong. And she didn't think she could fix them.

She went in to her bathroom, closed the

door and locked it. After listening for any footsteps, she opened the medicine cabinet and reached for solace.

CHESSIE STARED at Nick across the kitchen table. "Considering what teenagers face today, how could you think this couldn't happen to us?"

"Isabel never acted out." All traces of the sensuous man she'd parked with at the beach were gone. "I guess I thought we'd found the formula."

"There's no formula. And Isabel isn't the person Gabriella is." Chessie frowned. She thought Nick would know this. "Isabel's always been a loner whereas Gabriella needs people. Needs to belong."

"But we've talked to both girls about risky behavior."

"She wasn't drinking. You heard Ken say she was clean. So in her mind she wasn't engaged in risky behavior. She just wanted to be where her friends were."

"She could've ended up where Keri is."

How Chessie knew it. "But she's not in the hospital. She's safe. We need to focus on that."

"How could she be so reckless?" Nick stood and began to pace.

"I think we know now that she can be. That she might be again if Keri's situation doesn't serve as a wake-up call. We need to keep the lines of communication open."

"We need to keep a tighter rein."

When she looked at him now, Chessie saw not Nick the father, but the administrator. At school, however, he presided over the same four years of adolescence—different kids, but the same maturation level. At home he couldn't stop his girls from growing up. And away. It had to hurt him more than her because control was such a part of who he was.

"We need to be watchful, yes," she conceded, "but you can't keep them in a bubble. They need to learn how to face life and its challenges. That's what you try to teach them in school."

"Chessie, our job as parents is to keep our kids safe."

"No, Nick. Our job is to help them grow into independent adults."

He looked at her as if she were speaking a foreign language.

"They need more structure."

"They need guidance and help in making good choices, yes, but they need opportunities to spread their wings."

"Spread their wings? You make it sound as if tonight was no big deal."

"God, no! But I'm saying how we handle it is a bigger deal. We need to help Gabriella learn from this mistake."

He rounded on her. "They're teenagers. We're the adults. Or we should be."

"Oh, no." An awful realization began to dawn on her. "You're blaming yourself for not being home tonight."

"Don't be ridiculous. I have a job. We have commitments. We can't babysit them 24/7."

"But you're thinking we should have come right home after the pops concert." She stood to face him. "You're thinking we somehow behaved irresponsibly by driving around the beach and taking a little extra time for ourselves."

He didn't answer.

"Nick?"

"We have to focus on the big picture." He was stern now and unyielding. "We made a commitment to have a family. Until we've raised that family, we may have to put some of our needs on the back burner."

"I don't buy that!" Frustrated, she almost didn't recognize this stern, inflexible man. "We're parents, yes, but we're also individuals. Family life is a juggling act. I'm not going to give up being part of a couple to be a parent just as I'm not going to give up being me to be part of a couple."

"This week proves that."

And then it hit her. He was still upset with her for overturning the marital apple cart. She'd thought tonight at the beach she was beginning to get through to him, but that had just been physical. Any man would go along with the prospect of sex. But she didn't want just any man. She wanted Nick.

"Try to put yourself in my shoes," Nick said, his voice tired. "I found out we really didn't agree on how we wanted our marriage to unfold, and now I find out we don't agree on how we want to raise our kids. What's next?"

His words hurt Chessie terribly. "We're both tired. Stressed," she said at last, trying to break the staring contest they seemed to be having. "I think we should go to bed before either of us says something we don't mean. Something we'll regret."

"Fine. I'll check on the girls."

As he left the room, she wanted to call out that he was overreacting, but he sincerely believed she'd overreacted in her quest to fine-tune their relationship.

It seemed they'd reached a stalemate.

She stayed up until just before dawn, scrubbing the kitchen, replaying over and over again Nick's last question. *What's next?*

A week ago she'd thought she knew. Had seen a rollicking progression straight toward renewed marital bliss. Now, she didn't have an answer.

NICK GOT Isabel and Gabriella up at nine the next morning so they could have breakfast together before all four went to the hospital to check on Keri. The girls weren't happy about the reveille. Chessie hadn't come to bed at all. But she was in the very clean kitchen with the table set, cooking pancakes and sausage.

"I called across the street," she said, looking up from the stove. "Still nobody home. I don't like what that might mean."

"Don't go there, Chess. We'll find out the

whole story soon enough. And find out what we can do to help."

She looked so worried, he wanted to comfort her. But sometime last night, they'd lost the intimacy necessary for comfort. He hadn't figured out how to get it back.

"Why did you get us up so early?" Rubbing her head, Gabriella entered the kitchen behind him. "I have a headache."

"Late nights will do that to you," Chessie replied briskly, serving up breakfast. "Where's Isabel?"

"Hey, I'm not her keeper," Gabriella groused, reaching for a sausage.

Nick wrapped his hand around his daughter's wrist. "Now that's where you're wrong. We're a family. We look out for one another."

"I'm here," Isabel said from the doorway. It was a warm and humid morning, but she was dressed in cargo pants and a long-sleeved T-shirt.

Chessie eyed the outfit. "It's supposed to get in the high eighties today," she remarked as she placed orange juice at Isabel's place.

"It'll be air-conditioned at the hospital." Ducking her head, Isabel sipped at her juice.

They ate in awkward silence, which persisted on the ride to the hospital. Visiting hours had begun when they arrived, and the volunteer behind the desk told them there were no restrictions for visiting Keri.

"A good sign," Chessie said as they headed for the elevator.

When the doors slid open, Gabriella balked. "I'm feeling kinda sick. Maybe I should see her another time."

Chessie drew Gabriella to one side. "I can wait down here with you. Dad and Isabel can give us an update. Then—"

"No," Nick cut in. Gabriella needed to see the consequences of last night. Chessie shouldn't baby her. "We're all going up."

Chessie looked as if she disagreed with his decision, but she didn't say so. Instead, she urged Gabriella into the waiting elevator. The stiff set of his wife's shoulders told him loud and clear the issue was up for discussion later when they were alone. So what else was new? Lately, he said black, she said white.

On the fourth floor, they found Keri's room. Her door was open, but they hesitated in the hall before entering. Her back to the door, Martha sat by her daughter's bed. Keri looked so frail, hooked up to an IV and lying stiffly under a white sheet. Her eyes were open, but she didn't look at her mother.

Good God, that could have been his daughter.

"Martha," he said quietly, entering the room first. "How are you? Both of you."

Turning to look at them, Martha began to tremble. "Get out," she said, her voice unusually harsh.

"We just wanted to know how Keri was doing. What we could do."

"Keri's going to be fine, no thanks to you. You've done enough." As Martha spoke, Keri turned her head toward the window, closed her eyes.

"I don't understand."

"Why am I not surprised Gabriella didn't tell you?"

"Ken Nadick filled us in. He brought Gabriella home."

"Keri would be home now, too, if it wasn't for your daughter's bright idea." She looked hard at Gabriella who hung back in the doorway.

"From what I understand," Nick said cautiously, "this was a group idea. A very bad idea. Gabriella's grounded for her part in it."

"Her part in it? She was the ringleader. Keri told us everything. How Gabriella thought up the idea. How she convinced Baylee and Margot to go along. How Keri didn't want to do it, but Gabriella threatened not to be her friend anymore." Martha cast a withering glance at Nick. "You of all people should know how dangerous peer pressure can be."

"We're sorry," Chessie said, her arms around Gabriella and Isabel.

"Well, sorry doesn't cut it." Martha turned her back on them. "Now leave."

"Come on, girls." As Chessie urged them toward the hall, Nick could see the devastation in all three faces. After all, this was a friendship disintegrating.

Leaving the room behind his family, he saw George, still in uniform, coming down the hallway. "I'll meet you in the car," he said to Chessie, then waited for his neighbor.

George stopped reluctantly. "This isn't a good idea," he said.

"We're leaving," Nick replied. "But I need to know the score. What happened to Keri?"

"Someone put something in her soft drink."

"What?"

"We won't know till the blood work comes back. Maybe not then. They're keeping her for observation. I insisted."

"I'm sorry." Nick hesitated. "Martha seems to blame Gabriella."

"Keri told us everything. Considering how it played out for her, I don't see why she'd lie now."

Nick had seen more than one kid lie to the bitter end and more than one parent in denial. "I'll get to the bottom of it," he offered.

"You need to. With your daughter, I mean. In our lines of work, we both know how easy it is for a kid to get into trouble. And slide into more trouble if they're not straightened out."

"I thought the six of us could sit down and work it out. When Keri gets home, of course."

"Sorry. Martha and I have worked it out already. Keri's going to private school this fall. She won't be hanging around with Gabriella."

Stunned, Nick watched the man he'd counted a friend walk into his daughter's hospital room and shut the door.

WHEN DAD PULLED the car in to their driveway, Gabriella opened the door before he'd come to a complete stop.

"Don't go off the property," he warned. "Remember you're grounded."

As if she could forget.

She ran around the barn to where the back gardens met the marsh. There was an enormous cranberry bush that had grown so large it completely sheltered a granite boulder. Gabriella pushed through the tangle of branches to reach the rock. Once hidden inside, she let herself cry.

Keri hadn't even looked at her. And she'd lied. Big time.

Dad had said she was grounded until she told him the names of the guys who'd gotten the fake ID and where Keri could have gotten the drugs. She couldn't tell her father what she knew. He had too much power. As principal of her school, he could make life miserable for anybody. Not that she wanted to be friends with Danny or Kurt. They were jerks. But if kids thought she was a snitch to her father, she'd be cut so fast it would make her head spin.

As it was, Dad said Keri was going to private school next fall. Keri. The only real friend Gabriella had made since moving to Pritchard's Neck. And what kind of a friend had she turned out to be if she could stab her in the back to protect her own rep with her parents?

Now Gabriella was headed to high school with no friends, her father for principal, a mother who wouldn't act her age, and a dorky senior sister who was leaving for college in a year anyway.

So where did she fit in? Either in school or in her family?

For the first time in her life, Gabriella felt absolutely alone.

CHAPTER NINE

CELL PHONE IN HAND and pottery class roster in front of her, Chessie sat at the kitchen table late Monday morning and felt a deep empathy for George Washington at Valley Forge. Her revolution had hit the skids, too.

Nick had barely spoken a dozen words to her in the past twenty-four hours. Gabriella was supposed to be helping Isabel pick up, vacuum and dust the downstairs, but she'd done far more complaining than cleaning. And the fully enrolled pottery class Chessie was supposed to have taught this morning? Only half those enrolled had shown up, all of them summer residents. As Chessie had gone down the list, phoning those who hadn't shown, she'd been treated to a lot of chilly excuses. When she came to the bottom and Martha Weiss's name, it dawned on her. Martha had originally spearheaded a movement to pack the class with her considerable circle of friends and acquaintances. Now that Martha was no longer speaking to them, it appeared her friends weren't either.

Chessie couldn't even find solace in the newspaper and a cup of coffee. The new carrier had been on the job a week and hadn't managed to hit the driveway once. This morning's paper was so far up on the roof she'd have to get a ladder to retrieve it. The kid was supposed to collect today. She'd have to have a word with him.

Mondays sucked.

"You look as if you'd lost your best friend."

Chessie was startled to see Nick's sister-in-law Emily standing next to her. "Hey, Em," she said, brightening. "What brings you by?"

Emily glanced over her shoulder to her minivan in the driveway. Chessie could see Emily's four children, plus Alex bouncing so hard in their seats the van was rocking.

"Did Isabel forget?" Emily asked. "She promised to be mother's helper at the beach today."

"Oh my gosh, I forgot," said Isabel suddenly appearing in the doorway. This past week she seemed never to be out of earshot.

"Give me a minute to get a towel, and I'll be right with you."

"Teenagers." Chessie smiled weakly.

"How is Gabriella?" Emily, normally very self-assured, seemed tentative. "Brad listens to the police scanner."

"She's okay physically. She's in full rebellion, however."

Chessie expected Emily to say, *Like her mother.*

But she didn't. "I wanted to call yesterday. To see if there was anything I could do, but Brad told me not to."

"I don't understand." Chessie had expected the McCabes to descend *en masse,* and was perplexed when they hadn't. "Why would he not want you to call?"

"I…don't know exactly. Brad, Jonas, Sean and Mariah have always looked up to Nick because he had such a big part in raising them. But when you moved back to Pritchard's Neck…Brad said Nick seemed to distance himself. Seemed somehow unapproachable and self-contained. He was a little intimidating. Brad said he didn't think Nick would welcome help, would see it as a sign his family thought he couldn't handle his own affairs."

Chessie was stunned. "Do the others feel this way?"

"Pretty much. It doesn't help that we see you and the girls more than him."

So Chessie wasn't the only one who'd seen a change in Nick.

"I didn't mean to upset you," Emily quickly said. "And if there's anything you need—anything—you just ask."

"I will."

"I'm ready." Isabel reappeared in the kitchen with a towel.

"Honey, you're going to roast!" Emily exclaimed, looking at her long pants and long-sleeved tee.

"I don't want to get sunburned." Isabel headed to the car where the cousins set up a cheer the minute they spotted her.

"I have to run," Emily said, "but remember we're all here for you."

"I'll remember." Chessie tried to smile.

When exactly had they all lost the flesh-and-blood Nick?

"Gabriella!" She went in search of her daughter and found her in her room, lying facedown on her bed. "Isabel's helping Aunt Emily. I have to meet Dad at school. You're to finish the vacuuming, and you're not to go off the property."

"Where would I go? I don't have any friends."

"You'll make new friends."

Chessie hated how curt her answer sounded, but she needed to see Nick immediately, talk to him.

Gabriella waited until she heard her mother's car pull out of the driveway, then she headed downstairs. She grabbed a handful of cookies from the cookie jar and walked right by the vacuum cleaner and out onto the side steps where she plopped herself down in the sun to contemplate the rest of the world enjoying the freedom her stupid parents had taken away from her.

She looked at the cookies in her hand. They weren't even homemade. Because of her mom's stupid, stupid strike, they were eating cookies from the store. And cheap store brand, no less. Stupid, stupid, stupid.

Across the street Mrs. Weiss pulled her SUV into the driveway, followed by Mr. Weiss in his police cruiser. When Keri got out of her mom's car and walked into the house as if it was just a normal day, Gabriella felt glad her friend was home and seemed okay. But neither Keri nor her parents had even glanced across the street. It was as if Gabriella didn't exist.

Could her life get any worse?

A long shadow passed across her out-stretched legs. Shading her eyes, she looked up to see a kid on a bicycle. With the sun behind him, she couldn't see his features.

"Madison! You live here?"

The voice was strangely familiar. But why was he calling her Madison?

She moved only enough that she could see his face. It was the guy she'd danced with at the Surf Club Saturday night. Oscar or Olaf or Omar.

"Owen," he said as if reading her mind.

"What are you doing here?" Sure she sounded rude, but what was he, some kind of stalker? She'd had enough of Saturday night.

"I've come to collect. I'm your new paper carrier."

Gabriella tried not to let her jaw fall on the ground as she took in his words. And that… bicycle?

"Geez-o-Pete!" she said at last. "How old are you?"

"Fifteen." He grinned down at her as if it was a huge joke.

"But—"

"You thought I was twenty-one."

Gabriella didn't reply.

"I wash dishes part-time at the Surf Club. On my break I dance."

Just how weird was this guy?

"Did you have to go to jail?" he asked as if he had a right to know.

"I wasn't drinking. Officer Nadick just brought me home."

"Lucky you. Did you ever find your friend?"

Tears stung Gabriella's eyes. "She had to go to the hospital."

"So she was the one dehydrated from E."

"What are you talking about? Her father said someone slipped drugs in her soft drink."

"Right. If you're talking about Keri Weiss, I saw her take an Ecstasy tablet from Danny Aiken."

"You saw her take it? What else did you see?"

"Not much. She was dancing pretty hard, but she wasn't hydrating. Big mistake."

"Why?"

"'E dries you out."

Gabriella thought about how hot Keri had felt when she'd found her in the restroom. How she'd been hooked up to an IV in the hospital. Maybe this kid was right. Could he be right about Keri taking the drug voluntarily? Then she'd lied to her parents about Gabriella—sacrificed her—to save herself. How low could you go?

"You didn't take any, did you?" Owen asked.

"No."

"Smart move."

"As if that bought me any cred with my parents."

"What'd they do?"

"Grounded me."

"You'll live."

The matter-of-fact way he said it irked Gabriella. "Yeah, well, you know nothing about my stupid life."

"So, tell me."

"They treat me like a baby."

"Do you act like a baby?"

Gabriella clammed up. She didn't have to talk to this jerk. And she wasn't going to give him the satisfaction of getting up and going in the house. This was her territory. She wasn't about to surrender it to some stupid paperboy.

"Let's put it this way," he said as if he didn't get that she was ignoring him. "Kids are more grown up than their parents think they are and less grown up than we think we are."

"What are you—some kind of philosopher?"

"I'm going to be a playwright. I go to the School for Visual and Performing Arts in Portland."

So that's why she hadn't seen him around. Wouldn't have to see him around next year. Good.

"What else is so awful about your life?" he asked.

"You gonna put it in a play?"

"I might. That's what I like about working at the Surf Club. Good material."

"How about parents who turn their daughter into slave labor."

"What kind of labor?"

"Laundry. Dishes. Cooking. Cleaning."

"Grow up. I've been doing that since I was in elementary school. It's just my mom and me. She can't do everything. Plus I work at the Surf Club, run this paper route and mow lawns for money."

"A regular Boy Scout."

"I pull my weight."

"I can pull my weight."

"So do it."

"If I do, what's to stop me from going out on my own?" She thought of her sister leaving home in a year. How lucky was she?

Owen shrugged. "Nothing."

That was the smartest thing he'd said. And Gabriella filed it away for future reference. She didn't need this guy and his superior attitude any more.

"My folks aren't home." She indicated the money pouch he held in his hand. "If you're collecting, that is. And they're a little PO'd you can't hit the driveway."

"Hey," he shrugged, "it's my first week. I'll be back." He wheeled his bike out of the driveway. "See ya."

Not if she saw him first.

"CHESSIE!" Hattie looked up from her desk in the outer office. "You're just in time. Nick and a group of us were going out for lunch. Still planning for staff field day. Join us?"

Talk of staff field day was no inducement. As Nick appeared in the doorway, Chessie held up the takeout bag from Branson's deli. "I thought I might kidnap my husband for the lunch hour."

"That's an even better idea." Hattie moved to the door. "I even think there might be a clear corner of his conference table. But hurry. You know how nature abhors a vacuum."

Hattie left, but Nick remained in his office doorway, looking unsure. Chessie never invaded his work space. She knew he liked to keep his work and private life separate. But maybe he needed a reminder that he actually had a private life.

"Do you want to eat outside? In the senior courtyard maybe?" he asked.

"It must be ninety outside. I'd rather stay in the air-conditioning."

Reluctantly, it seemed, he stood aside to let her in his office. "How's your day been?"

"Not so great. Half my pottery class didn't show up. Martha's friends."

He didn't seem to hear her.

"Where are the girls?"

"Izzy's acting as mother's helper for Emily. At the beach. I left Gabby cleaning downstairs."

"Do you think it's wise to leave her alone?"

"Nick, she's fourteen." She placed the bag on a pile of papers on his conference table, and began to clear a space for them to eat. "Do you think we should get one of those parolee ankle monitors?"

He didn't appear amused. Very soberly, he reached for a sheet of paper in his computer printer tray. "Since you're here, you might as well take a look at my plan before it goes into effect."

Confused, she looked at what seemed to be a very detailed list. A professional document. Since when did he consult her on school matters? And then she saw the items on the list, articulated with bullet points:

•Curfew—10:30 p.m. unless prearranged.

•Must bring all friends home and introduce them; must provide parents' names and contact information.

•Will perform chores on a daily basis. Schedule to be posted.

•Will obtain and maintain part-time jobs that require no more than nineteen work hours per week or volunteer in one community organization.

•Will join at least one extracurricular club or school activity.

There was more, but Chessie stopped reading. "What's this?"

"It's a contract for the girls, to keep them out of trouble."

"Were you planning to discuss it with them first?"

"There's no discussion."

This wasn't like Nick. Sure, he was a strict father, but they'd always had a round table approach to parenting. As parents, they had final say, but the girls had always been part of the process.

Then an ugly thought hit her.

"Were you planning to discuss it with me before you put it before the girls?"

"You're here now."

"But you didn't know I would be." Alarmed, she held the paper under his nose. "Was this going to come as executive fiat?"

"We have a problem. I thought of a solution."

"In the past, Nick, when we had a problem, *we* came up with a solution."

"In the past I've pretty much left the girls

up to you." He took the contract out of her hands. "It's time I got more involved."

"You're saying I've done a lousy job of managing our daughters." She felt her blood pressure rise.

"I'm not saying that. But considering the events of Saturday night, we need to develop some new strategies." He held up the contract. "They're in here."

"And you were about to unilaterally set them in motion."

"If I recall, about a week ago, you went for a few unilateral changes."

"That was different!"

"How?"

"I made some temporary moves to get your attention and set up a dialogue."

"Temporary, huh?" He began to pace. "After a week, the situation's starting to feel awfully permanent to me. The house is a disaster. Gabriella's never behaved so badly. And you've slept in your studio as much as you've slept in our bed."

"Which should highlight the need for that dialogue." Chessie sighed deeply. "Sit down, please. Let's have lunch together."

He sat and perfunctorily began to eat one of the sandwiches she'd brought.

"I'm not saying those aren't good points in your contract," she conceded. "But I think the four of us need to discuss them. In a safe and neutral environment." She hesitated, knowing she was heading into sensitive territory. "Like family counseling."

"I have a counseling degree. We don't need to take our problems outside the family."

"Then let's keep it in the family. Emily wanted to know what they could do. You know how teenagers will often listen to other family when they won't listen to parents. Why not call a McCabe council—"

"No." He spoke the word so quietly that, at first, Chessie thought the sound had come from somewhere outside the room. "This is our problem. I've solved it."

"What is going on between you and your family?" she asked just as quietly.

"Nothing."

"Exactly. Emily says your brothers and sister don't know how to talk to you. That they think you've distanced yourself."

"She's got it wrong."

"She wanted to call when she heard about Gabriella, but Brad wouldn't let her in case you'd think they thought you were weak, or some such malarkey."

"Chessie, we've been away since we graduated high school. We've handled our own problems. My family knows that. They're just giving us a little privacy."

"The girls and I have spent more time with them than you have this past year. Privacy is not in their vocabulary."

"Whatever. I don't need their help."

"What is this *I* business? *We* need help."

"The girls need help, yes, but I'm the one with all the degrees in child development and education. Let me do what I do best, Chessie."

She was stunned. He'd never pulled rank on her before. "You won't let a counselor help us," she said when she'd regained her composure. "You won't let your family help us. You won't let me help us. You're taking everything on your shoulders."

"I can handle it. I signed a contract to manage a whole school full of Gabriellas and Isabels. I've shouldered heavier stuff than we're talking here."

"We're your family. Not a school system. You can't administer us."

"I'm doing what's right."

"I'm sorry." Hattie appeared in the doorway. "I never got to lunch. There's a shipment of science textbooks about to be unloaded, but they're definitely not the editions we ordered. We need you, Nick."

He got up with a look that clearly said, *At least someone does.*

"I'll see you at home," he said, and then he was gone.

Chessie wished she had some laundry to throw out the window. Or a trumpet to blast. Or some dishes to break. If she read him correctly, Nick had just laid down the law. And what did he expect her to do in response to his big counter-move? Run up the white flag?

Well, she wasn't going to. Somewhere in the craziness of the past week, she'd come to the realization that she couldn't return to the way things had been. They were going to have to find their way out of this marital trough, and, hopefully, together.

On the way home she stopped at the bakery and ordered two eclairs. When she'd eaten every last gooey morsel, she picked up ingredients for a healthier supper. Still eons away from realizing any benefit from her revolution, it was her night to cook. Whoopee!

CHAPTER TEN

Nick had something to do before heading home to supper. He didn't want to do it, but it had been bothering him all afternoon.

He pulled in to the McCabe lobster pound in search of Sean. Although Sean was nine years younger than Nick, Nick always felt the most at ease with him of all his family. Sean was a lot like Nick. Self-contained and least likely to stick his nose into another man's business. But Sean would tell him what family scuttlebutt was making the rounds about him, Chessie and the girls.

Parking next to a car with out-of-state plates, he saw a Help Wanted sign in the pound window, and wondered if it might be a job Gabriella or Isabel could handle. Inside, several customers stood around a tank pointing to live lobsters they wanted cooked while his father retrieved them with a large net.

"Hey, Pop. Is Sean around?"

"Out on the wharf."

As Nick made his way outside, his father called after him. "That's it? That's my visit for the month?"

Nick let the dig slide. Everybody seemed to want a piece of him, but there was only so much to go around.

Sean's lobster boat, the *Alexandra,* was pulled alongside the wharf where Sean was unloading a dozen or so traps in obvious need of repair.

"Hey!" his brother called out. "Lend a hand, will you? I need to load these on my truck."

Nick rolled up his sleeves. He was wearing a dress shirt, good trousers and leather loafers. The traps were still wet. Crusted with barnacles and dripping with algae, they were not street-clothes-friendly. But he wasn't about to sit around while his brother worked. He reached for a trap Sean had just slung onto the wharf.

"Good God, man!" Sean barked. "Get a pair of boots and a rubber apron from Pop."

Dry cleaning and a session with the shoe polish seemed a less involved option than going inside and listening to Pop's complaints.

"I'm okay," he said, hefting a trap and

heading for Sean's truck parked alongside the pound.

Sean shook his head. "You always were hardheaded."

As the two men worked silently unloading the traps from the boat, loading them on the truck, the physical activity began to clear Nick's head. It was strange how, growing up, watching his father try to make a living as a carpenter working mostly seasonal jobs for summer residents during some pretty tough recession years, Nick had vowed to get a steady profession—not manual labor—something with a salary, a regular vacation, benefits. And security. But now that he had all those, had them for going on fifteen years, he jumped at chances to escape the confines of his office to do something physical—run the cross-country trail at school or help at the loading dock.

"You're a mess," Sean said.

Nick grinned.

"Hop in." His brother climbed down the wharf ladder into the *Alexandra.* "Come with me while I moor her. You said you don't get enough time on the water."

Nick climbed into the big boat, undid the

lines, then leaned against the gunwale as Sean guided her out into the harbor.

"So I'm guessing this isn't just a social call," Sean said while the engine rumbled and the late-afternoon sun glinted off the high tide.

Might as well get to the point even though he'd like to just soak in the salt air and the gentle swell of the water. Enjoy the peace.

"What does the family have to say about Chessie and me? About the girls?"

Sean didn't speak right away. Instead, he brought the boat up smoothly next to his mooring float, next to the waiting punt. Snagging the line with a gaff, he secured the *Alexandra*. Then he opened a cooler. "Beer?"

A beer or twelve sounded good about now.

Not waiting for an answer, his brother opened two bottles, handed him one, then took a slow swig of his own. He looked long and hard at Nick.

"We'd like to know if there's anything we could do to help," he said.

"With what?" Nick didn't want to offer up anything that wasn't already floating on the McCabe airwaves.

"Mostly with Gabriella. Kit, especially, is worried. She knows from experience how much trouble a teenager can get into. Says she would have been a lot better off with a little more family interference."

"Gabriella's taken care of. She's grounded."

"And that will solve the problem for how long? A big family can provide a safety net—"

"Chessie and I will cope."

Sean raised an eyebrow.

"So you all think Chessie and I are in trouble."

"I didn't say that."

"You didn't have to."

"Nick, in my opinion, whatever's between you and Chessie should be worked out between you and Chessie, unless you tell us otherwise. But your girls…that's another story. We all know how hard it is to raise kids. The way I figure it, when Alex becomes a teenager, I'm going to enlist all of you for a tag-team event. There's no shame in taking all the help you can get. No weakness." He tossed his empty beer bottle in a plastic bucket for emphasis.

"You think that I consider asking for help a weakness?" Nick tossed his empty on top of Sean's.

"Why do you always have to go it alone?"

"I just have. It hasn't been a conscious effort." Was that a lie? "I went away to school. I got a job away. Now I've worked my way back here. My hometown. If I'm such a loner, would I return?"

"I don't know. You're here, but you're still acting as if you're away."

"How am I supposed to act?"

"Maybe as if you're glad to be back home. As if you're glad to see us."

"I am glad to be back. Glad to see all of you."

"But…?"

"No buts."

Sean eyed him skeptically. "Growing up, you were our second father. When you left for college, I was nine. Mariah was thirteen. Brad, eleven. Jonas, only seven. It was a huge loss. And then you chose not to come back… I, for one, certainly wondered if we were somehow to blame. I know Pop blamed himself for putting so much responsibility on you as a kid. Thought you only had bad memories of home."

It hurt Nick that his siblings and father thought that.

"No, I actually liked taking care of you guys," he admitted. He knew he could control the kids. What he couldn't control was Pop's fluctuating income. Even back then he sensed his father's fear of failure, sensed the high stakes. Hand-me-down clothes were a given. They ate Spam and nothing else at far too many suppers. And on more than one occasion, the utilities had been cut off. But whenever Nick confronted his father with his own boyish fears, Penn would tell him, "A show of emotion never put food on the table. Hard work does."

Sean smiled. "You know what I liked? Your grilled cheese sandwiches—"

"With maple syrup." He'd forgotten about those.

"Now Alex loves them."

Funny, he hadn't introduced them to Gabriella and Isabel.

"Sean…I followed the jobs to provide for my own growing family. And now…I'm not trying to keep any of you at arm's length. This job is a bear. You know the last principal got fired, and I was brought aboard to turn the building around. It's taken most of my time—"

"Hey, I'm not trying to add to your worries. Just know that we're here if you need us. We needed you, and you were there for us. Now we're in a position to help."

"Thanks." Nick felt a little guilty that Sean was being so open, while he'd not been absolutely honest. Returning to the fold as an adult dredged up that old fear of failure and the dire consequences of failure where family was concerned. And failure was not an option for him.

"We'd better get ashore. Kit and I are taking Alex to a minor league baseball game in Portland tonight." Sean slid over the side of the *Alexandra* and into the punt.

Nick followed. "Sounds like fun." He envied Sean the simplicity of parenting a nine-year-old.

When he drove the Volvo into his own driveway, the side door swung open. Isabel, dressed in one of his white, long-sleeved dress shirts, a black tie and black pants, stood at attention, a dish towel over one arm. It appeared she'd drawn a mustache on her upper lip. Now what?

Watching her dad climb out of his car and gather his briefcase from the back seat, Isabel hoped Aunt Emily's plan would work, but she had her doubts.

Earlier at the beach, she'd kind of had a

meltdown. While the kids had raced in the shallows, she'd sat on the blanket and blubbered to her aunt about how screwed up her family was. Surprisingly, Aunt Emily had really listened. And she'd offered a few explanations and suggestions as if Isabel was an adult who could understand. Not like Mom and Dad who were trying to keep everything a secret and pretending they were okay and handling things when Isabel knew they weren't.

Aunt Emily said even the best marriages weren't all happily ever after. That couples went through peaks and valleys in their relationship. She thought it was easier to climb out of the valleys if you could just get a little time alone to talk things through. But that was hard with jobs and kids. So she'd helped Isabel cook up an idea for a little romantic supper. Just something to show Mom and Dad that she and Gabby loved them, that they appreciated them. That's really all kids could do, Aunt Emily said.

After the beach outing, they'd picked up chicken breasts with wild rice and asparagus at Cape Catering. Isabel and Gabriella were to keep the meal warm and set a pretty table in the dining room. Of course, Gabriella had been a problem. She'd been sitting on the side steps sulking and refused to have any part of the project until Aunt Emily had given her a good talking-to. Cripes, if Isabel had any chance of having a kid like Gabriella, she was getting her tubes tied.

Finally, Gabriella had agreed to stay out of sight and work the kitchen while Isabel provided the continental wait-staff. Standing at the door, waiting for her father, she could hear her sister, just beyond the kitchen's closed door, thumping around, banging pots and pans. You'd think she was making the meal from scratch.

"Monsieur," she said as her dad approached, a puzzled expression on his face, "let me take your briefcase. Madame is waiting in zee dining room."

As he gave up his briefcase, she hoped her mom wouldn't be turned off by the green streaks down the front of his shirt. Opening the kitchen door a crack, she slid the briefcase through, then led her father into the dining room where her mother sat at the table, sipping cranberry juice from a wineglass.

"Your party, monsieur," Isabel said, pulling his chair out for him.

Mom smiled. "Apparently, while we were out, the town rezoned. We're now a French bistro." Right from the start, she'd seemed pleased with this idea.

When Dad sat, Isabel bent over him solicitously. "And would monsieur care for an aperitif?"

His mouth twitched. "What are you offering?"

Mom raised her glass. "I recommend the house cranberry."

"Cranberry it is."

Isabel might be wrong, but she thought she saw him relax just a little bit as she took the bottle of juice out of the empty utility bucket filled with ice. Maybe Aunt Emily had the right idea.

"Holy crap!" Gabriella's voice came from the kitchen.

"Zee chef," Isabel said, filling her father's wineglass, "eez new. And vurry temperamental. I must check!"

In the kitchen Gabriella was pulling the warming pan of chicken, rice and asparagus out of the oven. Flames were shooting from the dish. Without thinking Isabel poured the remaining cranberry juice over the flames which immediately disappeared only to leave an unrecognizable charcoaled lump.

"What happened?" Isabel didn't have to look far to see Gabriella had set the oven, not on warm, but on broil. The juice-soaked dinner was beginning to emit an acrid smoke. She hit the vent button over the stove. "Quick! Open the windows wider before—"

The smoke detector went off with an ear-splitting shriek.

"What's going on?" Dad stepped into the kitchen.

"Nothing! It is zee house specialty," Isabel insisted, reverting to role. "Poulet flambé. Your primitive American kitchen apparently is not up to zee challenge." She shoved her father back into the dining room. "Chat up zee madame," she said. "She is getting lonely."

Mom didn't look lonely. She looked worried. But let Dad handle her. Isabel had a poulet flambé to rescue.

Back in the kitchen, she pulled the battery out of the smoke detector to stop the infernal noise, then surveyed the damage to the dinner as Gabriella sulked.

"Told you this was a stupid idea."

"Shut up!" Isabel cut through what she thought was chicken. A very small core seemed unsinged. The rice and asparagus were toast.

Toast. That was it.

"Go pick some parsley out of the garden by the door," she ordered as she pulled out the toaster. "And any ripe cherry tomatoes from the pot on the top step."

As Gabriella slouched off, Isabel made toast from bread which seemed a little green around the edges. She cut off the crusts, slathered what remained with butter, then put slivers of blackened chicken on top. The arrangement looked pretty spare on the plates, but wasn't that par for the course with French cuisine? When she'd garnished the lot with a few sprigs of parsley and a sliced cherry tomato each, it didn't look half bad. But it needed something. Any fancy restaurant she'd seen on TV had plates with designs etched in sauce. "Go get the squeeze mustard."

"You are so bossy," Gabriella complained as she retrieved the yellow plastic jar. "I don't need a third parent."

Isabel ignored her sister as she garnished the edge of each plate with a thin design in mustard. Gabriella might not know it, but this was important. As to taste, well, she hoped Mom and Dad were overwhelmed by the romantic atmosphere.

Plates in hand, she pushed through the door into the dining room.

Chessie looked at the strange meal set before her, then up into her daughter's expectant face. "This looks…wonderful, sweetheart. Thank you."

Tentatively, Isabel smiled. "Dad?"

With a lopsided grin, Nick lifted his glass. "Here's to you, kid."

Their daughter let out a big sigh. "Call if you need anything," she said, brightening considerably. "Otherwise, our fine establishment prides eetself in providing our diners with privacee. Privacee and romance, that's our motto. Bon appetit!" With a flourish of her dish towel, she disappeared into the kitchen where she and Gabriella could be heard in muffled disagreement.

"Well," Nick said, prodding the thing-on-toast with his fork. "What do you suppose this is?"

Chessie used her napkin to suppress a giggle. "I don't know, but I hope the toast isn't from the moldy bread I was saving for the seagulls."

He put a blackened slice in his mouth, chewed, then swallowed. After a moment in which he looked as if he thought the morsel might detonate in his stomach, he said, "Chicken, I think. In a very former life." He took a big gulp of cranberry juice, then looked at the two remaining slivers on toast. "Lucky for us they went minimalist."

Chessie's heart melted. Obviously, the girls had worked very hard to make this meal. And on a night when she was scheduled to cook. And now Nick was willing to choke it down.

"Their hearts were in the right place," she said as she dipped a sliced and fanned cherry tomato in mustard. "And the sauce is fittingly French's."

It didn't take them long to finish everything on their plates.

"What happened to your shirt?" she asked as she tried to coax the last few drops of juice from her wineglass.

"I stopped to see Sean. He was transferring

some traps for repair so I helped. Sorry." He brushed at his stained shirtfront.

"That's…great." It was. That he'd made an effort to speak to his brother overrode any laundry issues. He didn't, however, seem inclined to tell her the gist of their conversation.

Isabel popped her head around the door. "I hope you have saved room for deezurt!"

"I don't know." Rubbing his stomach dramatically, Nick leaned back in his chair. "I'm pretty full."

"But," Isabel replied, clearing their plates, "zair eez always room for zee Jell-O!"

When she opened the door to the kitchen, the smell of smoke drifted out as Gabriella could be heard to mutter loudly, "Well, I'm just going to have to throw this pan away!"

The Jell-O had been scooped from individual plastic serving cups into bowls that weren't quite clean, but Chessie felt as if she were eating crème brûlée off bone china. Without prodding, her girls had prepared a meal with Nick and her in mind. Maybe, just maybe, they wouldn't need the behavioral contract she felt certain Nick had brought home in his briefcase. She might not be able to stop him from laying down the law, but she could delay him.

"Bra-a-vo, bra-a-vo, bravo, bravissimo!" She began to sing and clap the chant Nick had taught their daughters as little girls to tell the cook—always Chessie in the past—the meal was particularly appreciated.

Nick picked it up, and the two adults chanted like loonies until Isabel appeared in the doorway, dragging a soap-sudsy Gabriella. They bowed, Izzy more enthusiastically than Gabby, then disappeared back into the kitchen.

Kids. You couldn't live with them, and you couldn't ever figure out what they might do next.

"That came out of left field," Nick remarked, a bemused expression on his face. "What do you suppose got into them?"

"I'm not going to overthink it. It was… charming. Thoughtful and charming."

"But I'm starved," he admitted, keeping his voice low. "And there's no way we're going to raid the refrigerator without hurting their feelings."

"Come with me." Chessie took his hand and led him up to their bedroom. There she got down on her knees and fumbled under the bed. "I keep these for emergencies. Ah, yes!" She held aloft a half-empty can of mixed nuts.

"You keep these hidden, why?"

"I need them at the ready. When I need a PMS salt fix, even a trip to Branson's takes too long." She opened the can. Unfortunately, her periods had always been wildly irregular, and she hadn't seen one in quite a while, judging by the stale nuts. "It's the best I have to offer."

"Sold!" Grabbing a handful, he laughed and the flash of his white teeth was heartening. Of late he rarely got beyond a forced grin.

Like naughty children, they sat on the bed and greedily finished the nuts. Because he'd gone along with the girls even though he looked so tired, Chessie relented in her laundry prohibition. "Why don't you take a shower," she said, "and I'll presoak this shirt."

"You don't have to ask twice." He shrugged out of his shirt, and Chessie was struck by his physique. He'd taken care of himself. He would. He'd see it as a responsibility, think he couldn't take care of his family if he wasn't in A-one shape.

As he ran the water in their bathroom, she looked at his soiled shirt. This past week in particular, his wardrobe had taken a hit. But not because he was thoughtless. Just the opposite. He was a hard worker, her Nick. And a wonderful provider. But his focus worried her. She couldn't erase the memory of her own father, a classic workaholic, who worked himself to an early grave. After his death, her mother quickly remarried and immediately moved to Europe with her new husband. Because she didn't get along with her stepfather, Chessie begged to remain stateside. An arrangement was made with two elderly aunts, one of whom died while Chessie was in high school, the other when she was in college. The absence of family made Chessie readily agree to Nick's offer of a traditional family.

Chessie looked up from Nick's shirt to the photos framed and lining the dresser. As the girls grew and their flying-the-nest time neared, she worried what would become of her and Nick. After the childrearing was over, if he didn't see her as a woman attractive and worthy in her own right, would he, too, move on? If she were honest with herself, did she really want to be independent, or did she crave a closer relationship with Nick?

She put aside the soiled shirt, closed the

bedroom door, then headed for the bathroom, shedding her clothes along the way.

Some striker she turned out to be.

Nick was already in the shower.

"Want company?" she asked, sliding the door open.

The hard look of longing in his eyes gave her the answer.

Stepping into the warm spray, she reached for the soap in his hand. How long had it been since they'd showered together? Forever.

He turned to face the wall, and she soaped his broad back, his strong shoulders, his well-muscled arms. She loved how his back veed down to his narrow waist and tight buttocks. Avoiding the waterproof patch over the dog bite, she soaped his thighs and calves, then slid her hands back up his legs to encircle his waist. She leaned the side of her face against his back and let the water wash over her. Warm and healing.

As he turned in her arms, she stepped back. He faced her, solemn and watchful and fully erect. When she moved to soap his chest, he caught her wrists. It was obvious cleanliness wasn't foremost on his mind.

Roughly, he pulled her to him. The soap

dropped. He kissed her hungrily and she felt need rise from deep within her. She had missed him so much. Arching against him, she let out a soft cry. With a low growl, he cupped her bottom, lifted her and pressed her back against the cold tiles.

She wrapped her arms around his neck, her legs around his waist as he entered her. His movements were primitive and forceful and over far too soon. Not lovemaking, but urgent and possessive sex. Although she'd felt passion, she'd felt no release.

Breathing heavily, he held her tightly for a few seconds. There were no sweet afterwords although, when he let her down, he did it gently. And when he washed her, he did so intently as if he were marking her as his.

He turned the water off, then reached for towels. He wrapped her, and then dried himself. Silently. Watching her.

She wanted words—assurances—but he offered none.

After he'd dressed and gone downstairs, she felt cold. And alone.

GABRIELLA DUMPED the supplies she'd taken from the pantry onto her bed, then searched her room for her backpack.

She wouldn't run away tonight, but she was going to run away. She had to.

Earlier, while Isabel was taking out the trash and Gabriella was wiping down the kitchen counters, she'd kicked her dad's briefcase by mistake. It had opened and spilled his papers. When she'd started to stuff them back in, she'd seen the stupid contract.

She and Izzy were trying to do something nice for their parents, and they were planning to take away even more privileges. And here Mom had been going on all week about personal freedom and choices. Parents could be such hypocrites.

Gabriella hadn't shown Isabel the contract. Instead, she'd stuffed it in her pocket, betting it wasn't even designed for her sister. Miss Perfect. Miss Brown-Nose Suck-Up Perfect. She was sure Mom and Dad were going to lay down the law for her alone. Because she'd screwed up once. Apparently, the humiliation of being grounded wasn't enough.

That guy Owen had gotten one thing right. If she didn't like it here, she needed to strike out on her own. She could do it. Lots of other kids did. She just needed a plan so she wouldn't get caught. Getting caught only got you in more trouble.

Finding her backpack, she stuffed it with the granola bars and sports drinks she'd brought up from the kitchen. She added some clean underwear, a change of clothes and a few toiletries. The bag wouldn't hold anything more. That was okay. She was going to be traveling light.

Maybe she'd try hopping freight trains. She'd seen a special on the travel channel. It seemed exciting.

But she knew enough to wait for the perfect time. That would be hard, considering she was grounded. The only time their parents weren't breathing down her neck was when she was sleeping. So nighttime would be good. Not tonight, though. She had supplies, but no money. Tomorrow she'd find a way to lift a little bit each from Mom, Dad, Isabel and the emergency Mason jar. After that she'd be free.

ISABEL STOOD in front of her bathroom mirror and smiled before slathering cold cream across her eyeliner mustache.

Aunt Emily had been right. Despite the flame-broiled entrée, the meal had gone well. Mom and Dad seemed to get a kick out of it.

She and Gabriella had even had a few yucks as they'd cleaned up, although, when Isabel had come back from taking the garbage out, Gabby was back to her totally grouchy self. How could anyone run a marriage with kids?

And, over all, was the nice feeling that, if she couldn't talk to Mom or Dad, she could talk to Aunt Emily.

She wiped the cold cream off her face, closed the jar and opened the medicine cabinet door. When she slid the jar on a shelf, she noticed the familiar packet of straight-edge razors.

She hesitated.

No, the pain wasn't there. Not at the moment. And a poet should always try to stay in the moment.

She closed the cabinet door. She wouldn't need her little friends tonight.

CHAPTER ELEVEN

TUESDAY MORNING Chessie came downstairs to a clean kitchen. Dishes washed and put away. Garbage emptied. Surfaces cleared and wiped. Wonder of wonders. The laundry still needed to be done, but it could wait. She decided to let the girls sleep in. Call it positive reinforcement for their creative dinner last night.

As she was making coffee, Nick appeared, showered, shaved, dressed and ready for work. "Have you seen my briefcase?"

"By the door." After last night's encounter in the shower, she felt unsettled in his presence. As she imagined one might feel after a one-night stand. A little awkward in the light of day. Not that she'd ever had a one-night stand. Nick was her first and only lover.

Too, she was wondering if he considered last night a capitulation in her no-sex ultimatum. Did she? How could she not? This was a little more tricky than falling off a diet and starting back on the celery sticks the next day.

"I was sure I brought home the girls' contract," he said, rummaging through the mess of paperwork.

Oh, that. Chessie didn't care if that bit of heavy-handedness ever saw the light of day.

"I'll print out another copy and give it to them tonight."

Chessie chose to ignore the issue altogether. It was his idea. He could handle the fallout. "Coffee?" She really wanted to ask about last night, but he seemed securely locked in business mode.

"No. I'm having a breakfast meeting to finalize plans for the staff field day. I'm late." He started toward the door, but stopped. "About last night..."

"Yes?"

"It was...different. Sexy."

It had been, but it hadn't been intimate. She still craved intimacy. Watching him leave, she wondered if different meant progress.

And watching him leave, she realized his mention of the staff field day had surprised her. This year he hadn't invited her.

Perplexed, she grabbed a mug and the full

pot of coffee and headed through the utility room toward her studio, only to notice a Lexus pull into the spot in the driveway Nick had just vacated. Not looking forward to an interruption—she hadn't worked on her own pottery in over a week—but not wanting to discourage a potential customer, she put down the coffee to open the barn door. Ursula Delacorte, the woman who'd shown an interest in her free-form idea, emerged from the luxury car.

Oh, great. Chessie had no more than a title, a sketch and a very rough working model, barely more than she'd had when she and Ursula had spoken two weeks ago.

"Good morning," she called, hoping her potential patron understood the sometimes halting artistic process.

"Hello, hello!" Ursula trilled. "I was up bright and early and thought I'd take a ride down the coast to see how my piece is coming along."

"It's coming," Chessie replied, forcing the optimism.

"May I see?"

"Hmm…I usually like to wait to unveil the finished piece." That wasn't quite true. She'd only ever sold finished pieces. This was her first ever attempt at a commission. "A work in progress can be ambiguous. Confusing to—"

"Nonsense." Ursula breezed by in a cloud of rich scent. "I'm a sophisticated art lover. And a hands-on patron. I've been told I can be quite the muse."

Uh-oh. That sounded a lot like interference.

Chessie followed her up the barn stairs and into the studio.

"Now, where is it?"

"Over here." Chessie lifted the moist cloth covering the worked and reworked form on her revolving table. The rough sketch of the envisioned piece was tacked to a timber. Under Ursula's scrutiny the project looked pretty pathetic.

"When do you think you'll finish?"

"That's hard to say…"

Ursula now gave her a frank appraisal. "This is your first commission."

"Yes."

"You've never worked under deadline."

"No." Except for the classes she taught, she'd always worked when her family sched-ule allowed.

"A deadline helps." Ursula smiled, Cheshire-cat-like. "And I have the deadline for you."

"You do?" Chessie so wanted this commission, but her plate was full with family issues.

"I'm having my house redecorated. Lovely creams and sea green. I've told my decorator everything must be absolutely finished in a week and a half when I'll be having an open house. The invitations have already been sent. I'd like to highlight your piece in the foyer."

"A week and a half?" Chessie squeaked.

"Yes. But I've just given you an important jump-start. An idea, if you're blocked."

Chessie cocked her head in question.

"For your glazes. Now you know my colors. You certainly wouldn't choose anything that clashed. So your palette is a given."

Wishing she were wearing her "Real art does not match the sofa" T-shirt, Chessie stared at Ursula in disbelief.

"You do want the commission?"

"Y-yes." She did. Heck, even Michelangelo had his patron problems. "I do."

"Good." Ursula headed for the stairs. "Of course, I'll want to pick up the piece well before the party. Say, one week from today?"

Pardon? She had to get a major work ready

in a week. With the girls on her mind. And Nick. Moreover, she had to make certain "Her Head Was in the Goddess Movement, but Her Feet Were Firmly Planted in the PTA" blended nicely with a fresh cream and sea green décor.

Right. And this was all going to happen in what universe?

At least she didn't have to lie to Ursula. While Chessie was locked in shock, her patron had descended the stairs with a self-assured wave and a swirl of perfume. It probably never entered Ursula Delacorte's head that anyone might disagree with her.

Chessie wondered how it would feel to be a woman like that.

She glanced out the window and saw Martha and Keri getting into Martha's SUV. Although she sure could use a sticky bun session, she'd wait a couple days to approach Martha. She hoped their friendship hadn't been irreparably damaged. But in any event, they needed to talk as two parents.

Sighing heavily, Chessie turned to her work-in-progress. How could she show what she so passionately felt about relationships. Friendships. Family. Spouses. Business associations. They were all so tenuous, and maintaining them usually fell to women. But what about the relationship of a woman to herself? That concept, which too often got lost in the shuffle, was really what she was trying to portray in this piece. The title had come easily from her own experience, but the execution of the work itself was still frozen inside her.

Now, under a very tight deadline, she sat and smashed the project to a shapeless lump.

THAT EVENING Nick faced his unhappy family across the dining room table. He'd just finished explaining the new behavioral contract to Isabel and Gabriella.

"Why are you treating us like infants?" Gabriella complained, shoving her copy away.

"I'm not," he replied. "I'm treating you like mature individuals. Mature individuals enter into contracts. That's the real world."

"In the real world both parties have a say in what goes into the contract. I didn't have a say in this. Did you, Izzy?"

Isabel sat staring at him with big hurt eyes and said nothing. He did feel a little guilty including her in this. She was a year away from college, and lately it was almost as if she were trying to make up for Gabriella's behavior. But it was a tough world out there and getting tougher, and he was determined to keep them both safe. At least on his watch.

"What…did you all know about this?" Gabriella turned to Chessie. "Mom?"

Chessie had been as silent as Isabel. She hadn't gone against his plan tonight, but she hadn't endorsed it either. "If I may make one suggestion," she now said, ignoring Gabriella's question. "I think the contract should have a renewal date—in the near future—when all four of us sit down and evaluate it."

She had a point. He always tried to get his teachers to set realistic goals for their students. Realistic deterrents. And always with a very specific timeline. How come good management was easier with a staff of a hundred and a student body of a thousand than with one wife and two daughters?

"Okay," he conceded. "Girls, what would be a fair trial period?"

"Trial is right," Gabriella groused. "You're asking the convicted to pick their sentence."

He turned to Chessie for support—they'd always presented a united parental front—

but, for the first time in their marriage, she didn't offer any encouragement.

She seemed disengaged.

"Isabel?"

"I don't know what to say, Dad. I liked the open forum we used to use."

"We'll use it at the evaluation. In two weeks."

"Two weeks!" Gabriella smacked her hands on the table. "That's forever!"

"We'll see if time flies when you're busy. I called your grandfather. He needs a cashier at the lobster pound."

"Like I want to work with stinking fish all day."

"Then come back in two weeks with another part-time job or a good idea for volunteer work in the community."

"How can I look for a job when I'm grounded?"

"I told you the contract, when you sign it, stands in place of being grounded."

"The contract's worse than being grounded."

"No it's not," he insisted. "Except for the job or volunteering part, this contract is no different from the expectations your mother and I've had for you all along."

"Except now they're written in stone."

"No. Now they're spelled out so no one can misinterpret them." He signed his name on the first line at the bottom of the page, then passed the sheet to Chessie.

With a sharp intake of breath, she eyed the document as if it might bite. After a long pause, she reached for the pen, slowly signed her name next to his, then passed the paper along to Isabel. He was relieved she hadn't voiced objections in front of the girls.

Without looking up, Isabel signed.

"Traitor!" Gabriella shrieked, bolting from her chair with such force it tipped over. "Well, I'm not signing!"

"Gabriella," Chessie said evenly. "Go to your room."

"Gladly!" Without picking up the chair, she stormed out of the dining room and up the stairs. Overhead, her door slammed.

Chessie stood. "Isabel, honey, I need some input on a color scheme I've been developing. In my studio. Could you?"

"Sure, Mom." With little enthusiasm she rose to follow her mother out of the room.

"I think that went well," Nick muttered sarcastically to the four walls. He rose to pace the room.

No matter what Gabriella thought, the contract wasn't meant to be a punishment. He wanted his daughters to understand that society had rules, and their family was a microcosm of society. He hadn't intended to take any power from Chessie as a parent. Tonight he'd listened to her suggestion, and together they'd decided on a trial period. And he never intended to take the spirit out of his daughters. But when Isabel left the room just now, she'd looked pale and fragile.

Very simply, he'd wanted to do the right thing to ensure his family's well-being.

This afternoon Quentin, his band director, had come into Nick's office asking for personal advice. It seems Quentin and his wife had hit a rough patch in their marriage after the birth of their first child. Nick had urged him to remember that a couple existed long after kids grew up and went away. Quentin had thanked him for "his expertise." Expertise, hah! The man couldn't know that Nick felt like a charlatan as a family counselor.

LATER THAT NIGHT Chessie slipped into bed beside Nick who was, as usual, buried in paperwork. The logistics of moving a hundred staff members around the field on spirit day. An event she hadn't wanted to attend, but now felt somehow excluded from. She hated herself for being petty.

"The girls?" he asked, looking up.

"Gabriella's locked herself in her room. Morning will be soon enough to talk to her. I talked to Isabel. She actually liked the idea of a part-time job. Thought she might talk to your dad about the cashier position. She just wished you'd presented the whole contract idea as up for discussion."

"The way things have been going lately, they needed to see that we have a plan. In black and white. That we're not a family flying by the seat of our pants."

"I know."

"You do?"

She turned on her side to face him. "You think I'm fighting you in some way, Nick, but I'm not. I still want the same things you do, a strong family included."

"Then why does it feel as if we're at odds?"

"We're a family, but we're four individuals. With individual needs. It's not always a smooth combination."

"But you're willing to keep going." He looked unsure.

"Of course." How could he doubt it?

When she touched his face, his look turned hungry.

Without preamble he moved on top of her, scattering papers. Because she'd initiated the encounter in the shower, the subsequent quick, hot sex hadn't been a surprise. But this move from a sea of schoolwork came unexpectedly and she wasn't ready when he tried to enter her.

"Ow! Wait, Nick—"

Instantly, he pulled away, turning his back to her.

"I'm sorry I hurt you." He had lost control. To Nick, an unpardonable lapse in judgment.

"I wasn't ready, but…" She wanted to try again. She needed the closeness, too.

His silence told her there would be no second chance tonight. Why was he so hard on himself?

Sadly, she turned out the light.

GABRIELLA KNEW tonight had to be the night. She couldn't live in this house one more day.

Wide awake, she lay on her bed until her

bedside digital clock flipped to exactly midnight. No sounds came from either her parents' or Isabel's rooms. It had to be safe to make a move now.

She slung her backpack over one shoulder and picked up her sneakers. Tentatively, she opened her bedroom door. One of the cats immediately wound around her legs, throwing her off balance. Grabbing the banister, she clamped her jaws shut and waited until her heartbeat returned to normal before tiptoeing downstairs in the dark.

The moonlight pouring through the kitchen windows made the familiar room look weird. As if it wasn't any place Gabriella had ever lived in. Fine. It would make leaving easy. She made her way over to the Mason jar—she'd lifted five bucks each from Mom, Dad and Isabel—and emptied the emergency fund. A few singles and change. Bummer.

The phone rang and made her drop the change.

Who the hell was calling after midnight? Gabriella lunged for the phone, catching it before the second ring. Just her luck if the parents woke up.

"Hello?" she whispered into the mouthpiece.

It was a freakin' wrong number. Idiots. She was surrounded by idiots.

To ensure this particular idiot didn't call back, wake her parents and ruin her lead time, she left the phone off the hook. Stuffing the bills from the Mason jar in her pocket—she couldn't waste time picking up the change—she slipped outside, pausing only to put on her sneakers.

Pulling her bicycle from the side of the barn, she wheeled it out toward the road and freedom.

She had a plan. Although freight trains ran through the nearby towns of Kennebunk and Wells, they didn't stop at either place. She needed a freight yard, and Portland had the closest. She could get to Portland on the turnpike, maybe by hitching. And the nearest turnpike entrance was a few miles up the road. An easy bike ride, although she knew enough not to ride her bike right through the toll gate. When she got close, she'd hide it in the bushes and sneak on the highway.

That was the plan. It had seemed so simple as she went over it, lying on her bed. Now, however, it seemed a little daunting. For one thing, her bike didn't have a light. The moonlight should have been some help, but it cast such long, sharp shadows that depth and distance were skewed, making the landscape really creepy. For another, it was hot and humid, and the effort of pedaling with a heavy pack on her back made sweat trickle into her eyes. She wished she'd thought to bring a ball cap.

At one point a carload of teenagers raced by, stereo bass thumping. Someone threw an empty beer bottle at her, unnerving her enough that she took shelter in some trees.

Was this really a good idea?

Gabriella thought about how her mother was beginning to act like she had a life separate from the rest of them and how her father was acting like a dictator and how Isabel was becoming some weird Stepford kid and how Keri had betrayed her.

And how she didn't seem to fit in anywhere.

Peering out from the shelter of the trees and not seeing traffic in either direction, she wheeled her bike back onto the lonely road.

UNABLE TO SLEEP, Isabel slipped out of bed and headed to the kitchen for some of her mom's chamomile infusion.

She liked that Mom had asked her advice on

different glazes earlier that evening, in her studio, after Dad had gone all macho and laid down the law with that contract. She'd signed it so as not to make waves. Actually, he was right in that it wasn't all that different than what he and Mom usually expected, but he didn't have to spring it on them without a discussion. It made her feel as if he didn't have much confidence in her. Of course, Gabriella—

Something wasn't right.

She switched on the kitchen light to see the side door ajar, the phone off the hook and coins scattered all over the floor.

Oh, my God! It looked like the scene of a robbery.

She screamed.

And kept screaming until she felt her father and mother by her side.

"What the—" Dad began to check the rooms downstairs.

"Go see if Gabriella's all right," Mom urged.

She didn't have to ask twice. Isabel raced upstairs. It was horrible, just horrible, to think your family wasn't safe.

Gabriella's door was ajar. "Gabby! Wake up!" When she flipped on the overhead light, she squinted, trying to focus on the rumpled indentation in the middle of her sister's empty bed.

"Gabby?" Their shared bathroom was also empty.

She checked her parents' room, their bathroom and even her own room before heading back downstairs with a sinking heart.

"Well?" Mom turned to her as Dad came in from outside.

"Gabriella's bicycle's gone," he said.

"She's not upstairs." Tears stung Isabel's eyes. "I think...she's run away." Why'd she been so angry with her earlier?

"Did you know about this?"

"No!" Isabel stepped back as if stung. "She doesn't share stuff with me anymore."

"I should've seen it coming." Dad picked up the receiver that had been dangling off the hook and started to make a call.

"Wait, Dad! Hit star sixty-nine. Maybe you can find out who she was talking to."

"Good idea." It might have been, but he came up empty. "Unlisted number. Who the hell could she have been talking to?"

Both parents turned to Isabel as if she might know.

"Baylee Warner, Margot Hensley...? I

don't know. She was feeling pretty isolated from that whole crowd. Not Keri. Definitely not. That was over."

"Write me a list. Anyone you can think of." Her mother pulled her cell phone from her purse hanging on the kitchen doorknob. "I'll call the parents."

Part of Dad's contract, Isabel thought, was to provide a list of friends, their parents and the contact info. They sure could use something like that now.

"My cell's upstairs," her father said. "I'll call the police, then I'll head out to see if I can find her. Isabel, use the kitchen phone to start calling the family. Someone has to know where she might've gone."

Her fingers trembling, Isabel dialed her grandfather's number. Uncle Jonas, who wasn't married and still lived at home, answered. "Yeah?" He sure sounded as if she woke him up.

"Uncle Jonas, this is Isabel. Gabriella's run away. Is she with you and Gramps?"

"No, hon, she isn't. But I'll get dressed and start driving around. I'll call your grandfather, too. He's making the midnight run of lobsters to the Portland restaurant co-op. If your sister headed for the turnpike, he might run into her."

She could hear him fumbling, as if getting dressed. "Now don't you worry," he said. "We're going to find her."

"Thanks." She hung up. As she was looking up Uncle Sean's number, she could hear her mom talking on her cell. She didn't seem to be having much luck either.

Isabel called Uncle Sean, Aunt Mariah and Uncle Brad. None of them had seen Gabriella, but each of them promised to hit the road, searching. She couldn't believe it. It was one-thirty in the morning, and she'd called up a family posse just like that. How could you not feel optimistic when the McCabes had your back?

Her mom didn't look so optimistic. "No one's seen or heard from her," she said, her cell phone in her lap. She looked as if she were trying hard not to cry.

Isabel moved across the kitchen to put her arms around her mother's shoulders. "It's going to be okay," she offered. "She can't have gone far. She only has her bike."

Her father came back into the kitchen. "I talked to George Weiss. He says they can't file an official missing persons report till twenty-four hours after she's disappeared. But off the record, the officers will keep an eye out for her on their regular rounds. I'm going—"

The phone rang, making them all jump.

Dad got it first.

"Thank God!" He slumped against the counter. "It's Pop," he said, turning to Isabel and her mother. "He picked Gabby up just before the turnpike. She's okay."

"You'll bring her back?" he said into the mouthpiece, then frowned at her grandfather's answer. "No. Chessie and I will handle it. Pop—"

At that moment Martha Weiss came through the side door, carrying a pot of coffee. "George called," she said, hugging Chessie. "I thought you could use the caffeine."

Mom started to cry for real.

When Dad got off the phone, he didn't look happy. "Pop's making a run to Portland. He's taking Gabriella with him."

"Why?"

"He says he's had some experience with kids and he'd like to take a crack at her."

Isabel laughed out loud with relief.

Her father looked at her as if she'd lost it. "Geez, Dad, I'd think you'd be doing cartwheels." She gave him a big bear hug. "We're not alone any more."

CHAPTER TWELVE

GABRIELLA STARED across the cab of the truck at her grandfather.

"I got a full tank of gas and the night ahead of me, missy. We're gonna drive till I get the whole story." He looked like he meant it.

She glanced through the rear window at her bike—symbol of her failed mission— wedged in the truck bed between crates of lobsters. It seemed you couldn't get away with anything in a small town.

"Why'd you run away?"

"'Cause I can make it on my own," she declared despite the fact that she hadn't even made it to the turnpike entrance.

"You think so? How much money you got?"

"Eighteen bucks."

He seemed to think that over. Seriously. In fact, Gabriella had never seen Gramps so serious. With the grandkids he was all fooling around and fun. Always.

"Where'd you get the money? Earn it on your own?"

"No," she mumbled.

"Speak up."

"I said no. I got it from Mom and Dad. And Isabel."

"Ah."

That one syllable made her feel far more guilty than all the recent lectures, being grounded and that stupid contract. When he didn't say anything more, she made herself small on her side of the seat and stared out the windshield across the median at the headlights streaming by. Why couldn't she have been picked up by a trucker?

They drove all the way to Portland without a word. With every passing mile, Gabriella felt smaller and smaller. When they stopped at a waterfront warehouse, Gramps got out of the truck to unload the lobster crates. Several men helped him, all of them, Gramps included, talking and joking even after the bed was empty. Her grandfather didn't bother to introduce her.

When he got back behind the wheel, she was miserable.

"Hungry?" he asked.

"What?"

"Are you hungry? After my run I usually stop at this all-night diner up the way for breakfast."

"I could eat." In fact, she was starving.

A couple blocks from the warehouse, Gramps pulled the truck over again. The only light came from what looked like a hole in the wall in a long row of dark buildings. "Come on, sport."

Gabriella hustled to keep up with him. A neon sign shaped like a cup of coffee flickered over the diner's single front window, which was smeared with grease. This wasn't like the places where her parents took her to eat.

"Keep your hands in your pockets and your eyes to yourself," Gramps said as he opened the door. "Lot of wharf rats and sailors like this joint."

Oh, great. That was reassuring.

The room was long and skinny and none too bright, and the air conditioner over the door made a horrible racket. Gabriella was surprised to see all the stools at the counter and most of the booths along the wall occupied. Guys mostly. Dressed in work clothes or white uniforms.

"Penn!" the sole waitress said as her grandfather headed for the last booth in the farthest corner. "Coffee?"

"Ayuh. And a hot chocolate." He slid into the booth with his back to the wall.

Jeeze, Gabriella thought as she sat across from him, It's a hundred degrees outside and he orders coffee and hot chocolate.

But by the time the waitress came with their drinks, the air conditioner had her chilled to the bone.

"They make good waffles." Gramps poured five packets of sugar into his coffee.

"And bacon?" Gabriella didn't want to press her luck, but she was really hungry.

"Waffles and bacon. Make that two orders," Gramps said to the waitress with a wink.

Gabriella sipped her hot chocolate and tried not to make eye contact. She was waiting for the lecture.

"You know," he said at last, "you remind me of your dad."

Startled, she looked up.

"And a little bit of me."

Make that stunned. "How?"

"Well, for starters, I ran away when I was your age. And so did your dad. In fact, he was the only one of my five to ever try it."

"Dad ran away?" Gabriella couldn't picture it. Her dad wasn't the running-away kind. He faced things head-on. Always. And expected Gabriella and Isabel to do the same. "Why?"

Gramps looked sad. "When he was your age, his mom—your grandmother—had been gone two years. Your dad took care of his brothers and sister while I worked."

"He, like, babysat?"

"No." Her grandfather took a long, slow sip of his coffee. "He fed them, bathed them. Jonas was only a toddler. He helped them with their homework. And he watched them like a hawk. Kept them safe. He was my right hand man, and he did a helluva job."

Gabriella's eyes went wide. Dad had never told her this. Yeah, she knew he was the oldest, but…she couldn't imagine handling that much responsibility. Four kids to take care of every day. Once she and Isabel babysat overnight for Aunt Emily and Uncle Brad's four kids, and they'd slept most of the next day.

"It was too much for a kid," Gramps continued, "though it couldn't be helped. Not if we were going to stay together."

"What do you mean?"

"Social services was always sniffing around."

Gabriella couldn't believe what she was hearing. She'd been to school with kids from foster homes. She couldn't imagine her uncles and her aunt—her dad—having that hanging over their heads.

"Why'd he run away?"

Gramps shook his head. "I think he just needed some peace and quiet. He was only fourteen after all. About to start high school, like you. After forty-eight hours he came back home on his own. Picked up where he left off, only he was a little distant after that. I still don't know where he went."

"What did you do to him?" She sure was worried about what Dad would do to her after tonight.

"Nothing. He'd gone through enough. Losing his mother. Taking on the family."

Gabriella felt her throat grow tight. Even with all the weird things Mom had done lately, well, she didn't want to think about not having a mother.

"But I never told him…" Her grandfather screwed up his face as if he were in pain.

"What, Gramps? What didn't you tell him?"

He took a deep breath, then reached across the table to lay his big, rough hand over hers. His smile seemed forced. "You know, the best thing that ever happened to your dad was meeting your mom. Boy, could she make him laugh. And then you girls… Well, you made his life complete."

She looked at her grandfather and wondered what he hadn't told her dad.

Their waffles and bacon arrived, and the two of them ate in silence. When they were finished, she asked, "Do parents ever wish they didn't have kids? I mean, you said we made Dad's life complete, but I don't think he's too happy with us right now."

"I'd be a liar if I said he didn't want a bit of space now and again, but give you up? Never. It'd break his and your mom's hearts if anything ever happened to you. They'd never stop blaming themselves."

She trailed her fork in the leftover syrup on her plate. "You said I was like you and Dad. Did you just mean the running away part?"

"No." He looked her right in the eye. "I meant the chip on the shoulder part."

"I don't—"

"Yeah, you do. A real big heavy one. A chip's not all bad," her grandfather continued. "At first. It keeps you alert. No one can take advantage of you. But if you don't learn to deal with it, it grows and grows. And trying to keep it up there, you end up keeping everybody around you at a distance. And that's not healthy."

"It's Isabel that keeps everybody at a distance. Not me."

"No, you've got it wrong. Isabel might stick to herself with her poems, but she's got a big, soft heart. She wants to take care of people, and she knows she needs to be taken care of, too."

"And people with chips on their shoulders?"

"We think we can take on the world all by ourselves. But I'll let you in on a little secret. We can't. And the sooner we let others help us, the sooner we let them know we appreciate their help, the better off we'll feel. The lighter the chip will be. Pretty soon it's all gone. And we're a lot nicer people to be around."

The waitress came with the check.

"She's paying," Gramps said, pointing to Gabriella.

It took most of her eighteen dollars to cover the bill plus the tip.

ALTHOUGH CHESSIE AND Nick stayed in bed until the alarm went off, neither slept. Nick held her because she'd asked him to, but he was stiff and cold beside her. She doubted he took any comfort from her.

He shut the alarm off, then sat on the edge of the bed. "Why wouldn't he bring her home?"

"You said he wanted a shot at talking to her."

"Because he thought I hadn't handled her very well up until now."

"Did he say that?"

"He didn't have to."

"Why would you think your father doesn't approve of the way you're raising your daughters?"

"Because he didn't approve of the way I took care of my brothers and my sister."

Chessie was stunned by the vehemence in his tone. "Nick, your father has never said one word against the way you handled your siblings."

"You've got it. He never said a word to me about it. Period."

"And all these years you've interpreted that silence as condemnation?"

"How else should I interpret it?"

"That Penn was never one to express his feelings. He's not an effusive man, but he's not uncaring." She stroked Nick's bare back and felt him tense. "That your brothers and your sister have grown to be good people is testament to the care you gave them. Penn is proud of them. And you."

"If you say so." He headed for the bathroom.

It came to her in a flash. Jumping out of bed, she followed him. "This whole distance from your family is because you think you failed them in some way."

He didn't answer.

"And this control you exercise over your own family—Gabby, Izzy, me—it's because you're afraid of feeling that way with us."

"It's not a fear thing."

"Semantics."

"Okay." He inhaled sharply. "I always felt as if I was going to screw up back then. And the stakes were so high. We were always one step away from state care."

"But you made it through. Your brothers and sister are okay. Let yourself breathe now."

"Now I have my own family."

"And you have me. You're not alone." She put her arms around him and drew him into a kiss.

Responding with a passion she hadn't felt from him in a very long time, he groaned and pulled her closer yet. Kissed her with an insistence that made her think they might end up making hot, rough sex against the bathroom door.

But just as quickly as he'd drawn her to him, he stepped away. Although she could see longing in his eyes, his stance was wary, making Chessie wonder for the first time whether Nick had ever given himself totally to her. It was clear now that he'd set himself apart, emotionally, from the McCabe family to cope with the horrible possibility of losing them. Even today, when he was in a position to keep her and the girls safe, did he suffer from the double-edged specter of failure and loss? She'd always thought Nick-in-charge was simply who he was. Was it a front? If so, her Fourth of July rebellion would've looked like a direct assault.

"Nick—"

"I have to get going." He stepped into the shower. "I have an eight o'clock interview with a possible Latin teacher. At this late date, if she's breathing, she's got the job."

"You can't stay until your dad brings Gabriella home?"

"You'll be here."

The phone rang. Isabel picked up an extension just as Chessie answered. It was Penn. Gabriella was going to help him prep the pound for opening, and he'd bring her home in an hour or so.

Chessie and Isabel met up on the landing, Isabel in sweatpants and a long-sleeved sweatshirt despite the warm morning. "How'd you sleep?" Chessie asked.

"I didn't."

"Me neither. Let's go make some coffee."

As Isabel went in search of the newspaper, Chessie began to make coffee. When she opened the bag, the aroma of beans that usually gave her a lift made her downright queasy. Family turmoil and lack of sleep were beginning to affect her on an elemental level. This had to stop. She had to find her way back to her center, and her center was Nick.

There would be no working on that relationship this morning, however. Before Isabel could come back with the paper, Nick came downstairs ready for work. When he saw the coffee hadn't been made, he said he'd pick up a breakfast sandwich combo at Branson's, gave Chessie a quick kiss and headed out the door. It almost—almost—seemed as if he were avoiding the possibility of running into Penn and Gabriella.

"I can't find the paper," Isabel declared, coming in five minutes later. "Do you suppose anything will ever be right again?"

"Of course it will." Chessie gave her daughter a quick hug before the teenager flopped into a chair. "But I think you're mistaking right for perfect."

Isabel shot her mother a quizzical look.

"You're the poet. The wordsmith," Chessie said, pulling up a chair. "What you put on the paper is never as perfect as that thought or image in your head, but sometimes it comes out right. Or right enough. Like life."

"So Gabriella's running away is all right?"

"Not right as in the best choice, but right as in fitting a fourteen-year-old's developmental pattern. You've taken an introductory psych course. You know impulse control is both hardwired and learned. Well, Gabby's hardwiring is under construction. Just like every other teenager. Hers more seriously than some, it seems."

"And because of it, she gets off?"

"No. As a parent I need to understand, then help her learn to curb those impulses. To become an adult."

Isabel gazed at her hands. "You're an adult, but it didn't look as if you were curbing your impulses on the Fourth of July."

Ah, her daughter still hadn't reconciled that episode.

"Do you think I'm selfish for trying to be my own woman?"

Isabel looked up. Almost looked Chessie in the eye. "Don't you think you're a little old to be finding yourself?"

"Honey, we're always finding ourselves." Chessie took Isabel's hand. "Think like a poet, not like my daughter."

Enlightenment suddenly flickered in the seventeen-year-old's eyes before worry replaced it. "Does Dad understand all this?"

"Yes." Chessie thought he did. Hoped he

did. They needed some serious couple-time to confirm it.

At that moment Gabriella came into the kitchen with Penn close behind. Her younger daughter looked exhausted, but, at the same time, calm.

Penn put his hand on Gabriella's shoulder.

"Mom," Gabriella said, staring at a spot on the floor near Chessie's feet, "I'm sorry."

Penn cleared his throat, and Gabriella actually looked Chessie in the eye. "I really am." She sounded sincere.

Chessie couldn't remember the last time her fourteen-year-old had apologized. After the terror she'd put them all through last night, Chessie wanted to read Gabriella the riot act, but Penn caught her eye. With an almost imperceptible nod of his head he seemed to tell her things were okay. For now.

"Apology accepted," she finally said.

Gabriella exhaled as if she'd been holding her breath. "Where's Dad?"

"At work. He had an early interview."

Both Penn and Gabriella looked disappointed.

Penn patted his granddaughter's shoulder.

"Get some sleep, scout. You can apologize to your dad when he gets home."

"Thanks, Gramps." Gabriella threw her arms around her grandfather's neck before dashing upstairs.

"Thank you, Penn," Chessie said. "Words can't—"

"As the kids say, no problem." Penn grinned.

"Did she tell you why she ran away?"

"She said she could take care of herself. But my opinion? I think she just painted herself into a corner and couldn't think of a way out. You know how that sometimes happens."

Yeah. Chessie felt sort of painted into her own corner.

"I gave her a few things to think about," Penn added, "from a grandfather's perspective. But I have to shove off. The tourists will be beating down the pound door otherwise. Who knew lobsters were a breakfast food?"

Chessie tried to hug her father-in-law, but he brushed her off. "No mush!" He ruffled Isabel's hair, then left.

Isabel looked up at Chessie. "I know one thing that's right. Moving back to Pritchard's Neck where we have family."

Yes. If parenthood was easier in a tag team, the bigger the team the better.

GABRIELLA FELL into bed and let the tears flow. She was so, so tired, but when she closed her eyes and tried to sleep, all she could see was Gramps without a wife and Dad without a mother. The two of them working to keep the kids out of a foster home. The worry. If she thought she felt like crap when Keri abandoned her, how much worse had Mom and Dad felt when they thought she'd left for good? Would her running away mean they weren't fit parents? Would social services start sniffing around, as Gramps had said? Obviously, she hadn't thought things through. Her grandfather had made her see the stakes.

THAT EVENING Nick came home, eager to see for himself that Gabriella was safe and sound. And eager to talk to Chessie. He had big news. A major decision. A way, perhaps, to get their family back on track.

Isabel and Gabriella were in the kitchen, making salad and what looked like home-made pizza. He was surprised at the ordinary domesticity of the scene.

"Dad?"

Gabriella stood near the stove, uncertainty on her face. Pop had called him at work to fill him in, to urge him not to be too hard on his daughter. Their conversation was brief. Nick had been in the middle of a meeting, and his father had seemed irritated by that.

"Yes, Gabby?"

She flew at him and hugged him around his middle. Held on as if she had no intention of letting go. "Daddy!" she sobbed into his shirtfront. She hadn't called him Daddy since first grade. As he held her, he was amazed that his tough-as-nails daughter was so soft and small. "I'm sorry."

"It's okay." Gently he asked, "Where's your mom?"

"At her art class," Isabel replied as she grated cheese. "She should be home anytime now."

Was it Wednesday already? A whole week since he'd charged into that class and suffered a dog bite for his efforts? Unbelievable.

"Something smells wonderful!" Chessie burst through the doorway, sketch pad in hand, her face aglow.

"Pizza," Gabriella said, snuffling and stepping out of his embrace. "Homemade."

"And Caesar salad." Isabel untied the dish towel wrapped around her waist. "Ready to eat?"

"I'm starving," he said, wondering anew at the fluctuations of adolescence. One minute chaos, the next quiet accomplishment. "How'd your class go?" he asked Chessie.

She seemed taken back by his question, but quickly recovered with a smile. "Great! You remember Sandy Weston, the sculptor? Well, while we were drawing, he gave me some great technique pointers for my commission piece. I still don't have a real handle on the execution. Maybe his suggestions will help. How was your day? Did you get a Latin teacher?"

"Yes." And so much more. But he didn't want to disturb this rare, calm family moment. Not with talk of work or Gabriella's stunt last night. There'd be time for discussion later. He washed his hands, then sat down to a meal his daughters had prepared, apparently without setting off the smoke detector.

"This is fantastic!" he announced, taking a bite of crusty cheese pizza with fresh tomatoes and what looked like fresh herbs.

"Not like the chicken flambé?" Isabel asked with the most tentative of smiles.

"Izzy and I decided fresh from scratch was best." Gabriella's voice held pride, a trait not observed in his daughter of late, and the use of the co-operative *Izzy and I* did Nick's tired heart good. What had Pop said to her?

"Dessert's cantaloupe with sherbet," she added. "We figured it'd be pretty hard to screw that up."

"Oh, yeah, I forgot," Isabel said, reaching for a second piece of pizza. "Mrs. Weiss stopped by, looking for a plate of hers. She said she brought cinnamon buns over on it, sometime around the Fourth of July. But I think she just wanted to talk to you, Mom."

Nick watched Chessie's face. He knew she couldn't help being hurt by Martha's accusations after the beach club episode. Last night, after learning from George that Gabriella had run away, she'd brought coffee, but hadn't stayed long. A peace offering of sorts.

Chessie's expression remained noncommittal. "Did you find the plate?"

"In your studio. And Mom…? I looked at your new piece. I think you're trying to be too figurative. Maybe you should go more abstract. You're trying to get across a concept after all."

"Wow." Chessie put down her salad fork. "You might have something…"

Wow was right, Nick thought. This was his quiet Isabel. Talk about still waters running deep.

He hadn't wanted to talk about what happened today at work, but maybe now was the perfect moment, when both girls were acting so mature. He'd learned a lesson from the contract. No surprises. Besides, this decision was far too big.

He cleared his throat. "Actually…I have some news we should discuss. It could be really good news."

Three sets of eyes turned his way.

"A headhunter called today. Remember that associate superintendent job in Atlanta? The funding finally came through. The job's mine if I want it. Starting immediately."

CHAPTER THIRTEEN

CHESSIE STARED at Nick in disbelief. "Surely you're not considering this offer."

"I'm putting it on the table for family discussion."

The girls appeared stunned into silence.

"You have another year on your contract here," Chessie protested.

"And that contract releases me if I accept a better offer. The Atlanta offer is much better. A promotion. A big salary increase."

"But how could you leave here now? The school year's about to begin."

"We're as ready as we'll ever be. And Eleanor's ready to assume a principal's position. It's only a matter of time before some system lures her away. It would be better for Coastal High if she were promoted here. As for the assistant's position she'd vacate, there's a whole new crop of teachers who've acquired their administrative certificates since spring. There wouldn't be a problem filling her spot."

"It sounds like you've made up your mind." Isabel's voice was small, her eyes troubled.

"No, hon, I haven't. I want this to be a family decision."

Gabriella suddenly came to life. "I don't think it's a bad idea. We lived in Atlanta once before, and we liked it."

"Good attitude, Gabby. Very open," Nick replied, encouraged by the support.

Chessie wasn't happy about it. Not at all. "This last move was special, Nick. Your family's here."

"We've lived all these years with the idea that family was where the four of us were."

"But I like having a grandfather and aunts and uncles in the same town," Isabel protested.

"But you hate cold weather," Gabriella returned. "Atlanta has mild winters. Besides, we'd be halfway between Maine and Disney World."

"These are just some of the points we have to weigh," Nick interjected. "That's why I want you all to think about it."

"When do you have to give your answer?"

Chessie asked, suddenly very tired. She hated the exhausting process of moving, had hoped this move to Pritchard's Neck would be their last.

"It's a newly created position, so they're not pressed," he said, "but they want the new hire to start as soon as possible. I could probably stall for a week before they offer it to the next person on the list. If I accepted, I'd have to go on ahead. Get an apartment while you stayed behind to sell the house. The girls could live with me and start school."

Chessie looked hard at her husband, trying to figure out if he had an ulterior motive. Was he seriously considering this new job, or was this more of a power struggle? Had her Fourth-of-July rebellion sparked Nick's enthusiasm for a transfer? She didn't want to ask in front of the girls.

"This is Isabel's senior year," she said, instead. "She's had three different high schools so far. Heading into college it would be best if she had a couple years' stability. Two straight years in Pritchard's Neck."

"Through all our moves," Nick countered, "both girls have maintained excellent grades. Isabel isn't going to have any problem getting into a top college no matter what high school's listed on her diploma."

Isabel looked down at her hands and said nothing.

"I wouldn't mind moving," Gabriella interjected.

Sure she wouldn't, Chessie thought. Between junior high and high school, between friends and, at present, between a rock and a hard place, their younger daughter would jump at a chance for a fresh start.

"I would have to restart my pottery business from scratch," Chessie said.

"With the raise I'd be getting, you wouldn't have to work." Nick gave her that satisfied provider look, and she had to suppress the urge to scream.

"Being a potter—an artist—isn't work. It's part of who I am. Right here in Pritchard's Neck."

"You can be a potter in Atlanta, Mom." Gabriella's voice seemed far away to Isabel.

As the other three talked, Isabel kept thinking, *This can't be happening. It's all so wrong.* It was wrong to move when she'd just started to feel as if she belonged here. As if she had reinforcements in her grandfather and her aunts and uncles when stuff got too hairy at home. And now Dad wanted to pull that security out from under the four of them?

"I need an aspirin," she mumbled, then headed upstairs.

In her room she couldn't settle down. It was as if her arms and legs had a twitchy energy all their own. Pacing, she flipped through clothing and papers in search of her poetry notebook. Maybe if she tried to write...

Flailing her arms aimlessly, she bumped her desk, sending a stack of books, her poetry notebook included, crashing into her waste basket. When she went to fish them out, she found them among the shredded remains of her college applications.

She'd thought she could help her family by staying home, by commuting to college as a day student. How naïve she'd been.

She grabbed her poetry notebook and a pen. Tried to find images that might convey her sorrow. Tried to find something to say that would make her feel connected and minimize her loneliness. But the words refused to come. If she couldn't express herself, she had to escape.

She headed for the bathroom and the razor blades.

CHESSIE WONDERED at her daughter's absence. As difficult a topic as Nick had brought up, at least he'd presented it for family discussion. Isabel needed to be part of this, to make her opinions known.

"Gabby," she said, "would you check on your sister?"

"Sure." As Nick had pushed the pluses of the possible move, Gabriella had become quite perky in her support. It was obvious she was pleased to be in her father's good graces.

When she left the room, Chessie turned to Nick. "What's the real agenda here?"

To his credit, he looked genuinely perplexed. "No agenda, Chess. This is a serious proposal. We need to take a serious look at it. With Isabel in college a year from this September and Gabriella three years later we could use the extra money."

"I'm beginning to make extra money with my pottery. And now I want to settle down. Finally. Here in our hometown, with your family around us. I think Isabel—"

Her sentence was cut short by a blood-curdling scream.

Nick bolted from his seat with Chessie

right behind as they heard Gabriella frantically wailing, "Omigod, omigod, omigod!"

By the time she reached the landing, Nick was in the girls' bathroom, kneeling over Isabel, and Gabriella was pressed against the door frame, sobbing uncontrollably.

"Call 911!" Nick barked.

"No!" Isabel screamed. "I can make it stop, Dad. See!"

As Chessie peered into the bathroom, she didn't know what made her sickest—Isabel's forearms covered in blood, or her seventeen-year-old methodically stanching the flow with a hand towel as if she were an automaton without feeling or emotional involvement.

"Omigod, omigod, omigod…" Gabriella whimpered, hugging the woodwork and averting her eyes.

Instinctively, Chessie took her younger daughter in her arms where Gabby clung, shivering.

"It's stopping, Dad." Isabel held up her arms. The bleeding was reduced to thin red lines like bramble scratches… but there were so many. "Don't call 911. Please."

A wave of nausea swept over Chessie as she

stared at her older daughter while holding fast to her younger. "Isabel, what is going on?"

"I think I know." Nick scooped up Isabel, bloody towel and all, then carried her to her bedroom. "Take Gabby downstairs and put on some tea."

"Tea!" Was he crazy? Their daughter had just slit her wrists. "We need to get her to the hospital."

"Tea, Chessie." He laid Isabel on her bed. "Trust me."

He seemed so calm. In fact, so did Isabel. Unlike Gabriella, who still trembled in Chessie's none-too-steady arms.

"Chessie, please. Take Gabby downstairs."

She left, as much to protect her younger daughter as to show her trust in Nick.

In the kitchen she went through the motions of getting down the teapot, the mugs.

"Peach mango," Gabriella whispered as she huddled on a chair. "That's Izzy's favorite."

"Peach mango it is." To be sure, this was a nightmare, making tea while Isabel lay upstairs. She didn't know what was going on, but Nick seemed to. She was grateful for his self-assurance. If Gabriella didn't need her, she'd be beside him.

But Gabriella did need her. With wide, uncomprehending eyes, she watched Chessie move around the kitchen. A girl who usually spoke before she thought, she remained unnaturally mute.

When the tea had steeped, Chessie poured two mugs and set them on the table, then put two more on a tray. "Wait here," she said. "I'll be right back."

Gabriella hugged a mug of steaming tea to her chest and didn't argue.

At the top of the stairs, Nick met Chessie in front of Isabel's closed door. He took one of the mugs off the tray and nodded to the other. "Take this in to Izzy," he said softly. "Tell her you love her. Tell her everything's going to be all right. I'll go down to Gabby."

"But don't we need to take Isabel to the hospital?"

"She needs a doctor, but not a medical doctor. I called the school guidance counselor. She's recommended a family therapist."

"What—?"

"Just give her the tea. Sit with her a minute. If she wants to talk, let her. If she doesn't, that's okay tonight. Then let her rest and come downstairs. We need to talk to Gabby. I'll tell you both what I know."

"Oh, yes! Please. Gabby's terrified." As was she.

Nick kissed her gently on the cheek. "It's going to be okay, Chessie. I promise."

How could he promise that when everything seemed so awful?

Tentatively, she pushed open Isabel's bedroom door, expecting to see her daughter in some kind of agony, physical or emotional. Instead, she lay on top of the covers, her eyes closed, her features peaceful.

"Izzy," she said quietly. "I brought you tea."

Slowly Isabel sat up. "Thank you."

Although Chessie tried not to look at her daughter's arms, she couldn't help herself. With her sweatshirt sleeves pushed up above her elbows, Isabel made no effort to cover the pattern of cuts covering both arms. So this was why she'd been wearing long sleeves during even the hottest days. Chessie racked her brain to remember the first time she'd noticed the strange attire.

Sipping her tea, Isabel seemed almost relieved. Why? Had she wanted to be found out? Chessie didn't understand.

She sat lightly on the edge of the bed, and brushed the hair from Isabel's temple. Her skin felt cool, unfevered. "I love you, darling. Daddy does, too. And Gabby."

"I know."

"Things are going to be—"

"Okay. Dad promised."

"Do you want to talk?"

"Not now. I'm tired." She put the mug on her nightstand, then lay down. "Talk to Dad. He understands."

He did? Chessie fought back tears as she closed her daughter's door. Then why didn't she?

In the kitchen Nick was talking quietly to Gabriella, who now seemed calmer. Chessie wished she felt calmer, but, if anything, she felt close to hysteria.

"Will you please tell me what's going on?" she asked.

"Yes." Nick took her hand and drew her into the seat next to him. "The term for it is cutting. Isabel cut herself because, ironically, it made her feel better. Inside."

"How could she consider suicide and we never saw any signs?"

"Not suicide, Chess. This type of cutting—

painful, yet shallow—is rarely life-threatening."

"How do you know that?"

"I deal with suicidal teens and teens who cut. Isabel let me check her arms and legs. A good sign this was a cry for help. Her cuts are superficial. Enough to cause pain, not enough to do real damage."

"Girls do it to get attention," Gabriella mumbled, biting her nails. "But it's so gross."

"You know about this?" Chessie was shocked. Here she thought she was current with the issues in her children's generation.

"About cutting, yeah." Gabriella leaned into her father. "About Isabel, no."

Chessie turned to Nick. "What, outside of normal adolescent angst, is troubling Isabel?"

"I'd say normal adolescent angst would be enough to push a sensitive girl like Isabel to the edge. Plus, Gabby tells me Izzy thought the…discussions we'd been having lately might signal impending divorce."

"Oh, no. And then you talked of taking a job in Atlanta. Of getting an apartment by yourself…"

"Talk of moving might have triggered this episode, but there were other times, Chess. I saw healing cuts. She's been doing this a while. Not long, but a while."

"How could she do something so brutal?"

"As crazy as it sounds, there's a poetic sense to cutting that would appeal to a girl like Isabel. It's a display of strength—look at the pain I can bear—as well as sensitivity—look at the pain I am feeling inside. The operative phrase is *look at*. Eventually, cutters want someone to notice. To help bear or ease the pain."

"That's why she seemed almost relieved."

"Yes."

Feeling inadequate, Chessie leaned into Nick, who was now bookended by his daughter and his wife. What else did Nick know about kids that she didn't?

And then the epiphany hit her.

All three of them—Isabel, Gabriella and she—felt the desperate need to be seen and connected to the others. They also needed the others to help bear or ease any burdens along the way.

In the wake of this last upheaval, Nick had contacted a counselor. She hoped the sessions could include all four of them.

FOR THE FIRST TIME in…he couldn't remember how long, Nick took a day off work. A Thursday, no less.

He called in and took a personal day because Isabel, although she had her license, asked him to drive her to her morning appointment with the therapist who'd proposed a plan wherein Isabel would come alone at first. Then later, when she felt as if she could articulate her issues more clearly, the family would be invited to join the sessions. He sat in the waiting room and worried. Giving over control in this area made him very uneasy. Unease, however, was a small price to pay for his daughter's well-being.

After therapy, he and Isabel picked up Chessie and Gabriella, and he treated them all to lunch at The Breakwater restaurant, a place frequented by tourists who, more than likely, earned more than a high-school principal. Because his three ladies seemed to relax and enjoy the breathtaking view of the coast, the linens and extensive place settings, surprisingly, so did he. When the bill came, he viewed it as vacation money they hadn't spent. In trying to turn Coastal High around, he'd worked through any time he'd been slated to take off this past year. If he moved the family to Atlanta, he wouldn't get a chance to make it up to them for another year, at least. Why hadn't he seen the importance of vacations before now?

After lunch and a stop back home, he headed out alone to talk to his brothers and sister and Pop.

He caught Mariah at Wiggin's Landscape Nursery where, as manager, she was working on the order for fall bedding plants. He got Brad's whereabouts from the electric company, then tracked him down in the field. His brother took a break from replacing a section of line to talk. Sean was just pulling his lobster boat up to the pier for refueling when Nick arrived. He sat on the wharf and talked to Sean below just as the two of them had sat as kids talking to the lobstermen. Jonas was a little harder to track down. He was doing some custom cabinetry work on one of the summer houses on the point. The security guard at the gate didn't want to let Nick through, but Nick convinced him it was a family emergency, which it was in a way.

He didn't stay with any one sibling long, just long enough to tell them exactly what had been going on in his life. He didn't expect them to solve his problems; he wanted them—for the first time ever from his lips—to be aware he had his share. If they had suggestions, well, he was open to hear them.

The visit to Pop he saved for last.

By the time Nick got to the family lobster pound, Sean had arrived to give Penn a break. When Penn heard his son wanted to speak to him, he led Nick into the small back office. It was devoid of decoration, except for Alex's drawings, spare of furnishings and cluttered with paperwork, kids' books, half-filled coffee mugs and empty soft drink cans. A good spot for a long overdue father-son talk.

"What's up?"

It was difficult for Nick to find an opening. Finally, he said, "I don't know exactly how you handled Gabriella, but she seems to have taken your message to heart."

"I tried to give her a different perspective."

"Thank you." He paused to clear his throat. "I wasn't getting through to her."

"I don't know about that. You've had a lot on your mind. That's always when kids really angle for their share of attention. You were gettin' to her, but not in the way you wanted."

"I have had a lot on my mind. Too much work and not enough family, Chessie thinks."

"Well?"

"Work is how a man takes care of his family. Isn't that how it goes? And just putting in the hours isn't enough. You have to have a plan, and a backup plan, and a complete disaster plan…"

Penn watched him, but said nothing.

"You can jump in any time," Nick urged, "if you've got a better handle on this than I have. Because I'm down to my complete disaster plan and searching."

He stopped, fully expecting his father to tell him to suck it up. To tell him a show of emotion never put food on the table. Hard work did.

Surprisingly, Penn didn't resort to that oft-repeated credo. "After your mother died," he began slowly, "you took on a man's job, helpin' me with your brothers and sister. It amazed me, at times, how you, a kid, could worry the big picture while I was just sloggin' along day to day. I admired you for that."

"You did?"

"Still do."

Nick didn't know what to say. It was as if

he'd been holding his breath for years, waiting for his father's approval.

"But sometimes," Penn continued, "it helps to pull your visor down and stay in the moment."

"As in…?"

"Spend as much time as you can with your girls. They'll be grown up and gone before you know it. And let that wife of yours know how much she means to you. Lord knows there are too many days when I wish I still had the opportunity to tell your mother I love her." His father rubbed his whiskery chin, and the audible rasp was familiar and strangely comforting. "How does that old saw go? No tombstone ever read, 'He wished he spent more time at the office.'"

Nick let out a long slow breath and shook his head.

"So how do I get off this hamster wheel?" he asked.

"Figure out what's most important and start from there," Penn replied. "For me it was this town. I came home from Nam and never wanted to set foot out of Pritchard's Neck again. It just worked out that now I have my kids and grandkids around me. Color me lucky."

Nick paused. "I've been offered an associate superintendent's position in Atlanta. A promotion with a big raise. Any words of wisdom?"

Penn shook his head. "You're gonna have to think that one long and hard."

"That's it?"

"Nick, you'll do the right thing… What do you need? What do you want? Not as a man climbin' the ladder. As a man. Period."

Nick didn't know what startled him more—the fact that his father felt certain he'd make the right decision or the thought of making a decision based on what he wanted. Really wanted.

He wanted his wife and his girls happy. He wanted to love them and be loved in return. It sounded so simple when he put it that way.

"And somethin' else…" His father looked uncomfortable. "I was tough with you when you were a kid because that was the only way I knew to get you ready for what life might throw your way. Maybe, I was too tough."

"No, Pop. You did what you thought was best. That's all any of us can do. Thanks."

His father turned gruff. "Get on with ya. Sean will be dockin' me for takin' too long a break."

"I have to run anyway. It's my night to get supper."

"Don't tell me. Grilled cheese sandwiches and maple syrup."

Nick chuckled. "You know, I think it's time I introduced my crew to that treat."

Feeling twenty pounds lighter, he stopped at Branson's to pick up the ingredients for supper along with the biggest box of chocolates he could find.

As he pulled into his driveway, Chessie came out of the barn. The sun backlit her short auburn hair, making it seem like a halo around her head.

"Hi," she said quietly, coming up to him. "How'd it go with your family?"

"Really well." He held out the box of chocolates.

"Supper?"

"Uh-uh. These are for you. Just you. From me. Just me."

"Oh, Nick." She hugged him around his neck and snuggled close. "That is so sweet."

"That's not all," he murmured in her hair.

"What if I put a moratorium on new jobs? What if we stay put, right here in Pritchard's Neck until Gabby's in college, and it's just the two of us? Then we can decide where we go from there."

She stepped back to look up at him. "Do you mean it?"

"I never meant anything more in my life."

Clutching the box of chocolates, she kissed him so exuberantly someone driving by honked the horn and whistled.

CHAPTER FOURTEEN

MONDAY MORNING as Chessie readied her studio for the second session of the badly depleted pottery class, she stifled a yawn. Students would be arriving any time now, and all she could think about was crawling back into bed. She was exhausted…but, after many long sessions in her studio, the piece for Ursula Delacorte was complete. A day before the deadline, no less. The finished work was nothing as she'd first imagined, nothing like the sketch she'd shown Ursula, but it was everything she'd been trying to say and more, thanks to Isabel's suggestion she go more abstract. Just when you thought your seventeen-year-old might never grow up, amazing adult words came out of her mouth.

Surprisingly, the project had turned out to be a family endeavor of sorts. When Nick heard she was under a deadline, he said he might not understand art, but he understood deadlines. He then took the girls under his wing and gave Chessie space and time. Gabriella ran a regular lunch wagon between the kitchen and the studio, featuring a new McCabe treat—grilled cheese sandwiches with maple syrup dipping sauce. And when, in frustration, Chessie smashed her umpteenth false start, Nick insisted she take a break. He'd booked one of Kit's kayak eco-tours for the four of them. On that lovely, peaceful Saturday afternoon, Chessie found the driftwood that would jumpstart her stalled creative process.

"Hello!" The voice of her first student rang up the stairwell.

Chessie only vaguely recognized the older woman who entered her studio. "Do you think anyone would be insulted if I dragged out name tags?"

"Not at all," the woman replied brightly, circling the sheet covering Chessie's finished piece. "What's this?"

"Some custom work. The potential buyer's coming later today to see it. Hopefully, I'll make the sale."

"An unveiling. How exciting," the woman

said, accepting a tag and printing her name—Jess. "Will you show the class?"

"It's not the crockery type pottery you're working on. It's more mixed-media sculpture. I wasn't sure the class would be interested."

"Interested in what?" A familiar voice startled Chessie.

She turned to see Kit entering the studio with Alex right behind. "I hope you have a couple spaces. On Mondays I don't have any tours scheduled till afternoon. Alex and I thought it would be fun to take a class together."

"I wanna make a cookie jar," Alex declared with a big grin. "Aunt Emily's teaching the cousins how to bake."

"Do I hear my name?" Chessie hadn't reconciled the sudden appearance of Kit and Alex before Emily came up the stairs, followed by three women Chessie recognized as members of her sister-in-law's play co-op. "This is Olivia," Emily said, taking tags and passing them around to her friends, "and Diane and Lisbeth. We were wondering what we could do on the Mondays we're not in charge of our kids' play group, and I thought pottery. It would be a lot more productive than outrageously priced coffee and gossip at the mall."

Chessie was getting suspicious, but students from last week were arriving and settling at the long trestle tables set up for class. She could ask her two sisters-in-law what was up later.

"We only found out about this course a few days ago." Chessie looked up from setting out extra materials to see two of Nick's teachers. Susan taught English and Nora taught history, or was it the other way around? Chessie didn't know, but she knew from seeing them around town that they weren't teaching summer school. "Can we do a late registration?"

"Why…yes." Chessie thought at the time her flyers might be a little too low-key. "I had some people cancel, so I have room."

"Room enough for me?"

"Aunt Mariah!" Alex exclaimed. "Did Uncle Nick call you, too?"

"He sure did." Mariah looked at Chessie. "Mondays are my day off. Nick suggested I pick up a little culture."

Nick.

Chessie looked around at her full classroom. Nick would be the common denominator of all the new students. And she thought he hadn't been listening when she talked of the drop-outs and her disappointment. Unbelievable. She might just have to tweak her definition of romantic gestures.

"All right, class," she said, her fatigue slipping away. She put an upbeat reggae CD into the boombox. "Let's get busy!"

How she loved eager students, and this group was nothing if not eager. With laughter and rapid-fire chatter, the hour passed quickly.

As people were tagging their unfinished creations for storage till next week, Jess spoke up. "Will you show us your piece, Chessie?" she asked, indicating the covered work awaiting Ursula's approval. She looked at her own slightly lopsided bowl, not yet glazed. "Please, show us how the master does it."

A chorus of voices rose in agreement.

Suddenly, Chessie felt unaccountably shy. She'd stepped outside her comfort range in creating the piece for Ursula. She wasn't even sure some of the techniques she'd employed were all that regular. Although she loved the finished work, had she made something others would relate to?

As if sensing her doubt, Kit stood close to

her and said quietly in her ear, "You won't know what we think until you unveil it."

"All right." Chessie stepped up to the sheet. "I give you… 'Her Head Was in the Goddess Movement, but Her Feet Were Firmly Planted in the PTA'." She stopped short of removing the protective covering.

More than a few faces showed amusement at the title, but Kit made a silent tugging motion, urging Chessie on.

She removed the sheet and her creation was met by absolute silence.

The base of the piece was done in rough ceramic chunks and shreds and chips that tumbled over one another in a dull organic chaos that resembled freshly tilled garden soil. Out of this rose the piece of driftwood Chessie had found on the kayak outing. Strong despite the weathering it had endured, the wood— perhaps a branch in a former life—seemed to undulate, "arms" upraised, its natural silver finish giving it a look of elegance despite the heavy clods that anchored it. At the top a smooth knot looked amazingly like a face. Around this Chessie had fixed shards of pottery in pale opalescent colors, creating a shimmering crown that reflected light upon the "face". Her Goddess might be mired, but she was reaching for the stars.

Or that's what Chessie had intended. The silence of her students, however, unnerved her.

"Oh, my! That could be me!" Emily said, finally, her voice full of wonder. "Some days when I'm slogging through dirty diapers and smeared PB&J and pizza stuffed in the VCR, I take a look in the mirror and I think—I *think*—I can faintly see the former prom queen."

"For me," said Jess, "it's the two women I am. The one bogged down by arthritis and the one whose spirit won't be crushed, who dances to her own inner tango."

"What about work-woman and vacation-woman?" Susan exclaimed. "I can be literally buried under term papers that need grading, but I hold on to that sensuous creature who's saved up enough to lie on the beach for a week in Cancún and sip Mai Tais and flirt with the pool boy."

As her students began to talk of the dichotomy of their own everyday experience, Chessie's spirits soared. She had spoken and been understood. It was almost a shame that the Goddess would be moving on.

"What a great signature piece for your gallery," Kit said.

"I was thinking the same thing, but she's sold."

"Well, there's more great stuff where she came from."

Chessie gave her sister-in-law a swift, heartfelt hug.

As her class trooped noisily down the stairs—some of them swaying to the reggae beat—Chessie counted this as one of those top-of-the-world moments. How fitting that her family, who'd run her through the peaks and valleys of domestic existence all week, had been part of the support structure that made it possible. And what about Nick refilling her roster? Incredible.

As GABRIELLA SHOOK the dust mop out the side door, she saw Keri Weiss taking out the trash. Gabriella had to look twice because she'd never, ever seen her former friend help with any household chores. Come to think of it, for the past few days Gabriella hadn't seen Keri doing much of anything. She hadn't seen Margot or Baylee, either. What was going on across the street?

"Check it out," she said to Isabel, who was coming in from her first day as cashier at the lobster pound.

"Weird," her sister agreed. "Maybe Mrs. Weiss has taken a page from Mom's book."

"Maybe." Gabriella wondered what Keri could have done to precipitate the change, however. "Hey, how was the job?"

Isabel held up a large bag. "Gramps sent lobsters for supper. All cooked. And you would not believe the cute summer guys who come in with their parents to pick these out." She headed for the fridge.

Gabriella was sort of envious. She hadn't thought of the cute guy aspect of the job.

"Where's Mom?" Isabel asked, rummaging in the refrigerator.

"In her studio with that lady who's supposed to buy the Goddess."

"There's nothing to drink."

"Mom and I made a list of stuff we need. I was going to go to Branson's. I'll get you a soft drink."

"Thanks."

It was funny how nice that word sounded. How nice it was that Isabel and she had been decent to each other for the past few days. At first Gabriella was scared of her sister. Because of the cutting. It was too gross, and Gabriella hadn't wanted to do anything to set Isabel off. But after a couple days, it felt good just to chill and be, well, nice to each other.

Gabriella was also pleased to note Isabel now wore calf-length cargo pants and a tee with three-quarter sleeves. You could see scratchy marks on her forearms, but there were no new cuts. It was as if Isabel had nothing to hide. Maybe Dad was right and Isabel had wanted someone to stop her. Gabriella could relate. As ticked as she'd been that Gramps had picked her up when she was trying to run away, she'd been relieved, too. She wished she could find a way to put the brakes on her anger.

She picked up the shopping list and the money her mother had left for her and headed toward Branson's. Standing by the community bulletin board at the store's entrance, Owen was tacking up a flyer.

"Hey, Madison."

Why did he insist on calling her Madison? Oh, yeah. At the Surf Club she'd tried out that name. "What are you doing?"

He handed her a flyer. "We're putting on a production of *Grease*."

Gabby recognized the amateur theater group. "And you're in it?"

"I don't have a speaking part, but I'm one of the extras in the dance numbers. Plus I paint scenery."

"And tack up flyers." Gabriella wasn't impressed.

"Everybody does. It's fun. You should volunteer. We need extra dancers, and you're good."

She tried not to be pleased that he remembered.

"Just show up at our next rehearsal. Eight o'clock tomorrow night at the Atlantic Hall. You could walk from your house. I could walk you home."

She felt her cheeks go red. "I don't know."

"So what else do you have planned? Running away?"

Boy, was he a jerk. She turned to go into the store, but he caught her arm.

"I was just kidding," he said. "Last time we talked you were ticked with your parents and said you wanted to try it on your own."

"Yeah, well, I reconsidered."

"Good. It was a dumb idea. As a drama queen, you should channel your energy."

"Into being a dancing extra in a community play?"

"Hey, it's a start."

"You really think I'm a drama queen?"

"Actually, I think you have a chip on your shoulder." Owen grinned.

"Do you always say what you think?"

"I don't see any reason not to."

She gave a short, sharp laugh. What was it about this guy that appealed to her? "My grandfather says I have a chip on my shoulder, too. You'd get along."

"Hey, I get along with everybody. So you'll come tomorrow?"

She thought about the contract she'd finally signed with her parents and Isabel. About the job or volunteering part. "Okay," she said. She was doing it because it would keep her parents off her back, not because she wanted to see more of Owen.

NICK COULDN'T BELIEVE he'd gotten out of school before five o'clock, but as he pulled into his driveway, the church bell tolled the hour. And, as a reward, it seemed, Chessie rose from her seat on the side steps to greet him with a big smile.

"I like that happy expression," he said, getting out of the car. "Things going well?"

She took his hand and led him to the sidewalk. "Let's go for a walk."

"I need to put on sneakers."

"Oh, I don't mean a power walk. I mean a stroll," she said, waving her free hand dramatically. "Just look at this place." Before them the village activity was slowly winding down for the day. The boutiques and galleries in clapboard buildings painted traditional colonial colors were closing up, and the setting sun warmed the patches of marsh and sea that they could see from where they stood. "Tourists pay good money to come here. To stay in our quaint bed-and-breakfasts and to soak up the sea air. And do we appreciate what we see every day just beyond our doors?"

"I'm thinking this isn't a Chamber of Commerce tour," he said. "You're really saying you want to talk to me without the possibility of the girls interrupting."

"Yes. Although a pleasant backdrop can't hurt."

"Now I'm nervous."

"Don't be. Yes I want to talk, and, yes, I

want you to myself." She shot him a mischievous grin. "But just because I want you to myself."

How could he resist?

"It's a gorgeous afternoon for a walk, and supper's all taken care of," she said. "Your father sent lobsters. Any reason you know of?"

"Yeah, maybe. We had a talk a few days ago. Cleared the air. I think it's his way of saying he's glad."

"Then today is good." Short of the square, she stopped walking and turned to face him. "Thank you for rounding up a full class for me."

"Hey, I just put the word out that there was room."

"Why?"

"We know Martha yanked the plug, but word might get around that you weren't a good teacher. And that's not the case. I know how important your professional integrity is to you."

"Gosh, that is such a good answer." She leaned in and feathered his lips with a kiss.

"So…how did the class go?"

"Wonderfully well!" She began to walk again, energetically. "They wanted a sneak peak at the Goddess, and they got it. In so many different ways, they seemed to understand what I was aiming at."

"The piece. I forgot. Did your patron come and get it?"

"She came for it, but she didn't leave with it."

"I don't understand."

Chessie giggled. "It didn't match her color scheme."

"Now I'm lost."

"I departed from the original sketch, which Ursula liked based on how it would fit her décor, not necessarily on its artistic merits. The finished piece was 'too raw' for Ms. Delacorte's refined sensibilities. She was most upset. Seems she'll have to order a very large floral arrangement to fill the intended spot in her foyer. Her party must go on without me."

Nick was confused. "You don't seem particularly upset."

Chessie looked almost as perplexed as he was. "That's the thing. I'm not. That piece took a big chunk of my soul, as well as my time. I didn't want it going where it wasn't appreciated or understood. Every one of my students took more away from it than Ursula. Even Alex said it looked like her when she was knee-deep in the mudflats looking for treasure." Chessie chuckled. "A nine-year-old."

"But no one offered to buy it…"

"Someone, someday, will. When they walk in my gallery and meet her, someone will fall in love."

Nick saw his wife in a new light, self-assured, more attractive than she'd been with the haircut and the slinky dress on pops night. He felt that same first-date eagerness to get to know this woman. "And when do you think your gallery will be up and running?"

"Soon. This week the girls are going to help me clear the barn's first floor. Next week your dad and Jonas are going to put up some shelves using aged lumber they rescued from an old fish house. Brad's agreed to do the wiring. Kit's helping me set up the displays, and Emily's already planning an opening party."

"Wow." For a moment he felt left out.

"It's incredible the way it all went from concept to reality in a couple short hours this very afternoon. Everyone's schedules just meshed. I was going to call you at work to tell you the news, but I figured I'd rather break it to you when I had you all to myself."

He felt nothing but pride for this dynamo of a woman. "You are something else, Chess."

"Why, thank you." Was that a blush under the dusting of freckles across her cheeks?

"So are you getting out of the business of pots for the loftier realm of high art?"

"No…this is so extraordinary and why I wanted to talk to you…I learned something about myself with this commission process. I thought I wanted to move from crafts to art, but I don't. I want both—kind of like the Goddess herself. I love the domestic ramifications of a well-thrown bowl—the thought of friends and families sharing meals and more from my plates. And the fine art aspect? When I started working with Ursula, I was seduced by the idea of playing at being the artiste. I lost the focus on the art itself, on what I wanted to say with what I created. The women in my class today brought me back. In my free-form pieces I want to experiment with materials and technique and even with firing processes. I want to grow as I did with the Goddess. If someone buys, fine. If not, then the bread and butter of my business will be my pots and my classes as I grow as an artist."

Her eyes sparkled. "I learned that finding

yourself is a process of creation not a gift, perhaps a lifelong process. And as we create ourselves, we have to be careful to weave in and out of the lives of others."

As they rounded a bend in the road and came upon a tidal cove, the sea breeze picked up. Nick brushed an errant auburn curl from Chessie's eyes. "Something tells me, with an attitude like that you can have it all."

And he wanted to watch her achieve it. Not just watch. Be by her side. She was an amazing woman. He bent to kiss her, to show her just how amazing.

"Mmm," she murmured dreamily against his lips. "You see now why I wanted to have this conversation away from the girls."

It was only then that he realized he was kissing his wife on a public sidewalk…and he didn't care who saw.

"Excuse us, please." An elderly couple stepped around them. "How sweet," the woman commented to her companion. "Honeymooners."

Nick chuckled. As they'd walked and talked, just the two of them, there had been an element of honeymooning like eighteen years ago when they'd dreamed big and planned to make those dreams come true. It was too bad that as those dreams had started to come true, he'd forgotten to take little breaks along the way to savor the accomplishments.

He cupped her cheek. "I do love the girls, but I could get used to being a twosome again."

"Four years and Gabby's in college."

"Thanks for the time-out."

"You're most welcome. And thank you for the support of my work." She paused as if unsure. "When is your staff field day?"

"Day after tomorrow. Why?"

"I'd…like to participate."

"You would?" She'd never participated, and this year he'd given up asking.

"Yes. If it's important to you, it's important to me." She dimpled. "Now, are you ready for some lobster?"

"Nobody cooks them better than Pop," he said as they began a leisurely stroll home. What stroke of luck had brought him this close to his wife? "So…how was Izzy's first day at work?"

"She seems happy."

"And Gabby?"

"She dusted, did the grocery shopping and

volunteered with the community theater group."

"Pinch me. This is not the family of last week."

"Enjoy the moment." Chessie threaded her arm through his and pressed against him, happy with the day. Happy that Nick had taken the time to listen to her. He'd even seemed to understand her dreams. Her. "This probably won't be the family of next week."

It wasn't even the family of the next moment.

As they walked into their driveway, they saw Gabriella's distraught face in Isabel's window. "Mommmm! Daaaad!" Her face disappeared.

What new crisis loomed?

As Nick and Chessie rushed into the house, Gabriella thundered into the kitchen, holding aloft a fistful of shredded paper, with Isabel in hot pursuit.

"Give those back!" Isabel demanded. "They're private!"

"She's not going to college!" Gabriella shouted above her sister's demands. "Because of you! And me!"

While her two girls tussled for possession

of—what?—Chessie was relieved to see there was no blood, no physical injury.

"Sit," Nick ordered, pointing at the kitchen chairs. "Let's get to the bottom of this."

As Chessie's head began to pound, this once, she was grateful for Nick's administrative command.

"Gabriella, you first," he said.

Isabel retreated to a sullen silence.

"I bought Izzy and me soft drinks," Gabriella began. "We drank them in her room. I threw my empty in her waste basket, but she told me to recycle it. When I went to get the bottle out, I found these." She thrust a fistful of torn paper at her parents. "Her college applications."

Chessie was appalled.

"Isabel," Nick asked, "what is going on?"

At first it looked as if the seventeen-year-old wasn't going to answer. From mature art critic, she'd become belligerent adolescent.

"Tell them," Gabriella urged, not unkindly.

"I just thought…" Isabel seemed to fight back tears. "I just thought it might be better for everybody if I went to a community college. In Portland, maybe. I'd live at home and commute."

"Why?" Chessie couldn't believe her ears.

As private and sensitive a person as Isabel was, she'd been looking forward to the intellectual challenge of a bigger arena. Or so Chessie had believed.

"Money would be a good reason," Isabel replied without looking anyone in the eye.

"I don't buy that." Nick paused until Isabel looked at him. "What's wrong, Izzy?"

"With the way things have been going lately…maybe you don't need one more thing to worry about…like me living away."

"You're worried about us," Nick said.

"Yes."

"All three of us."

"Yes…but mostly you and Mom."

Chessie felt suddenly dizzy. What had Nick and she done to make this child-woman think she had to shoulder their issues? How could they explain that burden away?

"Isabel," Nick said, taking his daughter's hand. "Let me explain something to you about the nature of marriage."

Perhaps, Chessie thought, she needed to hear this as much as the girls.

"Your mom's and my relationship was strong before you came into our lives, and it will be strong when you move away. Maybe this sounds selfish, but the best thing we could ever teach you and Gabby is that you're not essential to our marriage. You're essential to our family, for sure. But your mom's and my well-being is contained within our private relationship." He smiled and squeezed Isabel's hand. "Now that gives you and Gabby full permission to venture out in the world and eventually find someone to share your life with."

He released Isabel to put his arm around a stunned Chessie. "Your mom and I are going to be just fine."

As Isabel offered up a faint smile and Gabriella settled back in her chair with an obvious sense of relief, Chessie nestled close to her husband. He got it. Maybe he'd gotten it all along and needed this mini-crisis to find the words. Maybe he knew it and had tried to show it, but she'd been focused on Nick the administrator and her rivalry with his job, neither of which made her feel safe or warm.

But Nick the man sure did.

She'd accused him of seeing her only in her role as wife and mother. Not in her capacity as a woman. Maybe she'd been a little guilty of dealing in stereotypes, as well. She planned to rectify that. Starting now.

LATER THAT EVENING Chessie stood in the middle of the barn's first floor, happily envisioning her gallery, when she heard a knock came at the open door. Martha stood on the threshold. "Am I interrupting?"

"No. Come in."

"What are you doing?"

"Thinking about the next stage in my career. The gallery."

"In addition to classes?"

"Yeah."

"That's quite an undertaking if the size of your class today is any indication. I saw the cars in the drive."

Chessie didn't respond.

"I'm sorry," Martha said.

"Me, too. I thought we had a stronger friendship."

"I went a little crazy. You know how that can happen when the welfare of your child is at stake."

"I do." Oh, boy, how she did. But she also knew you couldn't cope by lashing out at those closest to you.

"I've missed you," Martha offered tentatively. "So…how have things been going on this side of the street?"

"Okay." Chessie took a moment to filter her answer. She'd missed Martha, too, but if they were going to re-establish their friendship, she was going to start cautiously. "Today was an exceptionally good day. I think we're all at the top of the family roller-coaster. But I'm learning these peaks mean that a drop is just around the corner."

Martha chuckled. "I never thought of family life as a roller-coaster. I thought of it more as a giant Styrofoam peanut spill. You know, some aunt sends you a birthday present of one of her little glass candy dishes packed in gallons of static-y white peanuts. When you open the box, the peanuts fly all over the house. It takes forever to gather them up, and for years afterwards you're still finding a stray peanut here and there under the sofa or behind a bookcase."

Chessie eyed Martha in confusion. "I'm not sure I get what you're driving at."

"I always thought you started out your adult life with that spill to clean up. That you worked and worked at getting it under control until one day you finally managed to restore order—with only an occasional peanut to deal with—and for the most part life was all neat and tidy from then on."

"Hah!"

"Double hah!" Martha looked sheepish. "Keri's sure taken care of that illusion."

"Teenagers," Chessie replied noncommittally.

"You don't understand. I'm not talking in generalities. I…uh…Keri got picked up for shoplifting a couple days ago. With Margot Hensley and Baylee Warner."

Chessie's eyes widened.

"She tried to blame it on Margot and Baylee. But I know it was all three. Then I got thinking about how the whole Surf Club escapade was probably a joint venture, too. Not just Gabriella's idea. I can't believe my own daughter could pull the wool over my eyes."

"It happens to the best of us, Martha. Don't beat yourself up over it. Now you know."

"Gabriella was the best friend Keri ever had. Do you think…?"

"I can't speak for my daughter. She's done some growing in the past week-and-a-half. It's up to her to decide who her friends will be."

And although Chessie felt sorry for Martha when she saw the look of disappointment on her face, she also felt proud. She'd spoken the truth about Gabriella. Her girls were growing up.

CHAPTER FIFTEEN

GABRIELLA SAT in the Coastal High bleachers and watched her faculty for the next four years having the time of their lives down on the football field. Frankly, she and Isabel had been curious about an event that saw her mom and dad heading off together first thing this morning, smiling at each other as if they were dating. And Mom...well, Mom was acting weirder than usual, if that were possible. Before leaving, she'd given Isabel the keys to her Mini Cooper and had told them to have a good time today. No list of errands. No safety lesson. Just, have a good time.

They couldn't believe their good luck. She and Isabel had wheels!

So where had they gone after using up half a tank of gas driving around? To the high school to see what this staff field day was all about. They figured it was out in the open on public property. What was the worst that could happen? The security guards could tell them to leave. But they hadn't. As Isabel had pointed out, the security guards were down on the field with everyone else. Out of uniform, no less. And in the bleachers? Staff family members just as curious as them. It felt a little like a party.

"You kinda forget they're human." As laughter rose from the field, Owen climbed the bleachers toward her. "In school, I mean. Hey, I don't go here, but teachers are teachers all over."

It seemed this guy was showing up everywhere lately. But after last night, after the fun she'd had dancing at the rehearsal for *Grease,* and the way he'd walked her home at the end—like he cared she got home safely—she was glad to see him.

"So why are you here?"

"I was curious. My mom works here."

"What does she teach?"

Owen looked as if he didn't want to say.

"C'mon, you can tell me. I'll try not to give her a hard time if I catch her class."

"She's not a teacher. She works in the cafeteria."

A lunch lady? Gabriella thought how all last year Keri would make fun of the cafeteria workers. Of how dorky they looked in their aprons and plastic gloves and hairnets. And Gabriella hadn't been any better by laughing at Keri's jokes.

Owen stiffened. "You got a problem with that?"

"No. Why should I?" Not if it made her like Keri. "Everybody's here today. My dad wants it that way. When they're all wearing shorts and sweats, you can't tell who does what."

"Yeah, well, my mom says your dad is cool."

Her father cool?

"She says he treats everyone in the school alike. Fair."

"Are we talking about the same person? My father? The dictator?"

"Give him a break. When you think he's being unfair, isn't it really 'cause he's not letting you have your way?"

"Are you really an adult disguised as a kid?"

"Why do you say that?"

"Because you always take the adult's side."

"It's not about sides." Owen grinned, and Gabby noted that it was just a grin. Not a smirk. But real, as if he found life and people interesting. It was nice to be around someone who wasn't always trying to diss someone else. "I'm going to be a playwright," he said. "If I'm going to be any good, I have to put myself in other people's shoes."

"Then you're going to be one heck of a playwright, Owen."

He laughed as if he took it as a huge compliment. She guessed it was.

Isabel came up beside them. "The day's not over and we still have a half tank of gas. Let's get going."

"Can Owen come?"

"You want to?" Izzy asked him as if it was perfectly okay with her.

"Sure."

"Hey, Owen," Gabriella asked as they headed toward the parking lot. "How long have you wanted to be a playwright?"

"From the time my mom took me to see a library production of *Mike Mulligan and His Steam Shovel* when I was four."

"I knew I wanted to be a poet since I was in third grade," Isabel said, as if she didn't find Owen weird.

"Gosh. I have no idea what I want to be."
Gabriella wondered if that made her boring.

"Don't you think it's time you started to think about it?" Owen asked.

Yeah. If she was going to hang out with people like Isabel and Owen—which, surprisingly, wasn't turning out to be such a bad idea—she was going to have to learn to talk about things other than lip gloss and clothes.

"I do know one thing," she said. "I don't want to be Madison."

Owen looked confused.

"My name's Gabriella. My family calls me Gabby. I was thinking of changing it, though."

Owen laughed. "Well, you're no Madison, that's for sure."

"So who am I? Alexis? Taylor? Paige?"

"Brunhilda," he said with a grin. "Definitely someone with a helmet and spear."

She punched him in the arm. He punched her back.

STAFF FIELD DAY WAS nothing like Chessie had imagined. It was fabulous, and she was having a ball. Talk about misconceptions. This was about teamwork and creative thinking and…fun. And all this time she'd accused Nick of not knowing the meaning of the word.

As the staff took a break, she stood in the shade under the lunch tent and searched the crowd for her husband. She needed to tell him how impressed she was with this event. With the logistics necessary to pull it off. No wonder he'd spent so many hours in paperwork and preparation.

For starters, everyone went by their first names. Period. No one was to talk about their position in the school. That meant Chessie and the dozen or so new hires didn't know if they were on a team with professionals, paraprofessionals or nonprofessionals. It didn't matter. What did was the skill you could bring to the group task at hand, whether it was helping nine other people lower an eight-foot helium stick to the ground using only your fingertips and a great deal of patience, or crossing an imaginary river of stepping stones while maintaining continuous contact with one foot of both the person ahead of and behind you, or designing a protective covering for an egg so that you could drop it off the top bleacher without smashing it. With every exercise, the group members changed, as did their roles. There were bosses and there were worker ants, and it was all luck of the draw.

At the start of the day, Nick had given a few words of welcome, but then he'd blended in with the other participants. Chessie had yet to be on a team with him.

"Hey, Chessie!" Two guys trotted by. "Great solution to that tarp flip!"

She smiled. If she were ever marooned on a desert island with nine other people, and their survival depended on standing on a tarp and flipping it to the other side without anyone's feet touching the ground...she was definitely the go-to gal.

The whistle blew to assemble everyone back on the field. Someone—her name tag said Sylvia—read instructions into a bullhorn. They were to form two straight lines along the length of the football field, face the other line and pair off with the person standing opposite. After a few minutes of jostling and redistributing, the two lines came to a standstill. Nick stood across from her.

"What are the odds?" she whispered.

"I cheated. I know this exercise, and I wanted to make sure I partnered with you."

She smiled as she watched him take one of

the wide strips of cloth being passed down his line and felt as if they were back in junior high. In co-ed gym class. What was the activity she'd be doing with this cute guy?

"Listen up, folks!" Sylvia ordered. "People who have the blindfolds put them on the person across from you."

Oh, no. Blindfolds. This was not an exercise Chessie wanted to participate in. As an artist, sight was a very important part of who she was. Taking it away was a sort of visual claustrophobia she'd never been able to handle.

"We've been working all morning on mutual respect and trust," Sylvia read. "This, now, is an ultimate trust exercise. A lot more difficult than it appears. For the next five minutes, the sighted group will be leading their blindfolded partners around the stadium."

Chessie took a step back. Even with Nick leading her, this was too scary.

"Give your blindfolded partners instructions to touch various objects," Sylvia continued, "to walk over various terrain. Don't talk to them except to give them encouragement or directions. Don't be afraid to touch them to give them assistance."

"Nick, I trust you," Chessie said, a note of

pleading creeping into her voice. "Let's leave it at that. You know I hated blindman's bluff as a kid."

"This is diff—"

Sylvia eyed the two of them. "I'm going to pick a half-dozen people to be facilitators with me. We'll be circulating making unexpected noises. Sighted people, your job is to make your blindfolded partner feel safe. I'll blow the whistle in five minutes for you to switch roles. You may begin."

"No!" Chessie put up her hand as Nick raised the blindfold. "I'm sure I told you about the time I was in psych class and we had to close our eyes and fall back into a partner's arms. I couldn't do it. I sneaked out when the professor wasn't looking."

"Chessie, I know the fear you have of losing your sight. But this is role play. I'll be with you every step of the way. I'm not going to let you get into any trouble."

"I can't do it, Nick."

Hattie St. Regis happened to be in line next to Chessie. Before accepting her blindfold, she leaned over to Chessie and murmured. "How do you think it looks to the staff if Nick's own wife doesn't trust him?"

She was going to have to do this.

Gulping hard and blinking to squeeze back real tears, she nodded to Nick who gently tied the blindfold over her eyes.

And there she stood. Without her sight. A fear that ranked right up there with losing her family.

Nick took her hand and her elbow. At least she thought it was Nick. There wouldn't be any point to switching partners unawares, would there? But a lot could happen while she couldn't see. "Nick?" she asked nervously.

"I'm right here. You're okay."

The sound of his voice soothed her somewhat, but didn't stop a film of sweat from forming on her upper lip.

"Let's start walking," Nick suggested. "Remember we're on the field. It's reasonably level."

She balked. "What if I bump into someone?"

"It's my job to see that you don't."

"*See* being the operative word." She might actually cry, and thought the only good use for the blindfold was that it would hide her tears. From Nick. From his staff. This was a bad idea. This day was about the people of Coastal High, not about her and her phobia. She'd known if she participated today she'd somehow mess up. She began to tremble.

"Chessie." Nick spoke quietly in her ear. "I have to know. More than your fear of losing your sight for real, is this a control thing? Between us? Because you will have a chance to lead me—"

"No! It's the inability to see."

"It's only temporary. It's an exercise," he reassured her. "Let me help you work through it. I think it'd be good for you."

"Is anyone else freaking out, or am I the only one?"

"Don't worry about anyone else. It's just the two of us. Trust me."

For all she knew everyone else had taken off their blindfolds and was staring at the crazy woman. But, somehow, Nick's steady voice began to infuse her with, not calm, but a lesser degree of panic even while Hattie's words came back to her. What if it looked as if Nick's own wife didn't trust him? His professional integrity was so very important to him, as was hers. He'd shown that he understood and supported her by recruiting for her pottery class. She needed to show him support now even though she would rather do something less painful, like a Brazilian bikini wax.

"Okay," she said at last. "Lead me."

Surprisingly, he didn't move. Instead, he placed his hands flat under hers, palm to palm, waist high. She could sense him standing directly in front of her.

"Lean on me," he said. "Against my hands."

She did, tentatively at first, yet his hands didn't waver. He was so solid she felt as if she could turn and sit, using him as a chair.

"My strength is your strength," he whispered in her ear, his breath a soft tickle.

"Now wait," he said, grasping one of her hands firmly while releasing the other.

She strained to hear. His voice sounded somewhere near her knees, then rose.

"Inhale," he said.

When she did she could smell newly mown grass. She smiled. "One of my favorite scents."

"Now listen."

She did and heard quiet voices. Of sighted partners encouraging their counterparts. A low murmur like the distant sound of waves. Beyond that she could hear gulls, probably looking for handouts at the lunch tent. There was no chaos. Only calm.

"Open your mouth."

Without thinking, she did, and felt a hard peppermint slide into her mouth. She always slipped these candies into his pockets because they were supposed to make your senses sharper. Something a high-school principal needed. She never found them in the laundry—sometimes the papers, never the candies themselves—so he must eat them. Maybe even think of her as he did. The thought made her happy.

"Ready?" His voice was encouraging, his touch warm and steady. He was her Nick and he'd promised not to lead her into any trouble.

"Ready." As she'd ever be.

"We're just going to walk for a while. On the grass."

That was fine. She could handle that now without panic, and silently congratulated herself for the giant step forward.

"Focus on what you feel."

The strength of Nick's touch. One hand enfolding hers, the other guiding her elbow. The warm sun on her face. The soft cushion of grass under her feet. Surprisingly, there was a certain power in touch.

"On what you smell."

Peppermint. Behind that the smell of hot dogs and hamburgers the PTA members were grilling for lunch. Okay, that smell made her queasy for some reason. She tried to bring her thoughts back to the simplicity of peppermint.

"On what you hear."

Although she tried to focus on the soothing mantra of Nick's voice, she was distracted by someone approaching. Suddenly she heard the harsh jangle of keys right behind her.

Startled, she stumbled, but Nick caught her. Held her steady against his solid frame. "That was just a facilitator," he said. "They're moving between the pairs. Creating distractions."

"That doesn't seem quite fair," she retorted, strong enough to protest.

"Just the exercise's version of you-know-what happens." He chuckled and she could feel the sound in his chest as well as hear it. "Still trust me?"

"I always have," she replied and suddenly felt an overwhelming love for this man. And insight.

Here she thought his job was her competition, but she'd chosen him way back in high school for the qualities that ultimately made him so good at his job. The kind of thoughtful program he'd put together today, the kind of patience and understanding he'd shown her in this exercise. Strength. Empathy. Respect for others. The ability to instill trust.

She'd forgotten how simple it was to just close her eyes and trust those qualities in Nick she'd fallen in love with all those years ago.

"You're awfully quiet," Nick said. "Are you all right?"

"More than all right." She smiled and felt at ease, despite the blindfold.

The five-minute whistle blew. "Sighted participants stand close as your partners remove the blindfold." Sylvia's voice came over the bullhorn. "The sudden return of light may make them a little unsteady."

Carefully, Nick untied the knot at the back of Chessie's head. Despite the lesson she'd learned, she could barely wait to see again.

When she felt the strip of cloth fall away, she shook her hair and opened her eyes. And quickly felt the world slip away to black.

Nick watched Chessie slide to the ground.

"Water! Someone bring water!" Blood pounding in his ears, he leaned over the collapsed form of his wife to feel the steady pulse at her throat. "I think she's fainted."

He knew of her phobia and had clearly sensed her fear during the exercise, but she'd soldiered on. And it had been too much. He cursed himself.

The school nurse came running with the first aid kit while several hands offered up water bottles. Taking the smelling salts first, he cracked open the plastic vial and held it under his wife's nose. She flinched, then seconds later her eyes fluttered open.

"Chessie!" He cupped the back of her head in his hand. "Sip some water."

"What happened?"

"That's what I'd like to know. We're going to get you to the doctor."

"No! I'm fine. I just got worked up over being blindfolded."

"I don't think so." He held the water bottle to her lips, encouraging her to sip. "You're not the fainting kind."

As she accepted the water, she glanced warily at the crowd gathered around her. "Help me up. I'll sit in the shade. I'll be all right."

"Sit still. Please." He pulled out his cell phone. "If our family doctor can't fit you in, I'm taking you to the E.R."

"No!" She reached for the phone, but he turned aside. "You can't leave," she insisted. "Staff day's only half over."

Hattie knelt beside Chessie as Nick waited to be connected. He could hear Hattie assuring Chessie that the day was set up so that, once in place, it ran itself as a group effort. It didn't need a fearless leader. Nick didn't feel particularly fearless at the moment. Not with Chessie taking a nosedive on the turf. Why was it you could bear the pain yourself, but nearly came undone when a loved one was hurt?

He accepted the first appointment slot, then clicked his cell phone shut. "Come on," he said, lifting Chessie. "The nurse practitioner will see you as soon as we get there. If you need a doctor, she'll squeeze you in."

"This isn't right," she protested as they left the field to a chorus of good wishes. "You belong here. It's your job."

"No, Chessie. I belong with you. It's my life."

He placed her in the Volvo. Why did healthy

people faint? He racked his brain for answers, but found he could only focus on Chessie, sitting pale and unusually quiet in the passenger seat.

At the doctor's, he tried to carry her inside, but she wouldn't hear of it. Made him stay in the waiting room, too. She insisted she was fine. She had to be. He didn't like being left behind because it gave him far too much time to imagine all that might be wrong. Chessie didn't faint. Something had to have triggered it.

He counted the chairs in the waiting room. He paced. He sat and flicked through a two-year-old *Field and Stream*. He paced. He thought of calling Isabel and Gabriella, but decided against it. They weren't expecting Chessie and him home until after three. It was twelve-fifteen. Better not alarm them.

What was taking so long?

He paced.

Finally, he couldn't stand it. He pushed through the door that led to the examination rooms, and asked the first person he saw, "Where's Chessie McCabe?"

"I put her in room six, but the nurse practitioner's still with her."

Good. He had questions.

He opened door number six and found himself staring into Chessie's wide hazel eyes. She looked stunned.

"Mr. McCabe," the nurse practitioner said, "I was about to call for you."

He felt rooted to the floor. "What's wrong?"

"Nothing's wrong! We were just discussing good news." The nurse practitioner smiled broadly even as the color drained from Chessie's face. "You and your wife are going to have a baby!"

CHAPTER SIXTEEN

PREGNANT. Chessie couldn't find words to speak as Nick drove them home. She was thirty-seven years old, the mother of two teenagers. And pregnant.

Two months pregnant. Due in February. Valentine's Day.

Except for the very solid jar of prenatal vitamins she held in her hand, this might be a dream. She glanced over at Nick in the driver's seat. He seemed as shell-shocked as she.

At home they walked into the kitchen in silence. Nick rummaged in the refrigerator for something to drink while she sank into a chair, numb. She looked around the cluttered room and thought of everything that would need to be baby-proofed. After all these years.

Nick poured juice for the two of them, then sat across from her. The tension lines that fanned from the edges of his eyes were deeply etched. His mouth was set in a straight and serious line. A baby certainly threw a monkey wrench into all his well-laid plans.

How could this happen? Well, she knew. After Gabby was born, she didn't want to be on the pill indefinitely, so she and Nick had been vigilant about using condoms. Until the past few years. Maybe because she hadn't gotten pregnant, they'd grown lax. Two adults. And people expected teenagers to be responsible.

"We should talk." Nick sounded tired.

"I need time—" she felt tired "—to decide."

"What's to decide?" There was hurt in his eyes.

"Decide was the wrong word." She grasped for the right one. "I need time to let this soak in. Meanwhile, let's not tell anyone—"

"Not tell anyone what?" Gabriella asked as she and Isabel came through the door.

Chessie and Nick looked away from each other, and she felt like a kid caught red-handed.

Isabel stared at one parent and then the other. "Is something wrong?"

"No." Nick was quick to answer. "Your mother and I were just discussing…a change in plans."

Gabriella spotted the bottle in Chessie's lap. "Is someone sick?"

"Not at all," Chessie replied.

"Then what are these?" Gabriella snatched the bottle before Chessie could react. As she read the label her face flamed red. "Prenatal vitamins?"

"You're pregnant?" Isabel gasped.

"Yes," Chessie replied quietly.

"My thirty-seven-year-old mother is going to have a baby?" Gabriella shrieked. "Eeuuw! Gross! You're not going to have it, are you?"

"Gabriella! That's enough!" Nick started to rise out of his chair, but Isabel had already yanked her sister's arm and now held her with a steady grip and a steely-eyed glare.

"Are you going to have it?" Isabel asked, her voice filled with concern.

"Yes," both Chessie and Nick answered together.

Although Gabriella's eyes widened in disbelief, Isabel looked relieved.

"But I really don't want it talked about," Chessie said. "Not yet. Not even with the aunts and uncles. Or with Gramps."

"Why not?" Gabriella asked, astounded.

"If you're going to have it, what's the point of keeping it a secret?"

What was the point of keeping it secret for a little while longer? Nothing more than to let the reality of this bombshell sink in.

"Obviously, we need to make plans." Nick was already in schematic mode. Chessie could see it in his eyes. But was it for a child—their child—or a problem that needed to be solved?

"I'd say," Gabriella retorted. "This is a three-bedroom house. Where are we going to put this baby?"

"We have seven months to figure that out." Nick was fielding the questions, and Chessie let him. She felt as if she weren't a part of this scene, as if she were watching it from the wrong end of a telescope.

"Can we even afford a baby?" Gabriella sounded more and more like her father, but her question gave Chessie pause. How would Nick now feel about letting that lucrative job offer in Atlanta slip by? At her urging.

"Yes, we'll be able to afford this baby."

"Mom…?" Isabel looked worried. "Will you be able to do your pottery? The classes? The gallery?"

Wow. That was a whopper of a question. "I don't know," she replied.

Nick cocked his head as if he hadn't expected that answer. "Sure you can. It won't be exactly as you envisioned, but you can do it. We can help."

"Nick, we need to talk about so many things."

"Gabby, that's our cue." Isabel tugged on her sister's shirt. "Let's go get subs for supper. Mom, is there anything you can't have?"

Chessie smiled at Isabel's thoughtfulness. "Anything's fine. Thank you."

When the girls were gone, Nick took Chessie's hands in his. "I'm happy about this baby, Chess."

"You are?"

"Yes. I grew up in a big family. Lots of kids don't scare me."

"But after fourteen years, a baby…"

He inhaled sharply then exhaled hard. "I must admit the news came as a shock."

"But you're ready?"

"When are we ever really ready for what life throws us? I'd say, with your help, I'm as ready as I'll ever be."

"About help…" This was one of many

thoughts that had been scratching around in the back of her mind from the minute the nurse practitioner had spoken those fateful words. "I'll need more from you this time. This time around I'm more deeply into my pottery. You told Isabel you didn't think I had to give it up. I don't want to. But Gabby and Izzy are on the verge of having their own lives. You can't count on them to fill in all the time as babysitters."

"We'll work it out."

"And what about us? As a couple? We were just starting to make headway. Just starting to look forward to four years from now when we'd be a twosome again. Now we'll be fifty-six when this baby goes off to college."

"In eighteen years, right?" Nick smiled gently at her. "So, if this baby hadn't come along, how old would we be in eighteen years?"

"You know what I mean."

"I know. We'll have to work it out. Make time for each other. Like the pops concert. Like the walk the other day. Like closing our bedroom door."

"There's so much to work out. The last time I had a baby, I had a diaper pail. Emily has a diaper system for Eric. It's this big high-tech machine that shrink-wraps soiled diapers into odorless little packages suitable for party favors." She felt a fat tear roll down her cheek. "I feel like such a dinosaur, Nick."

With a chuckle, he stood and pulled her into an embrace. "Now I hear the hormones talking."

"I'm allowed," she snuffled into his shirt-front. "For the next seven months I'm allowed."

"So...can we tell the family?"

"Not yet. Please, not yet."

Nick worried at her hesitation. Her lack of joy at the prospect of a baby. Maybe she was afraid he felt obligated. Not committed. If so, he'd have to rectify that misconception.

He needed help to convince her, and, for Chessie, he wasn't afraid to ask for it. From Gabriella and Isabel. And from the rest of the McCabes. If they were going to raise another child, he needed to call in the tag-team.

IT TOOK HIM a couple days to set the stage, and as the plan unfolded in his mind, he wondered if it might be too over-the-top. But watching Chessie retreat into silence, taking long walks alone, he felt certain what he had

in mind would show her he could think outside a buttoned-down world and give her
what support and intimacy she needed.

On Friday he announced he'd asked Brad
and Emily if Chessie and he could "borrow"
one-year-old Eric for a day to get reac-
quainted with a baby.

Well, tomorrow was here. A rainy, gray
Saturday that could not have suited his plan
more if he'd been able to special order it.
He'd make sure Chessie took her vitamins.

Before she awoke, he was downstairs col-
laborating on the final few details with Gabriella and Isabel. The girls took off as he
readied a breakfast tray of tea and toast for
Chessie.

When he re-entered their bedroom, she
rolled over and opened one eye. "What's the
occasion?" she asked, indicating the tray.

"We have a minute alone. I thought we
could enjoy the peace and quiet."

She propped herself up against her pillows,
and he sat on his side of the bed, carefully
placing the tray between them.

"Thank you." She nibbled on a slice of toast.

It hit him that they weren't alone, hadn't
been for the past few days even when they

were the only two people in the house. With the prospect of a baby looming over their heads, the room actually felt crowded. By the end of the day he hoped they'd be able to get back to the two of them. For a few moments at least.

"So, when is Emily bringing Eric over?" she asked.

"Any time now. I told her we'd like a whole day's experience."

She offered him a tentative smile. "You know, when you mentioned this idea last night, I thought you were crazy. But I'm starting to look forward to the day...especially since we're doing it together."

"It looks as if it's just you, me and Eric, kid. Mariah called Izzy earlier. I don't know what that was about. And Gabby's spending the day in a special dance rehearsal. Seems she's got to learn some new complicated number by this afternoon."

He heard Emily's van pull in the driveway, followed by Pop's truck. Right on time.

"Our refresher course is here," he said, standing. "I'll go down to meet him."

"Give me a second," Chessie said, getting out of bed and opening the dresser drawer. "I don't think the day calls for anything fancier than sweats."

Truer words were never spoken.

By the time Chessie made it to the kitchen, Nick was balancing a very squirmy Eric on his hip while Alex, Nina, Noah and Olivia chased each other around the first floor. Alex had brought Nick's junior-high-school trumpet, which she was using liberally to lead the troop charge.

"Eric started walking last week," Emily said, "and he doesn't think he needs to be held anymore. He loves to go for a walk, but if this rain keeps up all day, that won't be an option. Sorry."

Through the side door Nick could see Pop and Jonas unloading the power tools from their truck to the first floor of the barn. "We'll be fine, Em. It's not as if we're first-time parents."

"Not at all." Chessie reached for Eric, held him aloft, then planted a big noisy raspberry on his tummy much to the one-year-old's delight. Nick didn't know how she could feel inadequate over having another child. She was a natural mother.

"Okay," Emily said. "Good luck."

When she turned to go and the four older

children didn't follow, Chessie shot Nick a questioning look.

"Uh, Em?" he said. "I thought we were going to just watch Eric."

Emily looked guilty, and for a minute he thought she might not go through with the plan. After all, she was the one who'd told him either Chessie would love his creative effort…or she would divorce him on the spot. But she took a deep breath and said innocently, "Oh, dear, I must have misunderstood. I thought you wanted all the cousins. That's why I had Alex sleep over. That's why Brad and I made a date to go to Portland to shop for a new car. I…I suppose we could cancel."

"Oh, I know how hard it is to find time for just the two of you," Chessie said as Noah ran by with Nina in hot pursuit. "Isabel doesn't go to work at the pound until later this afternoon. She can help entertain the older ones. You and Brad go and enjoy the day together."

"Are you sure?"

"Positive," Nick said emphatically.

"You won't have to worry about Eric being bothered by the chaos," Emily said, backing to the door. "He's used to it."

"Chaos," Chessie murmured as Emily

drove off. "Let's see if we can minimize it." She put Eric on the floor where he happily toddled right toward the cupboard under the sink. "Find something to secure those doors," she said, heading for the living room.

"Okay, gang," Nick heard her say as he grabbed some duct tape off the counter and quickly taped all the Eric-accessible doors shut, "who wants to work with some clay?"

"Me!" came the chorused reply.

"Well, follow the Pied Piper!" Chessie marched out of the living room and through the kitchen. "You can bring Eric," she said over her shoulder. "I bet he'd love to get squishy."

Nick scooped up his nephew and joined the end of the line. The only way he could keep the boy from fussing was by "flying" him with all the appropriate noises. This was better than a weight-lifting program.

When they hit the utility room, they could hear the screech of power tools coming from the barn's lower level. Pop and Jonas stopped when they saw the gang.

"Hey, Chessie!" Pop called out. "Jonas and I had a free morning, and we thought we'd get your shelves up. It'll be noisy for a few hours, but it shouldn't be too bad in the house."

"Actually, we were headed to the loft for a pottery class."

"You won't disturb us," Pop replied with a grin.

A dubious expression on her face, Chessie led the kids upstairs, but no sooner were they settled at a table than the din began in earnest. The power saw's high-pitched whine could etch glass. Jonas added his own touch by turning up his radio to a favorite heavy metal station. And the hammering—Nick was sure professional carpenters never needed that many strokes per minute—the hammering rocked the rafters.

"We can't work up here," Chessie yelled.

"Awwww!" The cousins didn't seem to mind the noise.

"He said they were only going to work this morning. We can come back this afternoon." She motioned for everyone to follow her. "Let's make cookies."

"Yaaaay!" The cousins were really getting into it.

As they trooped downstairs and back through the gallery, Pop winked at Nick.

No sooner had they settled around the kitchen table than Isabel came through the door with Mariah's big wet Airedale, Muffin. The cousins shrieked with glee as they rushed to manhandle the dog who stood in the middle of the kitchen and shook rain water all over everyone and everything.

From his perch on Nick's shoulders, Eric crowed his approval.

"What are you doing with that dog, Isabel?" Chessie was trying to get the cousins corralled.

"Aunt Mariah is getting her apartment painted this weekend. She needed a dogsitter. I offered."

"Well, put him in the utility room," Chessie ordered. "And all my bakers need to wash their hands. Again."

As Isabel led Muffin to the utility room, the cousins crowded around the sink, pushing each other in an attempt to be the one to use the spray nozzle. More water got on the countertops and the floor than on their hands.

"Yeowwww!" The caterwaul and hissing from the utility room and the subsequent barking were clear indications Muffin had discovered the cats. Nick handed Eric to

Chessie, then went to help Isabel. The cats were both on top of the furnace, and Muffin was straining against the hold Isabel had on his collar.

"He'll have to come in the kitchen," Nick said, grabbing an old towel from the rag bag. "He can't go out in the barn with all those power tools."

"We'll put the cousins to work drying him," Isabel said with a big grin. "That should be fun."

Oh, it was. The dog loved it. The cousins loved it, especially Eric who crawled all over Muffin, helping dry the dog with his tiny overalls.

"You, mister, are soaking wet," Nick declared, picking up the baby. "Let's see if your mom packed you a change of clothes."

Muffin plopped down under the table and fell asleep.

"Here's the carry bag," Chessie said. "You might as well change his diaper while you're at it. Izzy and I will start the cousins on cookies."

"Cookies, yum!" Gabriella exclaimed as she burst into the house with three teenagers in tow. "Hey, guys! This is Owen, Grady and

Allie. We have to learn a new dance by rehearsal this afternoon, but the quilters are
using the Atlantic Hall. I said we could use
our living room."

"Now isn't a good time," Chessie protested
as she tried to supervise Alex opening a five-
pound bag of flour. Nina, Noah, Olivia and
Isabel were helping themselves to the chocolate chips.

"We'd do it in the driveway, but it's rain-
ing," Gabriella explained. "And we really, really have to learn it by two this afternoon."

"Honey," Nick said, "we wanted her to get
involved in a community project."

"Okay." Chessie wiped a smudge of flour
from her nose and sneezed. "Far be it for me
to stifle creativity."

As Nick laid Eric on a changing pad on the
dining room table, Gabby and her friends
headed for the living room where he could
hear them pushing back furniture and rolling
up the rug. Within minutes the whole house
was pulsing to the rhythm of rain on the roof
and the music of *Grease*.

He looked in the kitchen to see Chessie's
reaction. It was a fine line he was walking,
and he didn't want to push her over the edge.

But Isabel was helping keep things chaotically fun. She'd started to sing along to the music and had gotten the cousins to join in. Soon their little fannies were waggling to the jitterbug beat as they knelt on their chairs to put their mark on the cookie-making process.

The house sounded like a YMCA on a Saturday and smelled like a kennel.

Isabel boogied into the dining room and picked up Eric, now freshly diapered and sporting a dry pair of overalls. "Ask Mom to dance," she nearly shouted in his ear.

He needed no further urging.

Coming up behind Chessie, he spun her around and began a bump-and-grind he didn't know he had in him. The cousins stood on their chairs, applauding. When Chessie threw back her head and laughed, the sound filled Nick's heart with joy.

If family life was messy, this was the best possible mess.

At noon his plan began to unwind on schedule. Pop and Jonas stopped in to say the shelves were built. A little later Mariah came by to say she'd take Muffin. The "painters never showed." Kit stopped by not long after to say she'd take the four older cousins off their hands. Midafternoon, Isabel went to work at the lobster pound, and Gabriella and her friends traipsed off to their rehearsal. At three-thirty, Emily came to retrieve Eric.

And then there were two.

With a look of astonishment on her face, Chessie stumbled into the living room and collapsed on the sofa. "What a day!"

Nick sat beside her. "Listen," he said.

"I don't hear anything."

"Exactly."

"Oh, this is lovely." With a tremendous smile, she lay back against the sofa cushions and plopped her legs in his lap.

He took off her sneakers and her socks, then began to massage her feet.

"And this is divine!" She closed her eyes.

"It's nice. Just the two of us."

She opened one eye. "But for how long?"

"Doesn't matter," he insisted. "If we can sneak only ten minutes for ourselves out of a crazy day does it mean those ten minutes are less intimate than, say, a night out?"

She opened both eyes. "Are you finding a lesson in today?"

"Maybe. Was the experience so bad?"

She laughed. "Actually, it was fun."

"And now?" He deepened the foot massage.

"This is heaven. Even if the whole gang bursts back in here in five minutes, these two minutes have been worth it."

"I'm beginning to think intimacy isn't quantitative. It's comparative."

She sat up, her expression suspicious. "Why, Nick, when did you become a philosopher?"

"Well, I—"

Unexpectedly, she straddled his lap and skewered him with those intense hazel eyes. "Or should I say scriptwriter?"

"What are you talking about?"

"Today." She smiled and there was mischief in the tilt of her head. "Today reminded me of Gabby's favorite bedtime story when she was little. A man seeks advice on curing the awful noise in his house. Seems the bed squeaks, the floor creaks and the tree branches rustle against his windowpane." She settled on Nick's lap in a way she had to know tormented him. It wasn't a bedtime story he wanted now.

But she continued in mock innocence. "The man was advised to get a cat, a dog, a chicken, a goat, a donkey, a cow and a horse and house them in his bedroom until the chaos nearly drove him crazy. But when he got rid of the livestock, the squeaky bed, the creaky floor and the rustling branch seemed oh, so peaceful." She tweaked Nick's nose. "Does that scenario sound familiar, oh, great philosopher?"

"I seem to remember it…"

She pressed her forehead to his. "Did you engineer today?"

"Some people throw laundry out the window to make a point…others create morality plays."

With a whoop of laughter, she bopped him over the head with a sofa cushion. "That is so unlike you!"

"Did I make my point?"

"Which was…?"

"Actually, Pop reminded me when I talked to him a few days ago about deciding whether I should take that Atlanta job. He told me when things get complicated, clear away the clutter to the essentials."

"So you thought you'd dramatize the process for me today?"

"Hey," he brushed a lock of hair behind her ears, "you're an artist. I thought you'd respond to a demo."

"You surprise me. Every day." Her look turned wistful.

"So what's wrong?"

"Not wrong. But…throughout the chaos today, you were with me. When we have this baby, you'll still be working six days a week."

"Not necessarily. I talked to Richard Filmore about getting the board to fund a second assistant principal or administrative assistant. When Eleanor and Hattie heard, they promised to look into federal grant monies to fund what the board couldn't." He smiled and felt an old weight lifting from his shoulders. "That got me thinking. I have a highly capable staff. I need to delegate more. That's my new resolution."

"Wow."

"Not only that, Emily gave me a list of reliable teenage babysitters plus the name of an agency that supplies part-time nannies. If you need more time for your work, we can budget."

"Did Emily ask why you needed this list?"

"To get everyone's help, I told them we'd be making a big announcement. Soon. They don't officially know, but they *know*. Are you upset?"

She looked at him with love and admiration. "You've really thought this through."

"Like it or not, you and baby McCabe are going to be seeing a lot more of me."

"So you think you'll be around for the sticky parts?"

"Many of them." He crossed his heart. "Promise."

"You'll make time for the two of us?"

"Did I not get the entire cast to exit stage left and leave us these few minutes?"

"Dear Lord—" she raised her eyes heavenward "—what else is there to learn about my husband?"

"Chessie, I want us to raise this child together."

She flung her arms around his neck and hugged him hard. When she looked him in the face, the worry lines across her forehead had disappeared, and her expression was filled with joy.

"So," he asked, "can we officially tell the family about this new rugrat?"

She grinned. "Give me five more minutes of foot rub, and you've got yourself a deal."

LATER THAT NIGHT Nick came up behind Chessie as she stood by the rain-drenched window and put his strong arms around her.

She inhaled his freshly showered scent and thought back to the Fourth of July when she'd stood on this very spot and jettisoned the family laundry. When she'd struck what she'd thought was a blow for separating and distinguishing her wants and needs. How naïve she'd been. Nick had helped her realize that fulfillment came, not from separating ourselves from others, but from finding moments of strong connection to those we love and cherish.

"What's the status on that no-sex ultimatum?" Nick asked, his voice low and husky in her ear.

"I wasn't very good at it, was I?" She thought back to her willing participation in the shower days earlier.

"Then why'd you hit me with it? Just curious, in case you ever decide to use that strategy again."

"I won't." She turned in his arms to face him. "I thought I was getting to what was fundamental to a man. To make you sit up and take notice. I'm ashamed to admit I tried to use sex as leverage to focus on me. But I underestimated you. And me. I love the intimacy of married sex. Need it. I nearly cut off my nose to spite my face."

He chuckled. "So…ready for bed?"

"Yes and no." She felt a tingle of excitement at the prospect of loving him. Of offering herself without strings, or baggage or ulterior motives. "That depends on what you're planning to do there. Now, sleep would be a no…"

The smile that lifted the corners of his mouth was for her. The desire in his eyes was for her. There was no doubt in her mind that right now Nick saw and wanted her, only her.

"I love you, Chessie," he said.

There were no simpler words. No sweeter declaration.

"I love you, Nick."

He drew her away from the window and toward the bed. Slowly as if time had no meaning. With assurance he slid his hands under her T-shirt, skimmed her sides, lifted her arms and removed the bit of fabric in one fluid motion. The humid night air caressed her skin.

He sat on the edge of the bed and very deliberately pulled her to stand between his knees. His hands on her hips, he trailed kisses across her stomach, lazily unzipped her shorts and let them fall to the floor around her ankles. He pressed the side of his face to her abdomen. Above the baby. Their baby.

She wound her fingers in his thick dark hair and leaned against him, realizing fully that sex between a wife and her husband should not be a favor, a tool or a weapon. It was a mutual gift. Somewhere over the years, she'd lost that insight. She bent to kiss Nick's brow.

He lay back on the bed, bringing her on top of him where she could gaze into his face. Trace his beloved features with her fingertips. The worry lines at the edges of his eyes were all but gone. She would safely bet he wasn't thinking of work.

With a grin and a hungry glint in his eye, he turned his head quickly and caught the tip of her little finger with his teeth. Licked the pad with his tongue. Made her shiver. This was like the first time only better.

She moved on top of him. The towel around his hips fell away, leaving only the silkiness of her panties between them.

He pulled her into a kiss that began in languorous exploration and soon escalated to passion. Chessie felt seen and desired. Cherished. And that gave her the power to reciprocate, withholding nothing.

She kissed him for the past and for the present and for their shared tomorrow.

He entered her and with his body made a silent, indisputable promise that in everything that might happen the two of them would take refuge in each other.

Finding release, she cried out softly—for his ears only—and held him tightly as he shuddered then came to rest in her arms.

"I love you," he breathed against her skin.

And wasn't that what she'd wanted all along?

EPILOGUE

One year later

"TAKE THAT!" Wielding a cardboard sword, Gabriella lunged at the papier-mâché head of the dragon whose blanketed body undulated on three pairs of feet across the makeshift stage set up on the McCabe cottage's lawn. The large audience of mostly four, five, and six-year-olds seated on the grass with their parents howled their approval.

Owen and Gabriella had devised the perfect summer job—adapting children's books to plays and selling matinee tickets to the performances. Owen did the adaptations while Gabriella made the costumes. Both worked on scenery and acted, pulling various members of the McCabe clan in for minor parts. Today cousins Alex, Nina and Noah were playing the dragon, and, by the way in which they were cavorting on stage and drawing out the final confrontation scene, they seemed determined to milk every moment in the spotlight. Gabriella, upping the intensity of her attack, appeared to relish the improvisation. The production was *The Paper Bag Princess,* in which the princess rescued not only herself but her prince as well.

Chessie, leaning back on her elbows in the cool grass next to Sophie's carrier seat, smiled her approval. Sometimes the princess needed to take matters into her own hands. Gabriella certainly had this past year with her passion for the stage positively channeling most of her raging hormones. Most. There were occasional flare-ups just to make sure her parents hadn't lost their edge.

Sophie reached over the side of her carrier seat and plucked a dandelion. Before it could reach her mouth, Chessie scooped up this daughter, who was such a daily surprise. And joy.

She nuzzled the baby's soft, fragrant neck. "Are you hungry?"

Sophie cooed.

"Let's go get you a bottle and see if Izzy needs anything."

With a big grin Sophie pulled Chessie's nose.

Leaving behind the sold-out crowd, Chessie danced with her five-month-old daughter in her arms, up the driveway to the gallery where Isabel was presently minding the store. Isabel had applied to and been accepted by Boston University where she'd be living in an apartment with five other girls, no less—in the fall. This summer she was working the gallery for Chessie during the days and, in the evenings with a select group of friends, frequented the Portland cafés that held open mike poetry readings.

As they entered the gallery, the bell above the door tinkled, making Sophie's eyes go round with wonder. That was one of the many blessings of this child—the reminder to find delight in the minute particulars of each day.

"How's our girl?" Isabel came forward to take Sophie.

"Ready for her bottle. Can we bring you anything?"

"I'm fine." Isabel cradled her baby sister, gently blowing on her wispy curls, making Sophie squint and wriggle in pleasure. "You go fix the bottle. I'll wait here with Miss Squish."

Chessie looked around the gallery with a sense of satisfaction. "How's business?"

"Good. I sold a set of blueberry bowls, a hemp textured vase—the biggest one—and a birdbath."

It hadn't been easy finding time to care for an infant, create her pottery, conduct classes and run a gallery. But Nick and the girls had pitched in to make it all happen.

"And I could have sold the Goddess," Isabel added. "Again."

"Never." Chessie smiled on the piece that held court on a pedestal in the center of the gallery. A constant reminder of the wide spectrum of her existence. From the pedestrian to the sublime. The challenge lay in savoring it all. "I'll be right back."

She was in the kitchen only a few minutes when she heard the side door open and close. "I'm home!" It was Nick.

He'd been home a lot this past year. He, Eleanor, Hattie and Richard had engineered some extra money from the board as well as some federal grant funding to get another administrative assistant.

He lifted her off her feet and spun her around. "And beginning right now, I'm officially on vacation. Two weeks. Cell phone's off. Eleanor's in charge. I'm yours. Can you stand it?"

"I'll try!" She laughed, then kissed him soundly, reveling in the few moments they could steal alone before they stepped out into the ever-widening concentric circles of love called family.

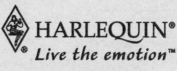

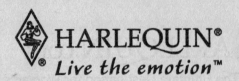

AMERICAN Romance®

Upbeat,
All-American Romances

flipside

Romantic Comedy

Harlequin Historicals®

Historical,
Romantic Adventure

INTRIGUE

Romantic Suspense

HARLEQUIN ROMANCE®

The essence of
modern romance

HARLEQUIN® Presents

Seduction and passion
guaranteed

Super ROMANCE®

Emotional,
Exciting, Unexpected

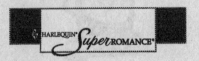

Temptation

Sassy, Sexy, Seductive!

HDIR204

eHARLEQUIN.com

The Ultimate Destination for Women's Fiction

**Visit eHarlequin.com's Bookstore today
for today's most popular books at great prices.**

- An extensive selection of romance books by top authors!

- Choose our convenient "bill me" option. No credit card required.

- New releases, Themed Collections and hard-to-find backlist.

- A sneak peek at upcoming books.

- Check out book excerpts, book summaries and Reader Recommendations from other members and post your own too.

- Find out what everybody's reading in Bestsellers.

- Save BIG with everyday discounts and exclusive online offers!

- Our Category Legend will help you select reading that's exactly right for you!

- Visit our Bargain Outlet often for huge savings and special offers!

- Sweepstakes offers. Enter for your chance to win special prizes, autographed books and more.

**Your purchases are 100%
guaranteed—so shop online
at www.eHarlequin.com today!**

INTBB104R

From first love to forever, these love stories
are fairy tale romances for today's woman.

Modern, passionate reads that are powerful and provocative.

Emotional, compelling stories that capture the intensity
of living, loving and creating a family in today's world.

A roller-coaster read that delivers romantic thrills
in a world of suspense, adventure and more.